Mr Right for the Night

Marisa Mackle

POCKET BOOKS

TownHouse

First published in Great Britain and Ireland
by Pocket/TownHouse, 2002
An imprint of Simon & Schuster UK Ltd
and TownHouse and CountryHouse Ltd, Dublin

Simon & Schuster UK is a Viacom company

1 3 5 7 9 10 8 6 4 2

Simon & Schuster UK Ltd
Africa House
64–78 Kingsway
London WC2B 6AH

www.simonsays.co.uk

Simon & Schuster Australia
Sydney

TownHouse and CountryHouse Ltd
Trinity House
Charleston Road
Ranelagh
Dublin 6
Ireland

A CIP catalogue record for this book is available
from the British Library

ISBN 1 903650 27 5

Typeset by Palimpsest Book Production Limited,
Polmont, Stirlingshire
Printed and bound in Great Britain by Cox & Wyman Ltd, Reading, Berks

ACKNOWLEDGEMENTS

Thanks to:
God, without you there wouldn't be a book
Sheila Collins for being my Granny, best friend and inspiration
Dr Tara Mackle for the wonderful title
Dr Naomi Mackle for the mad weekends away
Eamonn Mackle for the amazing cooking – my parties wouldn't be the same without you
Daphne Mackle for bombarding me with all those books and for dragging me out that cold winter's night that happened to change my life
Roxanne Parker for being my friend and 'personal trainer'
To all the writers who gave me advice and encouragement: Deirdre Purcell, Maeve Binchy, David Rice, Sr. ni Riain, Susan Schreibman and Niamh O'Connor
To the friends that supported me: Angela and Eileen Jones, Barbara O'Donnell, Marjorie Parker, Lisa Warren, Niav and Emer O'Reilly and Anita Murphy (from my Dundalk days)
To: Suzanne Tuthill for the legal advice

To: Jim Fitzpatrick for the photos
To: my editor Treasa Coady and also to Helen Gleed, Lucy Curtis and everybody at TownHouse
To: my UK editor Kate Lyall Grant and everybody at Simon and Schuster
And most of all to: St Jude and St Anthony for answered prayers

This book is dedicated to Sheila Collins with all my love

Chapter One

If you ran after men they ran away.

They were like dogs, Anna's granny had once said.

If you chased a dog he ran off.

If you stopped he stopped.

If you turned slowly so did he.

If you ran away he panicked and ran after you.

Apparently.

Anna Allstone had chased her mother's dog once for five hours up and down Sandymount Strand. People had stared at her like she was some kind of dog thief. He'd glared at her from a safe distance pretending he'd never seen her before in his life. And even when she bought a tin of Chum in the garage across the road and rapped it with her pocket-knife like a madman, he still refused to cooperate. It was only later, when she finally gave up, got into her mother's car and prepared to drive off, that he ran after her like his life depended on it. If only she'd used the same tactics on Emmet Dirave last week. If only she hadn't called round to his house with a bottle of red wine and the Sunday papers to find an unfamiliar blue Fiat parked in the drive. If only she hadn't rung the doorbell seven times, eventually shouting desperately through the letter box, 'I know you're in there, you prick.' If only she hadn't left several life-threatening messages on his answering machine telling him he'd be sorry, that he'd never meet anyone like her ever again. If only she hadn't changed her tone later on in a tearful 'call me please and we can talk about this' message. If only . . .

Anna dutifully blew out the thirty candles her mother had clumsily stuck on a strawberry flan. She smiled into her dad's camera. CLICK. There, captured on camera for ever. It would be placed carefully on the sitting-room wall along with all the other twenty-nine.

'Will you have a piece, Anna?' Her mother slapped a generous slice onto a plate in front of her. With a huge dollop of cream. Anna gave it a disdainful look. There were at least a thousand calories in that.

'Your mam went to an awful lot of trouble so she did,' Grandad croaked from behind the *Irish Times*. 'She's been baking all afternoon.'

'That was very nice of her,' Anna tried to look cheerful. She glanced from her overweight mother to her lean father to her live-in grandfather. 'So any other news?'

'Your brother got promoted,' her mother said proudly.

'Didn't he just get promoted recently?'

'Yes, and he just got promoted again,' her father added, looking like he was about to explode with pride.

'Great, he must be nearly running the bank by now,' Anna's voice was dry.

'Have another piece of cake, Anna.'

'No, honestly I'm full and er . . . it's getting late. I don't want to be wandering the streets late at night. Dublin's becoming quite dangerous, you know.'

'I'll drive you home so.' Her father stood up wearily and picked his car keys up from the kitchen table.

'Are you sure you don't mind, Dad?' Anna grinned.

He shook his head. 'I know you've just turned thirty, love, but you haven't changed a bit. You'd still do anything for a lift. When are you going to get your own car?'

'Soon, Dad, soon,' Anna promised as she kissed her mother and Grandad goodnight.

Thank God that was over with, she told herself as her father drove her home to Ranelagh. Next year she'd organize something more exciting. Like a party, say. Not with her family though. No, with young people. Then again thirty wasn't very young. Not if you wanted to be a ballerina or a model or something. Or a tennis star. But it didn't matter because she didn't want to be any of those things anyway. You had to think positive in life. Thirty was very young in some professions. Like thirty would be extremely young for a bishop. Or a chief executive of a major company. Or a famous poet or professor. Or a headmaster or, God forbid, a grandmother! Stop it, she scolded herself. There was no point in going round in circles about this. She could weigh up the pros and cons till the cows came home but nothing could change the fact that she'd hit the big three oh. Period.

Chapter Two

Anna,

It's hard to believe it's been twelve years! Are you still as mad as ever? I'm sure you're wondering what this is all about. Well, Vincent and I (we tied the knot in June) are throwing a joint thirtieth bash. Sounds so old, doesn't it? We'd be absolutely thrilled if you and your partner could come along, Saturday, 8 April, 8.00 p.m.

Victoria Reddin (née Reilly)

Anna stared at the note before attacking the second half of her King Size Mars. The pot of pasta had just started to boil but she couldn't possibly wait another twenty minutes to eat. She read the note again. And again. Then she washed the rest of the Mars down with Diet Coke. The whole thing was bizarre. Damn this silly note. It was mind-boggling. She turned the pasta down to one, half wishing she hadn't eaten the entire Mars. It would take a good few *Mr Motivators* to work all that off. She blamed Victoria. It was all

her fault. The invitation had completely thrown her.
She dialled Claire's number. Claire was always great
in a crisis. Sensible and settled, married to a solid
man called Simon who sold shares, Claire would
have all the answers.

'Claire, you won't believe what hap—'

'Oh Anna, can I ring you back, this isn't a good
time.'

'But it's an emergency.'

'Your house is on fire?'

'No.'

'Someone's dead?'

'No, nothing like that . . .'

'Well then, Anna, it's not an emergency. I'll ring
you back, bye.'

Anna sighed, the phone feeling like a dead weight
in her right hand. What had happened to good
old friendship? Huh! They said a friend in need
was a friend indeed. Well, Anna was in need and
indeed Claire was not being supportive. But since
Claire had got married, the only thing she loved
to talk about was other people's marriages. Recent
marriages. Broken marriages (that was a favourite).
Annulled marriages (though to be honest you didn't
get too many of them in Ireland). Yet. Gay marriages.
Hello! marriages. Second and third marriages . . . It
was just oh so dull.

Anna couldn't understand it all. She supposed
it made Claire feel part of the most dangerous
and furiously fast-growing society in Ireland – the

ARMPITTS – Annoying Rich Married People In Their Thirties Society. Anna missed the old Claire. The one who got plastered every Saturday, fired every second Monday, stood up every Thursday and dumped every Friday. God, she used to be so much fun! These days Claire was an ARMPITT with an armful of advice for her few remaining single friends. And although she meant well, all the 'tips' got to you after a while. The phone rang suddenly. Anna cleared her throat.

'Hello?' she answered softly in case it was a man.

'Anna, it's all right it's me, we can talk now.'

'Oh good. Am I being timed?'

'Wait till you have kids and you'll know all about time management.'

'You'll never guess who got in contact with me.' Like a crime correspondent Anna spoke in a low throaty voice.

'Victoria Reilly.'

'Oh, how did you know?' Anna could hardly contain her disappointment.

'She sent me a card as well.'

'Did she?'

'Apparently she sent one to everyone in the class.'

'So it's like a reunion.'

'Something like that. What else did you want?'

'That's it.'

'God, Anna, you're the biggest drama queen,' Claire laughed.

'She asked in mine if I was still as mad as ever?'

'That's weird, she must be mixing you up with someone else.'

'I bet she doesn't even remember me,' Anna sniffed.

'Well, it's been twelve years.'

'I don't care how long it's been. I haven't forgotten how she made our lives hell. Don't you remember the way she called us *Little* and *Large* to make the others laugh?'

'Oh kids will be kids.'

'It wasn't as traumatic for you.'

'Huh?'

'You were *Little*, I was *Large* . . .'

'Oh God, Anna, stop being paranoid. Was there anything else?'

'Anything else? I don't think you quite understand what's going on here.'

'Listen, Anna, it's really not such a big deal. Now I really have to go, I . . .'

'You can't go.'

'I've something in the oven.'

'Bullshit.'

'I'll call round later.'

'Great, I'll open a bottle of wine.'

'Yes, that should solve all our problems.' Anna removed all her clothes, including shoes and under-wear. She stepped on the weighing scales as slowly as she could and peered at the dial. Oh God, that couldn't be right. She discarded her earrings and hair clip. It still didn't make any difference. Sugar. This was bad. She got dressed again and ambled towards the kitchen. She was starving and, besides, a few more bars of chocolate wouldn't make a difference. She reached for a packet of Maltesers. They were light, weren't they? Remember the ad with the thin girl rowing the boat?

She was looking forward to Claire coming over. It was about time Simon babysat for a change. Claire was like a prisoner sometimes. *Not that it was such a terrible complaint.* Anna frowned. After all being as free as a bird wasn't all it was cracked up to be either. She uncorked the bottle of red just as the doorbell rang. Great. Perfect timing.

Claire looked super for a mother, Anna thought. Her long dark wavy hair was shining and her cheeks had a healthy pink glow. Anna let her into the freezing communal hallway.

'Mind the bicycles,' Anna pointed out. 'They belong to the lads downstairs.'

'Oh yeah, you said one was cute, didn't you?'

'One's cute, one's not. They're students.'

They climbed the stairs and were soon seated in Anna's minute one-bedroomed flat. It was ensuite in that it had a shower, a toilet with an ice-cold seat that didn't encourage you to sit for very long, and a ridiculously small basin dribbling cold water. But the rent wasn't ludicrously expensive and at her age she needed privacy. It was comfy, and she rented it by herself. It was untidy most of the time except for about three evenings a year when she entertained friends and was forced to throw most of her stuff under the bed before the first guest arrived.

'So how's little Andrew?' Anna asked politely. Best to get the baby talk out of the way before moving on to more important things.

'Oh, he's as good as gold. Not like other babies who cry all the time.'

'Good, great.' Anna poured herself a generous glass of wine and put her feet up. 'I'll babysit for you any time.'

'Yes, thanks er . . . that's very generous of you.' Not in a million years would Claire let her best friend look after poor Andrew; God, it didn't bear thinking about. Andrew would probably be force-fed tins of Chum while bottles of luke-warm milk would have to suffice for Blackie.

'Anyway,' Anna continued cheerfully, anxious to hurry things along. 'About that note from Victoria. Isn't it extraordinary? And I mean it's a bit ridiculous sending out invitations at this stage. The party isn't for nearly four months!'

'Oh, I suppose she's giving people who live abroad the chance to fly over for the reunion. I shouldn't get too worked up about it,' Claire said mildly. 'It was probably meant as a kind enough gesture.'

'Kind, me foot!' Anna tugged at a long strand of fair hair. 'That one was never kind. Can't you see the only reason she's invited us is to torment us with stories about how well she's done.'

'Maybe you're right.'

'Of course I'm right. Well, we're not going. She can shove her stupid party,' Anna said firmly.

'It mightn't be too bad.'

'Too bad? It'll be terrible. God, Claire, wild horses couldn't drag me along to something like that. First of all I'm very much partnerless at the moment, and second of all I'm not prepared to go along and sing Happy Birthday to a girl who made my teenage years hell.'

Anna picked up a box of Pringles and began to munch defiantly. Claire sipped her red wine slowly. Neither girl spoke for a while.

'You know if you don't go it will be worse,' Claire said eventually.

'How?'

'She'll think you haven't made a success of your life.'

'Don't care.'

'You don't want her saying "Poor Anna", now do you?'

'I never thought about it like that.'

But it was true. That's exactly what Victoria Reilly would say. Anna could imagine her standing in the dining room surrounded by antiques and chandeliers, clinking her champagne glass and laughing loudly. Suddenly conversations would hush and Victoria, the beautiful bitchy hostess, would exclaim, 'I *knew* someone didn't show up. Anna Allstone didn't. Remember that very peculiar girl . . .' and everybody would remember and shriek with laughter. God, it was a horrible thought.

Anna drained her glass and promptly refilled it. 'Right,' she said, 'so I'll go.'

'You might as well.'

'But only under one condition. I must, absolutely must, find myself the perfect partner for the night.'

'That's the spirit.' Claire raised her glass for Anna to refill.

Anna frowned. 'Do you think it would be difficult meeting the perfect partner in Dublin?'

'Have you ever tried looking for a needle in a haystack?' Claire asked unhelpfully.

'Mmmm, you could have a point. I mean he'd *have* to be decent though. I'm not dragging some small balding dingbat salesman along to meet the victorious Victoria and Vince.'

Claire laughed. Anna could really get herself worked up over the most insignificant things. People changed as they grew older. True, Victoria and her gang had been particularly nasty at school but that was years ago. It was time to let bygones be bygones.

'He'll have to be the right mix, of course,' Anna continued. 'No NYCDs.'

'Sorry?'

'Not in your class dears.'

'Right.'

'He'll have to be good looking, of course ... in a classy way ... without sideburns, cheap leather jackets, rings on thumbs, et cetera.'

'Why don't you make a list?' Claire hooted with laughter. This was great fun.

'Good idea.' Anna didn't laugh. This was serious business. Her reputation was at stake here. 'Give me a pen.'

Claire took another sip of her wine. She was really beginning to enjoy herself. It was great getting away from Simon and Andrew for the night. Mind you, when she got back home and saw the pair of them fast asleep, she'd be cooing in her drunken state and thinking she was the luckiest woman in the world. She *always* did that.

'Right,' said Anna after a while, 'I've made one. It's quite short though.'

'Show us.'

Anna reluctantly handed over the list. Claire read aloud.

1. No moustaches.
2. No shirts with horses on them.
3. No stunning exes.
4. No overdrawn credit cards.
5. No clingy loser friends.
6. No female friends who are *like a sister* to them.
7. No hairy backs.
8. No problem spending money.
9. No control over the relationship.
10. No daft ideas about settling down.

'There's a lot of noes here,' Claire said.

'Well, the yeses are obvious. Yes, he has to have a high-powered job. Yes, he has to be tall, dark and handsome or tall, blond and handsome. Yes, he has to have a decent car (preferably 02 reg). Yes, he has to be hysterically funny without being crude. Yes, he has to respect his mother and sisters (without quoting them the whole time) and yes, he has to think Cindy Crawford's looks are only average compared to mine.'

'And seriously, what do you suppose your chances are of finding this . . . wonderful specimen?'

'Nil and none,' Anna answered matter-of-factly. 'But hey, there's no harm in aiming high.'

'You should have no problem meeting someone,' Claire said kindly. 'Everyone I know thinks you're very attractive . . . not to mention extremely funny.'

'Well, don't mention it please. My mother always told me that funny women invariably end up being funny all by themselves. Or end up telling jokes to the cat who won't laugh unless he knows he's being fed soon. Men hate funny women.'

'Do you reckon?'

'Of course. Victoria didn't have a funny bone in her body and all the guys loved her 'cos she was blonde with big boobs.'

'Maybe you're right. Look at the girls in *Friends*. They're funny and they're always having men trouble.'

'Exactly.' Anna stood up and opened a second bottle of red. She was beginning to perk up. The list had given her some perspective on life. It was important to focus on what you wanted. You had to see the dim light at the end of the tunnel. But there was only one problem. Where in the world was she going to meet this man?

Chapter Three

Anna sat at an empty checkout trying to figure out her life. Of course she wasn't being paid to do that. She was being paid to tot up the previous week's sales in ladies fashions and make a list of the top ten sellers. But all that stuff seemed pretty trivial compared to her most recent crisis. Her head was throbbing a bit after last night's wine and the bright lights in the store seemed especially bright. Thank God it was Tuesday morning and there weren't too many customers about. The place looked like a bomb had hit it. Anna hated the sales when everything was thrown into big metal bins near the doors under gaudy red lettering: EVERYTHING 99p. Of course you got the odd punter who claimed she'd found one of the new bright-blue £20 shirts in one of the bins. But Anna was well used to those types. After four years in the retail business she'd met them all; pregnant shoplifters who weren't pregnant at all, women who swore blindly they hadn't worn the silky black and pink 99p knickers and were therefore demanding a refund, women who'd bought pedal pushers in the seventies only to find out now they didn't fit. Women! They were a frigging nuisance.

June Nelson would be around after lunch to discuss the sales report. Anna was trying to force herself to get motivated before the woman arrived. June lived for Lolta's and seemed determined to become head of the company no matter what the cost. A manless, childless, lifeless woman; Anna had an inner dread of ending up like her. Of course Anna had ambitions of her own. She'd love to head a store eventually. After all, there was nothing she didn't know about retailing. But she had her own private ideas about how a store should be run successfully. And she certainly wouldn't live or die for this company. No way.

Elaine appeared at the desk. Elaine was manager of footwear and also company mad but not as mad as June. But at least June had an excuse – she was middle-aged and discontent. Elaine wasn't even thirty! She was far too young to be married to Lolta's. Not of course that you'd ever mention marriage to poor Elaine. It was a sore point. Elaine had married young. She was now a deserted wife. Wasn't that a horrible image? It always reminded Anna of a half-naked, starving woman in a desert! Ugh!

'How's the old head?' Elaine gave a slight smile. 'Anna, you're a million miles away.'

Anna sighed. There was no point telling Elaine about her silly search for a man. Elaine would only scoff at it and remind Anna that happiness could only come from within and until you loved yourself no one else could love you and all that crap. She'd suggest that Anna take up spinning classes on a Monday, yoga on a Tuesday, pottery on a Wednesday and so on. At any given time Elaine was doing about five different evening classes, which meant that she had absolutely no time to meet men, *which was exactly the point*, as Elaine would point out. But she was a good sort and a dedicated and non-aggressive department manager.

'I'm trying to sort out this sales report.' Anna frowned. 'Sales are up on last year but are not matching budget figures. It's a bit worrying.'

'It's not like you to worry so much.'

'No, but *June* will worry and therefore *I* worry that my head will end up on a platter after lunch.'

'Don't let her bully you,' Elaine said matter-of-factly. 'You know your stuff.'

Anna sighed, 'That's the problem. I *do* know what I'm talking about but I often feel I'm bashing my head against a brick wall. All June ever does is talk down to me and slam my suggestions. I'm getting pretty sick of being treated like a clown.'

'Coffee?' Elaine asked hopefully.

'Absolutely, let's go.'

She could always invite Mark from across the way. He was good looking in a God-don't-I-know-it kind of way. He was well educated – boarding school, commerce degree, masters in finance. And was sociable – well, he was with women anyway judging by the amount of female traffic going in and out of his front door every weekend. Anna lived across the road from Mark in Ranelagh. She had done for years. The only difference was he owned his own house, which by now was worth a small fortune, and Anna rented hers along with four other people she didn't know. That's because Mark had been a good boy in UCD, playing his rugby, attending all his lectures, evenings spent in the library, two summers in Nantucket, Saturday nights in Kiely's and the rugby club. Perfect.

Anna, on the other hand, had studied Philosophy and Greek and Roman civilization (very interesting subjects but not ones that got you a lucrative job in Finance), got completely sloshed in the UCD bar four days a week (not including nights), hung around alternative people who'd since disappeared off the face of the earth, and then fecked around Europe for two years before securing herself a pensionable punishing position at Lolta's.

Anyway perhaps Mark wasn't the best bet. Anna wanted someone sociable but not too sociable. Imagine if he copped off with one of Victoria's single friends at the party. God it would be too humiliating by far. No, Mark was not a good idea. Besides, he'd only think she fancied him which would be absolutely ridiculous when they both knew they were strictly friends.

'But you see people are far more fashion conscious these days. And they're also insisting on quality. People know the value of a good pair of shoes.'

'Yes indeed.' Anna nodded vigorously as Elaine wrapped up her ten-minute speech on modern footwear. 'I completely agree, Elaine, I think you've hit the nail on the head there.'

They went downstairs to find the staff gathered in a circle chatting about their current flings. God, you couldn't trust them an inch. As Anna and Elaine marched towards them the crowd dispersed. Wow, the power of being a department manager!

Jeans were the most consistent sellers, Anna noted. In fact they sold so well they were never reduced in the sale. That made sense, didn't it? Only the crap was reduced, and to think grown women actually fought over it! Mind you, June wouldn't be impressed by that fact alone. Anna went through the list.

Party wear was incredibly slow. Coats had shot up since they'd been slashed to half price the week before. The new spring collection hadn't exactly taken off, which wasn't too surprising when you considered it was still January and too cold to be buying flimsy cotton twinsets.

'What about knitwear?' June barked, her beady eyes bulging.

'Knitwear's fine,' Anna was managing to remain remarkably calm.

'Be more specific.' She picked up a chenille turtle-neck. 'What about these, how many units were sold last week?'

'Eighteen,' Anna made a wild guess.

'Twelve is the figure I have.'

Well, if you already knew why did you ask me, you stupid frustrated cow?

God the woman was so negative. Always looking for a chance to catch Anna out. If she'd listen to her suggestions about merchandising, it would be more to the point. Anna knew she had a great eye for what drew the punters in.

'I want you to ring around Navan, Drogheda, Dundalk and Kildare and find out how their knit-wear is selling in comparison. I'll expect that report on my desk by five.' She stormed off.

Anna stared after her skinny little frame. She was tempted to raise two fingers but was aware of her position of responsibility as a department manager and therefore refrained. June seemed to be on some kind of mission recently to make Anna's life hell. It didn't really matter how many polo necks Kildare sold. There was much more to life. There was bound to be a war going on somewhere in the world. Or an earthquake. She was still single at thirty. Now that was more serious than a few polo necks. The retail business, which she normally thrived on, was beginning to get her down. Oh how nice it would be to win the lotto and set up her own fancy boutique in somewhere like Spain, say, where she could dress elegant women. Pick out clothes that would really really suit them. To live in such a warm sunny place would be bliss, wouldn't it? Marbella, say. Lots of Irish people were buying places down there. A place where you couldn't see your breath every morning in the chilly hallway, where goddam students didn't let down the state of the place with their bicycles, where fifty-pence pieces didn't run away with your hot water, where strangers couldn't listen to your phone calls because the communal phone was placed strategically in the hallway within hearing distance of all and sundry and where people didn't have parties full of other people who didn't have to get up in the morning.

Anna rang Kildare and waited for the department manager to come back with the knitwear sales. Oh to turn up one morning with sunglasses perched on top of her head, a suitcase under her arm and a one-way ticket to the sun. Then she'd tell June Neelane to get all her knitwear and stuff it up her you know what.

By the time the cleaners had gone Anna was exhausted. It had been an excruciatingly long day with constant deliveries and staff shortages. She set the shop alarm and let herself out of the side door. It was a dull damp winter's night and the thought of sitting in her dark damp dreary flat did nothing to raise her spirits. God, she hated January. It should be abolished from the calendar altogether.

She'd love to pop over to Claire's. Claire's house was always lovely and warm with a friendly fire crackling in the grate. Claire's kitchen presses were always stacked with good food, and expensive wine was always chilling in the fridge. Andrew would be lying peacefully among his teddies in his little yellow cot and Simon would be sitting on the sofa fidgeting with the *FT*.

No, she wouldn't call in. If she called in she wouldn't want to leave and Simon would start yawning in a desperate attempt to get her to go. Or offer to drive her home before it got too late. She couldn't call in to Elaine either. Elaine would have finished her yoga by now and would be preparing for a sensible early night in preparation for another early start. And anyway Elaine thought anybody who drank alcoholic units on a weeknight was definitely an alcoholic. And at that very minute Anna would almost kill for an alcoholic unit.

It was unfair when you thought about it, Anna decided as she walked the main street in Ranelagh and passed its many busy pubs. If she were a man she could quite easily go in, prop herself up at the bar with a pint, and either watch the match of the day or enjoy an aimless chat with the barman. But as a woman, she'd do nothing but attract unwanted stares and, God forbid, if she chatted to the barman, he'd probably presume she was gagging for it. No wonder so many women drank at home on the QT.

Anna popped into Centra and bought *OK*, a walnut whip, a tin of spaghetti hoops, a low-fat yoghurt, two scratch cards, the *Evening Herald* and a two-litre Diet 7-Up. Was she imagining it or did the young Chinese chap behind the counter look at her pitifully as he placed her goods in a white plastic bag? Oh, maybe she was just being paranoid. Surely Ranelagh was full of women living on their own. She wasn't any different. Anyway there was nothing *wrong* with being single. Single was sexy. Better than separated. You only had to look at poor Elaine. Be positive, Anna told herself and quickened her step, remember you're one of those uptown girls everybody's talking about.

Anna jabbed her key into the big green door. Well, it used to be green in its day, but it could surely do with a lick of paint. She looked in the cubbyhole beside the phone for her post. Nothing for her. Only a flyer for Pizzaland and a brochure on central heating. It's a pity the landlord wouldn't take note, Anna thought ruefully as she closed the door behind her. Suddenly there was a big bang. She found herself in darkness. Shit, the bulb in the hallway had blown. That was all she needed. She shuffled along in complete blackness, keeping close to the wall. She hit something. It fell. There was a crash. She screamed. Her leg hurt. The door of the downstairs flat swung open allowing light to flood into the hallway.

'Are you all right?'

She looked up. She blinked hard. No, she wasn't dreaming. No, she hadn't hit her head, only her leg, so she couldn't be hallucinating. But something was clearly amiss for the guy holding her hand as well as holding her gaze with huge dark-brown eyes, was the cute student guy from downstairs. Good God, he really looked the spitting image of Johnny Depp up close. Not the way he looks now, but remember him in *21 Jump Street*?

'I'm so sorry about the bike,' the vision spoke. 'The light to the hall seems to have blown. Is your leg hurting?'

'It is a bit,' Anna mumbled. Actually it wasn't really sore at all. But still, that didn't mean she was about to hobble up the stairs and out of the vision's life for ever.

He and his flatmate (whose name turned out to be Martin) helped her into the downstairs flat. A small fire was lit and empty wine bottles cum candle-holders were placed around the room. A stunningly beautiful girl with straggly brown hair was sitting on the sofa, dressed in something that looked like a carpet. She was obviously a student. The walls were decorated with pictures of your man from *The Doors* and the guy from *Nirvana* who committed suicide. *The Charletans* were playing (on the radio of course). The place was strangely comfortable except for the girl. Not that she was deliberately making the place uncomfortable, but still she was a girl and a very pretty one at that.

'I'm Suzie,' she smiled. 'Can I get you a cup of tea?'

The last thing Anna felt like was a cup of tea but she was afraid that if she said no she couldn't justify staying in the flat a little longer. So she agreed.

'Maybe Anna would like a beer?' the vision suggested.

It was exactly what Anna preferred. She wondered how he knew her name.

'From the phone,' he explained. 'Your mother's always looking for you.'

Great, Anna thought, that will be terrific for my street cred. But why would her mother be ringing her when she knew she'd be at work? Checking up on her as usual, the nosy cow. Making sure Anna was at work and not 'pulling a sickie'! Typical.

'I'm Steve.' He shook Anna's hand. He'd the longest, darkest eyelashes she'd ever seen. He looked her up and down, taking in her smart navy suit and briefcase. 'We just moved in a few weeks ago, so excuse the state of the place. We haven't exactly got round to buying furniture and stuff.'

'That's okay,' Anna said coyly. *She could always sit on his knee.*

'So what do you do with yourself?'

'Retail manger.' She blushed without knowing why. 'And you?'

'Student,' he laughed, 'in case you hadn't noticed.'

Anna laughed too. 'Er, what year?' she asked cautiously. If he said first or second she'd be out of there so fast, sore foot or not.

'Fourth year,' Steve said as Anna breathed a short sigh of relief. 'Actually I should have finished already but I took a year out to travel around France.'

'Do you speak French?' Anna was delighted.

'*Bien sûr.*'

'Do you like Paris?' Anna was wildly conjuring up images of the romantic city, leisurely walks along the Champs-Élysées, sipping *café au lait* in Montmartre.

'Oh yes,' Steve said dreamily, 'my girlfriend lives there.'

'Oh right.'

Anna turned towards the beauty on the sofa.

'Not me,' Suzie giggled, 'I'm Steve's cousin, Martin's girlfriend,' she explained.

'Oh right,' Anna said again a bit more enthusiastically. So the girlfriend was in Paris. Oh well, not to worry. Out of sight, out of mind and all that. Anna began to relax. The beer was very good.

'Actually we're having a party tonight,' Martin said brightly. 'You're very welcome to come along.'

'Thank you,' Anna grinned. Tuesday night. Of course they *always* had parties on Tuesdays. She might as well stick around. No point in not going to it. Sure wouldn't she only be tossing and turning upstairs trying to block out the noise?

Martin handed her another beer. He was very

plain, Lord love him. She wondered how he got together with the lovely Suzie. Maybe he'd an engaging personality. He seemed pretty decent anyway.

'Do you want me to stick your groceries in the fridge?' Steve went to pick up her stuff.

'No, I er . . . no thanks, honestly.' *God, no!*

'Shall I take your coat?'

'Oh all right so.' She handed it over reluctantly. She wondered did her legs look big in the short skirt. At least she was wearing thick black tights. Marvellous!

There was a knock on the door.

'That must be Grainne.'

'Who's Grainne?' Anna asked.

'Don't you know her?' Steve went to answer the door. 'She's one of the nurses upstairs.'

Great.

Grainne was a plump girl with wild black curls and a cheeky face. She bounced into the room with a six-pack. 'Hey, folks!'

She looked curiously at Anna. 'Your face is awful familiar,' she said.

'I live underneath you.'

'Oh right. You do the *Mr Motivator* video sometimes, don't you? I'd know his voice anywhere.'

This created a bit of a laugh.

Another knock. Sandra. Another nurse. Where were the men? What kind of party was this?

'I didn't realize the party was semi-formal,' Sandra said snidely, referring to Anna's suit.

'I've just come from work,' Anna said, 'I'm a manager, I don't wear a uniform, you know.'

'Turn off that shit and stick on Britney,' Grainne shrieked. 'Or ABBA.'

'They always do this to me,' Steve chuckled. 'They're always bossing me around.'

And you obviously enjoy it, Anna thought. If it was my flat I'd have booted them out long ago.

Two more guests arrived. Eddie and Greg. Both engineers. The party began. Conversations flowed. Beer flowed. Anna relaxed. The nurses relaxed. Maybe they weren't so bad after all. Steve relaxed but not as much as Anna would have liked. He kept his hands to himself. Maybe he did fancy this bird in Paris after all. Foreign women had a habit of snatching vulnerable Irish men. It was their sallow skin. And skinny hips. And the way they were totally uninhibited about their sexuality.

'So, are you going out with anyone yourself?' Suzie asked sweetly. She seemed that sort of girl. Sweet.

'Not at the moment, no,' Anna answered. 'I'm concentrating on my career.'

It wasn't exactly the type of thing you'd normally say to another woman. But she was a cousin of Steve's, which meant that anything she said could technically be repeated to Steve.

'I'm also very fussy,' Anna added. Fussy was good. It meant that she wouldn't go with just anything. She hoped that one would get back to Steve. She noticed

Suzie looking a bit miffed. Uh oh! *Fussy* wasn't a good word. After all, Martin was no oil painting. Sugar! Best to change the subject. Fast.

'So what age are you?' Anna asked.

'Twenty,' Suzie smiled, all sweet again.

Good God! Twenty! Almost ten years younger than herself. That meant that when Anna had been twenty, Suzie had been ten. What age was Steve then? What age were they all?

'What age are you?' Suzie wanted to know.

'Twenty-six,' Anna lied.

'Are you serious?' Suzie's eyes opened wide. 'And you never married? No kids or anything?'

'Don't kill me off just yet,' Anna gave a short laugh. 'Why, what age is er . . . Martin?' She didn't want to be too obvious.

'Twenty-two. Steve's twenty-three,' she added much to Anna's relief. Thank *God*. Twenty-three was young but better than say . . . eighteen. Still he'd probably look too young at Victoria's party. Unless he wore a suit. And pretended he was a real engineer. Then again, what if he met a real engineer?

It was all a bit complicated.

She'd think about it again in the morning. When she was sober. She looked at her watch. Midnight. The party showed no sign of slowing down. The two nurses were dancing to Samantha Mumba. The two engineers were smoking something with a strong smell. Suzie was passing round a bowl of peanuts. Steve was just sitting there. Divine!

The beer had run out and so had the fags.

'I've some in my flat.' Anna jumped up. No point closing the party down just 'cos the ciggies had run out.

She legged it up the stairs, grabbed the cigs and a cheap bottle of wine someone had brought to her last party. She was all set. She felt her way downstairs, carefully. No point falling and breaking a leg. Something grabbed her waist. She screamed.

'Sssh,' a soft sexy voice whispered. His breath was warm against her face. His hands felt strong around her waist.

'Steve?'

'Mmm.'

She pressed herself against him and ran some fingers through his hair. It felt short. Steve's hair wasn't short.

'Who is this?'

'Eddie . . . God, you're gorgeous, so voluptuous, so . . .'

'Get lost would you,' Anna pushed him out of the way. The bloody nerve!

'Sorry,' he mumbled and slunk back down the stairs.

Anna pulled herself together. This was a bit of a disaster. She didn't really feel like going back down to the party now. Her head was spinning. She *should* go back down though. To Steve. She shouldn't leave him down there with those raunchy nurses. But then again, she couldn't turn in to work tomorrow with a hangover. She went back into the room and lit a cigarette. Steve was really something. If only she looked like Brigitte Bardot and spoke in a seductive French accent. If only she wasn't pissed out of her head. Sure no wonder she was feeling groggy. She hadn't had a bite to eat since lunch.

She kicked off her shoes and put her feet up on the bed. She flicked her cigarette ash into an empty teacup. She couldn't think straight. For a second she wished she was a student and didn't have to get up in the morning. Or a nightwatchman. Or a nurse who worked the nightshift.

Somebody knocked on her door. God if that Eddie hadn't got the message, he'd soon get it now. She jumped off the bed, stuck her shoes on and flung open the door. It was Steve. Anna opened her mouth and shut it again.

'Are you making the cigarettes up yourself, or what?' He leaned on the doorframe and grinned.

'Er no, not at all, I was just about to bring them down.'

'What's the wine? Is it French?'

Anna checked the label quickly. 'Yes it is,' she whispered, mesmerized, taking in his perfect mouth, high cheekbones and dark eyes all at once. 'And I've two glasses,' she added.

'Have you any objections to drinking the wine up here . . . together?'

'Well no . . . But what about the others?'

'They're all right. Suzie and Martin have called

it a night. Eddie is snogging Grainne. Sandra is just about to pass out and Greg has gone home.'

'OK. Have you got a corkscrew?'

He produced one from behind his back. She removed her jacket. He hung it up. They both removed their shoes. He poured the wine. She drank it. He lit her cigarette. She smoked it. He turned out the lights. She . . .

Chapter Four

They stood on top of the Eiffel Tower. She wore a long, flowing, white viscose dress. He wore black tie. She was thin. Very thin. And tanned. He held her tight in case somehow she might escape from him and shatter the lovely illusion. Somewhere in the distance a phone rang . . . and rang and . . . JESUS CHRIST!

Anna jumped out of bed like a shot. What time was it? Oh no, oh God, no this wasn't funny. Where was her bloody watch? Her heart was racing as she tore the sheets off the empty bed, desperately searching for her watch. Steve was gone but that didn't matter right now. The sun was streaming through the crack in the curtain letting her know that it was very, very late. The phone rang. Jesus, her ass was really on the line now. Eventually she caught sight of the watchstrap sticking out from under the bed. She picked it up. Oh Jesus, no! Ten past ten. An hour and forty minutes late. The phone kept ringing. She threw on her old dressing gown and slippers and headed downstairs, trying to think of a good excuse.

'Hello?' she croaked into the phone. Her voice sounded dreadful.

'Anna?' It was Mr Evans's voice. Evans was the store manager and reasonable enough most of the time. But this morning *he* sounded none too impressed.

'Oh Mr Evans, is that you?'

'Anna, are you sick?'

'Mr Evans, I hardly got a wink of sleep,' she said truthfully, 'I feel wretched.'

'Is it something you consumed?'

'Very possibly.' Anna couldn't believe how well she was doing and she didn't even have to lie.

'Do you feel well enough to come in?'

'If I really had to I would, but to be honest . . .'

'Listen, Anna, if it's a bug I don't want it going around the store. Take today off and we'll see you tomorrow if you're feeling better then.'

'Yes, Mr Evans, I'm so sorry about all of this. I promise to rest myself, don't worry.'

The door of the downstairs flat opened and Steve appeared in a black T-shirt and boxers. His hair was all messy and cute. He winked at her. 'That's right, Mr Evans, I think I'll head back to bed right this minute. Goodbye, Mr Evans.' She hung up.

'Nice one,' Steve grinned.

'Did I sound convincing enough?'

'I almost believed you myself. Anyway why would he doubt you? It's Wednesday. People don't usually ring in with hangovers on a Wednesday.'

'That's true.'

'And you promised your boss you'd do something straightaway. Now I'm going to see to it that promises don't get broken.'

Herbert Park was quiet apart from the ducks and a couple of joggers. Anna and Steve strolled hand in hand across the grass. Anna was wearing his red woolly hat in case anybody from work recognized her. They sat on the deserted kiddies' swings and talked about life. He'd travelled a lot. As had she. He loved animals. Anna also loved animals. He loved art. So did she *now*. Neither of them mentioned the French girl and Anna had no intention of bringing her up.

It was late when they got back. The house was quiet. He made her tea. They listened to music. He was still too young to go to the party, Anna decided, but not too young to fall in love with. For a while.

'Anna, what a surprise!' Claire held the door open with one hand, Andrew was supported by the other. 'Why aren't you at work?'

Anna leaned forward and planted a kiss on Andrew's soft baby cheek. She stepped into the hallway. 'Sorry to butt in like this but it's an emergency.'

'What's new?'

'I would have phoned but I couldn't. Long story.'

'You should get yourself a mobile.'

'No way, I can't stand the things. I really don't

understand why people want to make themselves available twenty-four hours a day. Do you know what I saw the other day? This couple walking down Baggot Street hand in hand, both talking on their mobiles. It was so sad.'

'Come into the kitchen and relax. It's nice and warm in there.'

They sat down. Andrew tugged his mother's hair and gurgled. It was as if he knew something was up.

'Well?' Claire raised her eyebrows.

'I met a man,' Anna announced, pleased as punch.

'Where?'

'At home in Ranelagh.'

'I knew it!'

'What? You couldn't possibly . . .'

'You always sort of had a thing for Mark!'

'I did not.'

'Did too. You were always going on about how good looking he was.'

'I was not,' Anna said indignantly. 'I still think he's good looking, but I would certainly not get involved with him. God, no. Anyway, it's somebody else. His name's Steve. He's a twenty-three-year-old engineering student who looks like a God and has the sensitivity of an angel.'

'Oh please, I've heard it all now.'

'I'm serious, Claire, this could be the one.'

'The one? Anna, *I'm* serious, I'm beginning to think you're a burger short of a Big Mac. You're old enough to be his mother!'

'Age shouldn't be an obstacle in the path of true love,' Anna spoke solemnly.

'It'll never work.'

'You always say that.'

'And I've been right . . . so far.'

'Well done.'

'Listen,' Claire wiped Andrew's dribbling mouth with his bib, 'I don't want to be the one to put a dampener on things, but seven years is too . . .'

'You're right, I'll go straight home and tell him to stay the hell away from me.'

'Just be careful, that's all.'

Steve held the big green door open, a deep-red rose between his teeth.

'How did you know it was me? It could have been the landlord,' Anna giggled.

'I was watching you come down the road. Hungry?'

'Starving.'

'It's just as well I'm cooking.'

'Is there anything you can't do?'

She followed him into his flat; a rich smell of curry came from the kitchen. Yummy. The phone rang outside.

'Can you get that?' Steve asked. 'By the time you come back in dinner will be served.'

Anna stepped out into the hallway and picked up the phone.

'Hello?' *Please let it not be my mother*, she begged.

'Allo?' The voice seemed very far away.

'Hello, yes?'

'Allo, ees Stephan zere?'

'Er no . . . he's not here at the moment. Who's this?'

'Claudine, 'ee told me ee'd be 'ome zees evening.'

'Did he now?'

'Can you give message?'

'All right.'

'Tell 'im I 'ave bought my plane teecket and I will be in Irlande zees Friday.'

Chapter Five

The silver Mercedes convertible screeched to a halt, soaking Anna's silk stockings.

'Jesus Christ,' she cried as she spotted the dirty spatters all across her Pretty Polly legs.

'Would you like a lift?' Mark Landon stuck his head out of the driver's window.

'Oh, I might as well,' Anna muttered ungraciously and opened the passenger door. 'And could you stop off at a shop so I can replace my stockings.'

'Now you're pushing it,' Mark laughed. He looked well. Mark always took care of himself. Today he wore a sharp charcoal-grey suit, a crisp white shirt and a royal-blue tie. His aftershave was strong and he looked exquisite. He edged his way into the thick Dublin traffic.

'You're looking well,' Mark said. It was always the first thing he said to her. It didn't matter if she was posting a letter with a face full of spots and a head full of chip grease or if she'd just spent four hours in the hairdressers.

'Thank you,' Anna replied dryly. 'So do you.'

'How's the love life?' That was always Mark's first question. God, she could read him like a book.

'Great.'

Mark gave her a puzzled look. This wasn't the answer he usually got. And he wasn't going to be satisfied with a monosyllabic answer.

'Who is he?'

'That's for me to know and you to find out.'

'You're very annoying. I will find out, you know.'

'Oh I know.'

'Is he . . . he's not famous or anything?'

'No.'

'Thank God for that.' A pause. 'Was he at UCD?'

'Actually . . . yes, kind of.' *He's there now.*

'I'd probably know him then, wouldn't I?'

'No.'

'I give up.'

'So how's your love life?'

'I'm still going out with Sally.'

'Still?' Anna knitted her eyebrows. 'Last time I spoke to you it was Elourda.'

'Oh yeah, it didn't work out between Ellie and myself.'

'You mean you dumped her?'

'You know I've no intention of answering that.'

'So Sally is girlfriend of the month. Let me guess, what does she look like . . . tall, blonde, busty, vacant-looking?'

'Don't be nasty, I wouldn't be nasty about your man.'

'You should meet him.'

'Where does he live?'

'With me.'

'What!' Mark nearly crashed the car.

'He lives in the flat downstairs.'

'You mean he's one of the students?'

'Yep.'

'Cradlesnatcher.'

'See, I knew you'd be nasty.'

He stopped the car outside Lolta's. She got out and smiled, 'Thanks for the lift, Mark. See you soon.'

'Sure and good luck with the student.'

'Yeah and good luck with silly Sally.'

'She's not silly.'

'What is she – a nail technician?'

'A doctor.'

Anna closed the passenger door firmly, waved brightly and walked away quickly. Shit, she really put her foot in that one. She hated Mark to outsmart her. And she hated him to be going out with someone intelligent. The bimbos she didn't mind – she could ridicule them privately and know that Mark would soon get bored. But a female doctor? Now she didn't like the sound of that. Doctors were very serious about everything.

As a department manager the trouble with a day off was that you'd twice the workload the following day. Because no one else could do your work for you. Elaine only knew about footwear. Conor only knew about household and Maggie only knew about children's wear. That's the way things worked in Lolta's. Nobody knew anything about anything. Except June. And she knew too much.

June was a funny creature. Not funny as in ha! ha! But as in weird. And sad really when you thought about it. Because although June had donated her whole life to Lolta's would she ever get thanked for it? Never. And neither would Elaine. And that was the truth. Manager or not, you were still another number on the payroll and the day you left that number would promptly be deleted from the computer. Fact.

Anna had entered the retail business after stints at working in shops and bars all across Europe. People often questioned her choice of career – the long hours and constant dealings with the public. But Anna could not even imagine working in, say, an office with people constantly breathing down her neck all day. At least in Lolta's she was given a good bit of responsibility and no two days were ever the same. One day she'd have her own store and run it the way she wanted to. But there was no point leaving Lolta's until she had as much experience as possible. Her main issue with Lolta's was her dislike of the clothes; the head buyers there had a penchant for poor quality clothing that would soon be found in heaps in fields all around Ireland whenever the travelling community decided to move on.

'Anna!' A piercing shriek broke her thoughts. June

was looking for sales of the hideous flowery skirts brought in yesterday.

'We haven't sold any,' Anna explained. 'It's too early. People aren't going to buy that stuff in January.' *Or any time unless they're colour blind.*

'I suggest you stick one in the window display. Match it with a catchy top.'

Here we go again, Anna thought. 'Do we have a catchy top?'

June gave her a cold, hard stare. 'I'll leave it to you,' she said frostily.

'Bridget, can I have a word?'

Bridget was one of the part-time girls. A pleasant, hard-working girl with bobbed brown hair and glasses. She hurried over to the desk looking terribly anxious.

Anna gave her a huge smile. 'Would you ever get a good spot in the window for that new flowery skirt – you know the hideous one with the flowers?'

'Oh yes.' Bridget nodded solemnly.

'Maybe you could dress it up with one of our catchy tops?' Anna said hopefully.

'Catchy tops?'

Anna was delighted to find Bridget looking as bewildered as she felt. 'I trust you, Bridget.' She gave her an encouraging wink.

Oh the joys of delegation! Anna didn't have time to be fretting over ridiculous-looking garments. It was mad putting stuff like that in the window. It would scare your granny so it would. If you put up a *Pickpockets are Welcome* sign, you'd probably draw in more punters. Anyway she had to sort out this whole mess she'd got herself into, namely Steve (or Stephan) and this mademoiselle from Paris. The more she thought about it, the more she wished she'd told him straightaway. That Claudine was coming this weekend. This weekend! The timing couldn't be worse. If she didn't tell him at all then he might go home to Kilkenny and Anna could answer the door and tell her he'd emigrated or something. Could she live with the guilt? Probably. Could she risk the fact that he might find out and hate her for ever? No. Then again, she'd be doing Claudine a favour.

He wasn't worthy of her love. Or a £159 return ticket. He'd cheated on her, for God's sake. He'd do it again *if Anna had anything to do with it.*

Claudine must be stopped. She mustn't make that wasted journey. Anna would save her much heartache in the long run. God, could somebody please inspire her and tell her what to do?

Chapter Six

'Anna, we've got to talk.' The familiar glint had disappeared from Steve's dark eyes.

'I know,' she said, aware that the talk mightn't be great fun. Men never wanted to talk. Unless of course it was trying to talk you into the sack. But, more often than not, when men tried to talk it usually meant they never wanted to talk again. To you. Or see you ... Or snog you. Well, maybe snog you. Occasionally. If there was nobody else about. But only if you understood that the snog wasn't going to lead to anything else. *Anything more meaningful.* 'Okay, shoot,' she told him.

They were sitting in Steve's flat, which was now significantly less inviting than it had been the night of the party. The expression on Kurt Curbain's black and white face was painful. Probably as painful as the look she herself was sporting, Anna thought glumly.

'Would you like a cigarette?' He held out a near empty carton of Marlboro Lights.

'No thanks,' she shook her head, 'I'll probably need one more after the talk.'

'Remember I told you about the girl in Paris?'

'Vaguely,' Anna sniffed. 'As far as I remember you mentioned her the first night we met, but I don't recall any reference after that.'

'I'm sorry.' Steve stared at the ground. He looked perfectly stunning tonight. And younger than usual, but perhaps that was just an illusion. 'I'm racked with guilt.'

'Oh.'

'She's coming to Dublin tonight.'

'Oh.'

'I only found out this evening. Apparently she rang on Wednesday but one of the nurses must have forgotten to give me the message.'

'Oh.' It was now Anna's turn to feel guilty.

'So . . . God, I hate doing this . . . but we can't see each other again.'

'Oh.'

'I'm sorry.'

'Yes.'

'Do you hate me for doing this?'

'No . . . but to be honest it's a bit silly you telling me you can't see me again when I live upstairs.'

Steve gave a short laugh. 'I know, it does sound silly.'

'Right then.' She stood up. 'I'll be off.'

'Do you mind terribly?' He looked beautiful. She wanted to kill him but she was too upset.

'Mind?' she shrilled. 'Mind? I couldn't give a shit.'

'Oh.' It was Steve's turn to look hurt.

'Well, good luck.' She made for the door.

'Sorry.'

She closed the door gently. Paused for a moment. Contemplated going back in and abusing him.

Decided against it. Gave his bicycle an almighty kick. And stormed upstairs.

The flat was cold. It was always cold. And cheerless. She didn't turn on the light. Turning on the light might be interpreted as a positive action. And she didn't feel positive at all. She turned on the little fan heater and dragged it over to the window. She sat on the tiny stool there and stared numbly through the draughty window. The light in Mark's front room was on and she could see a table was set. For two. How nice. And Steve and Claudine would be two tonight. Also very nice. And she, Anna, would be one. Eating for one, sleeping as one and feeling miserable as one.

She had to ring Claire. Claire would be so sympathetic and wouldn't say, 'I told you so.' She never did. At least not straightaway. But she couldn't ring from the phone downstairs. Not while Steve was still in the building. God, it was very annoying. She should get herself a mobile. Even if it did do damage to your ear and irritated the life out of strangers all around you. Eventually she heard him leave. It was upsetting to hear him go. It meant that he wasn't going to change his mind and come up the stairs to tell her he'd made a terrible mistake and beg her forgiveness.

She ran downstairs and rang Claire.

'He's gone,' she wailed.

'Oh you poor pet.' Claire sounded appropriately distraught.

'It's so unfair. I thought I was falling in love with him.'

'Yes, but you have to remember you didn't know him very long,' Claire reminded her.

'Will you come out with me for a few consolation drinks?'

'I can't, Anna, I'm in the middle of cooking. Simon's got some friends calling round.'

'Who?'

'John, Richard and Jake.'

'All married?'

'Jake isn't.'

'And he's the ugly one, I suppose.'

'He's not bad, I don't really know him that well.'

'Can I come round and help out?'

'You mean . . .'

'No, I don't mean just to eat all your food. I'd love to help out . . . genuinely.'

She wore a black velvet dress to the knee, black patent shoes with a slight heel, small diamante earrings and twisted her fair hair into a high ponytail. She eyed herself doubtfully in the mirror. If these guys were hotshot traders, they'd probably admire glamorous, chic-looking women. Anna pulled on her black wool, full-length coat and wrapped herself in a grey cashmere scarf. This was about as glamorous as she got.

Simon nearly died when he saw her standing at the door.

'Don't worry, I'm here to help.' Anna pushed past him into the hallway. Simon would be mortified by a woman showing up on a lads' night out. Simon was a man's man, and although Claire raved about him, he wasn't exactly Anna's cup of tea. Anna was way too independent for the likes of Simon.

Claire was completely freaking out over chicken à la king.

The doorbell rang loudly.

'Oh God,' Claire panicked, 'they're early. Oh no, Simon's gone up to have a shower. You wouldn't entertain them in the drawing room, offer them a drink or something?'

'No better woman,' Anna grinned. 'Do I look okay? Has my ponytail fallen down or anything?'

'No, you look fine. Go on, run.'

Anna braced herself at the hall door. She took a deep breath. Calm, cool and sophisticated – her image for tonight. She opened the door. A well-built man of average height with a nicer than average face, a short haircut and a smile, stood there. He was holding a plant. He looked mildly confused.

'Oh you shouldn't have,' Anna giggled as she stretched out her hand to receive the plant.

'Er . . . this is Simon and . . . ?'

'Yes, Simon and Claire's house, only Claire has

been replaced by a younger model called Anna.
I'm Anna.'

'You're . . .'

'Joking, yes of course I'm joking. I'm Claire's best
friend, come in.'

Jake, yes it must be Jake (because he wasn't wearing a ring), threw back his head and roared with
laughter.

'You're brilliant,' he yelled enthusiastically. 'God,
you'd almost got me there, ha ha!'

Anna was delighted. She'd made a good impression already. She hadn't meant to be funny. The
thing about the plant had come from nowhere.
Probably something to do with the glass of white
wine she'd gulped down behind Claire's back.

'If I'd known you were going to be here I'd have
brought a second plant,' he laughed.

'Oh well, next time.' Anna took his coat. 'Drink?'

'Yes, and I smoke too.'

They both laughed.

'Seriously though, I could murder a G&T,' he
said.

'There's ice in the fridge.' Claire fingered the
chicken and frowned. 'It seems to be all right now.'

'So, where have you been hiding Jake all these
years?' Anna demanded as she poured a generous
measure of gin.

'Ah, leave Jake alone, he's not so bad. Stop being
so sarcastic,' Claire scolded.

'I'm not being sarcastic. I'm serious. He's a good

laugh. He'd be perfect for Victoria's party. He'd know Simon so I wouldn't have to look after him for the evening. Perfect.'

Claire stared at her friend suspiciously. 'You *can't* be serious. Jake's not your type at all.'

'Well, let me be the judge of that.'

'You're on the rebound, Anna.'

'Ah, don't be daft. Steve – stunning as he was – lasted little longer than a one-night stand. Besides he was too immature for me.'

Anna was tired of Claire's pessimistic attitude, this firm belief that Anna couldn't make anything work with anyone, that she was a walking disaster with an 'ABUSE ME' sign firmly painted on her forehead. Jake mightn't be Russell Crowe but he wasn't bad.

The doorbell rang again.

'You get that,' Anna told Claire, 'while I bring Jake his drink.' There was no point making small talk with the married ones. They might think she was charming but who cared? They were taken!

'Do you know that gin can be a depressant?' Anna handed Jake his drink.

'No way.'

'Seriously, it's a medical fact I think. People can get angry because of gin.'

'Ah nonsense.' Jake knocked back half the glass. He swallowed hard and blinked twice. 'Get lost, Fatso.'

Anna stared, completely stunned.

'Jesus, you're right,' he laughed unselfconsciously, 'It's having a terrible impact on me.'

Anna gave a surprised laugh. Jesus, that wasn't much of a joke. If he'd called her *Bony* or even *Thicko* it wouldn't have been so bad. But *Fatso*? No, that was way too rude. That's what Victoria had always called her. God, on second thoughts maybe it wouldn't be such a good idea to invite Jake to Victoria's. They might gang up on her!

She gave him a watery smile. 'Perhaps you should have a beer,' she whispered.

John and Richard entered the room and shook Anna's hand formally. They were all business. Both wore glasses. John's hair was badly receding. Richard was grey all over. Shocking. And these guys were only in their mid-thirties! Well, Jake looked very handsome indeed beside his two colleagues. Anna decided she'd give him a second chance. After all she shouldn't be too quick to jump down people's throats.

'Drinks, gentlemen?' she offered.

'I'll have a white wine spritzer.' John was folding his grey rain mac.

'And I'll have a Ballygowan,' said Richard, 'No ice.'

She fled the room.

'I'm not going back in there.' Anna slumped down on one of the kitchen chairs and zapped the remote control. 'Oh, *Fair City*. Great.'

'You don't watch *Fair City*.' Claire prodded the

Black Forest Gateau ice cream to see if it had begun to thaw.

'I do now.'

'God, Anna, you have to make more of an effort. You can be very unsociable at times.'

'I'm sociable when I meet interesting people.' Anna popped a cherry tomato into her mouth when Claire wasn't watching. 'It's just that those guys in there . . . well, they'd put a bloody insomniac into a coma. I mean, I can't understand it, they're ugly men, right? But they've good jobs and therefore probably had no difficulty getting two wives for themselves. But if you took two equivalent women, say, they'd have a much harder time getting two husbands because a lot of men prefer good-looking women to women who have good careers. Do you see what I mean? Women get a pretty raw deal when you think about it.'

'Listen,' Claire moved the bowl of cherry tomatoes out of Anna's reach, 'I don't have time to be contemplating life and all its faults. I've Simon and Andrew to keep my mind full.'

'Ah Claire, you're becoming one of those women we always swore we'd never become – you know, babies, husbands, nappies, Volvos, bills and washing machines.'

Claire feigned sudden shock. She peeled off her apron, threw it on the table and placed her fists defiantly on her slim hips. 'I should throw you out,' she threatened playfully.

'I'll only leave if you absolutely promise to come on a girls' night out tomorrow.'

'It's just that . . .'

'I'm serious, now or never.'

'Right, if it will shut you up.'

Anna stood up. 'I'd stay and help you clean up and that . . . but it's been a long day and I don't want to get in anyone's way . . .'

'Go,' Claire ordered and opened the kitchen door into the hall.

'Goodnight.' She kissed her friend's cheek. 'Should I go in and say goodnight to the lads?'

'Better not,' Claire said wisely. 'I'll give them your regards. And eh . . . don't worry about the student. He didn't sound that great to begin with.'

Anna closed the door behind her and the icy January air immediately bit her uncovered skin. She delved deep into her coat pockets to retrieve her gloves. It was true. Steve wasn't any great shakes. And had never realistically been a contender for *Ideal Date of the Year* award. But still she wasn't looking forward to going back to the empty flat knowing that the man who'd just rejected her was living under the same roof. She began the walk home.

As she neared the house she noticed the lights in the downstairs flat were on and the curtains hadn't been drawn. She wondered if the beautiful Claudine had already flown in from the French capital and whether she was now murmuring sweet nothings into smitten Steve's ear.

As she neared the front door, keys dangling in her right hand, she heard loud voices. The door opened slightly. Anna's blood ran cold. Oh God, what was she going to do?

She could always dive into the long grass that was supposed to be a garden, but that would look pretty pathetic. Desperate even. She took a deep breath and a bold step forward.

Steve's face appeared. He caught Anna's eye like a rabbit caught in unexpected headlights. They both froze.

'Er . . . Anna. How are you?'

'Fine.' Anna's voice was stilted. She craned her neck for a view of the buxom Brigitte Bardot. Instead she was greeted by the sight of a slight, mousy-haired girl of about five foot, dwarfed in an unflattering dun-coloured coat. The girl smiled awkwardly, revealing Bugs Bunny teeth.

'Anna, this is Claudine,' Steve introduced the two girls without emotion.

'*Enchantée.*' Claudine held out a bony, ice-cold hand.

Anna was flabbergasted. Surely . . . surely this wasn't her? She shook the French girl's hand automatically.

'I live upstairs,' she said.

'Superb.' The foreign accent sounded bizarre.

Anna wasn't sure what was superb about living in a dingy little lifeless flat in Ranelagh but she said nothing. If Claudine thought it was superb, let her.

Then again Anna might think it was superb herself if she was here to visit the seductive Steve. And didn't realize he was a cheat. She caught his eye. He looked guilty as hell. Good.

Anna bid them a frosty farewell and marched upstairs to her own accommodation. Christ, she couldn't believe it was Friday night and once again she hadn't a damn thing planned. She wondered where Steve and his amour were heading. Somewhere really unromantic probably. Like a walk around the block. Or a boring old drink in one of the local pubs. *Thank God she was rid of him*, she told herself half-heartedly. She turned on the fan heater and the radio. Nothing but dance music. Damn. They always put on dance music on a Friday evening to put people in the mood for going out. Why weren't there any stations geared towards lonely thirty-year-old women who preferred to sit in? Maybe she'd get ready and pretend she was going out. Sure, didn't they say half the fun was getting ready? Yeah right!

The phone rang. Oh God, she really didn't feel like answering it. Let one of the nurses get it – it was usually someone looking for one of them anyway. It rang and rang. Oh no, just suppose it was someone for her? But who could be ringing at nine o'clock on a Friday night? The house was obviously empty. The person on the other end of the phone was being very persistent. Oh maybe she should answer it. It could be an emergency. Reluctantly she made her way downstairs.

'Hello?' she whispered, as though it could be a nuisance caller.

'Anna?'

Heavens! A male voice! Anna quickly racked her brains to figure out which of her desperate exes had the nerve to call her so late on a Friday evening and presume she'd be in.

'Who's this?' she asked warily.

'Mark,' the voice answered casually. Relief flooded her. Thank God it was Mark and not some pervert looking for one of the nurses. But relief soon turned to indignation. What did he mean by ringing her so late? Did he think she hadn't got a life or what?

'Hello, Mark,' her voice was politely cool, 'what can I do for you?'

'Are you up to anything?'

'I'm just getting ready to go out,' she lied.

'Oh where to?'

'Into town and then off to Club Anabel to meet some friends,' *Another lie*.

'Oh! A few of my mates are heading there.'

'Right.' Oh Jesus! 'Right, well I'm not one hundred per cent sure if that's where we are going. We might go to Renards instead. Or Spy. Or straight to Leeson Street. It depends how things go.'

'I see,' he sounded subdued. 'That's a pity because I thought we could do something tonight. We haven't met up in ages.'

'Well, if I'd had a bit more notice maybe . . .'

'Right. Well, listen I'll give you a lift into town, it's raining.'

'Oh no!' Anna practically shouted, 'I'll get the bus.'

'Don't be ridiculous, I insist.'

'But what about Sally? Aren't you meeting her tonight?' Anna was panicking.

'She's on call tonight.'

'But someone might see us together and get the wrong impression. It might get back to her.'

'Don't be daft,' Mark laughed. 'Anyway, Sally doesn't get jealous,' he added.

Sally doesn't get jealous, Anna repeated spitefully after putting down the phone. Isn't she great altogether? God, what kind of a mess had she gone and got herself into now? She should ring him back and tell him she'd made the whole thing up. Or that Elaine had cancelled at the last minute. No, he'd think she was sad. She went upstairs and started to get ready. Had she a screw loose or what? she seriously began to wonder as she smudged pink lipstick on her cheeks to give them a healthy glow. Did her image really mean that much to her? Or to Mark? After all she didn't fancy him and he didn't fancy her so what was the big hoo-ha all about?

'By the way,' she said to him half an hour later as he stood in the doorway, 'how did you know I wasn't out with Steve tonight?'

'Oh that was easy,' Mark grinned, 'I saw him leaving with some sallow-skinned bird a while ago.'

He opened the car door for her and she sat in the passenger seat, fuming. 'Seat belt on?' He flashed her a gleaming smile. He looked annoyingly good this evening. And smelled even better.

'Yes.' Anna glanced at her watch absent-mindedly.

'You're not running late, are you?' Mark looked concerned.

'No, no I'm meeting Elaine at ten.'

'Elaine . . . have I met her now?'

'No,' Anna said firmly.

'Is she single?'

'Well . . . yes.'

'Is she good looking?'

'She certainly wouldn't be interested in you,' Anna snapped. Immediately she regretted it. Sure wasn't Mark only trying to do her a favour? It wasn't his fault that she was leading him a merry dance. She'd have to stop behaving like a pitbull terrier in his company. It was terribly gauche.

He pulled up outside the Shelbourne Hotel. 'Are you sure you'll be okay here?'

'Fine,' Anna grinned broadly at him, 'honestly, you go on. I'll be just fine.'

'Enjoy your night.' At that moment Mark looked totally stunning. She couldn't believe she was about to let him drive away because of some silly facade.

'I will,' she said. 'Bye.'

She walked purposefully up the steps of the Shelbourne Hotel, past the crowded reception area and straight to the Ladies. She took a long hard look at herself in the mirror. She hadn't looked this good in years. What a pity she was all dressed up with nowhere to go. She opened her little black handbag and took out her brush. Well, she had to do something, hadn't she? She couldn't exactly turn around and walk straight back out again. She began to brush her hair. The Ladies was full of ARMPITTS all vying for the mirror. Anna felt like she was really in the way. Hair done, she fished out her foundation and needlessly applied it. That lasted about ten minutes. She brushed her hair again and then wondered what to do. Was it safe to go back out again? She stared hard at her image. She now looked like a hooker who'd dumped her face into a bucket of foundation. Excellent.

Eventually she marched out of the hotel and hopped into a nearby taxi.

'Where to, love?' the taxi man enquired.

'Er . . .' God, where was she going? She could hardly go back to Ranelagh. No, that would be ridiculous. First, she didn't want to bump into Mark again, and secondly she couldn't bear the thought of sitting alone in her flat knowing that Steve and Claudine were making out underneath.

'Stillorgan,' she said suddenly, 'Stillorgan please.' And before she had time to change her mind, the taxi driver had taken off like a grand prix contestant.

Ah well, Anna thought, at least her parents would be pleased to see her. She hadn't seen them since her birthday and life must be so dull for them at the moment, stuck with Grandad rabbiting on about the good old days.

Anna's parents were not as pleased as she'd thought they'd be. Mr and Mrs Brown from next door were round playing bridge.

'What are you doing here?' Her mother frowned.

'Just thought I'd pop in.' Anna forced a smile.

'On a Friday night?' She was definitely suspicious. 'Really, Anna, you should be out mixing with people of your own age. You'll never meet a man round in your parents' on a Friday. Grandad is in the kitchen. I suppose you can go in and keep him company.'

She disappeared into the good room. Anna was left alone in the hallway. God, what was the point in being a dutiful daughter when nobody appreciated it? She wasn't in the mood for listening to the entire history of County Roscommon. She slumped into one of the kitchen chairs and shut her eyes. Was there any woman in Ireland quite as sad as she was? She wondered what Victoria Reilly was up to. No doubt frolicking with fickle friends in a famous hot spot. Consuming champagne from crystal. Goading her friends in her latest Gucci get up. So what? Anna wouldn't like that kind of lifestyle anyway. It was all so pretentious. She preferred the simpler lifestyle. Like . . . a night in with Grandad, say.

Chapter Seven

'I didn't go in the end, Mark.'

'Where did you go?'

'Listen, Mark, I wish I had all day to chat but I'm up to my eyes, so I'm putting the phone down now, right?'

'Talk to you later so.'

'Yeah, yeah, bye.'

She cut him off. God, he'd a bit of a cheek, Anna thought as she made her way over to the checkouts. She should start ringing his office at the IFSC with all kind of obscenities. That would soon put an end to the fun and games!

The checkout queues were building up. She marched over to prevent two of the gum-chewing staff from describing their hangovers in great detail in front of paying customers. A headache was approaching fast, streaking past all traffic lights and stop signs. But she couldn't leave the shop floor. It was manic. God, roll on seven o'clock.

A pram collided with the back of her heels. Ouch!

She swung around ready to attack but the worn-out-looking woman with the double buggy didn't even know she'd hit her. Anna hobbled over to the fed-up security guard. 'Everything in order?' she checked.

'None of our regulars yet,' he said with a deadpan face. "Regulars" meant shoplifters. They usually appeared on Saturdays along with the crowds, heading straight for the sportswear. Nightmare stuff. The bell at one of the checkouts rang loudly. A customer was whingeing about being short-changed a fiver. Damn!

That meant opening the register and checking all sales for the afternoon against cash in the till. It would take at least fifteen minutes. Oh to work in a quiet little library. Or a church. Or in the fields as a goddam shepherd. What was that Jean-Paul Sartre had said? Hell is other people.

'Oh Claire, I'm knackered.' Anna leaned against the communal phone booth in the hallway. How she was going to motivate herself to get upstairs, shower and make up, and face the howling wind, she just didn't know.

'Get ready, Anna. Seriously, the babysitter is on her way. I'm practically ready to go.'

'Is Simon not babysitting?'

'No, he'll probably join us later.'

'Oh right,' Anna said.

'That's not a problem, is it?'

'Well . . . would Simon not think of going out

with some of his own friends? You know . . . like a lads' night out, since this is supposed to be a girls' night out?'

'Er . . . er . . .' Claire couldn't think of a suitable answer.

'It's just it might be more craic you know, just us, the girls.'

'I never thought about it like that,' Claire mumbled, 'but surely you can't expect me to behave like a woman on the pull. Simon is well known on the Dublin social scene.'

'I completely understand,' Anna sounded sympathetic, 'I wouldn't dream of asking you to let Simon down. I completely understand how important he is.'

'Yes,' Claire agreed uncertainly. 'Oh by the way . . . Jake said he thought you were extremely good looking.'

'Did he?' Anna was pleased. It was always nice when someone thought you were good looking. Unless of course it was some lecherous drunk in a nightclub when the lights had come on. Or down in the chipper, say. Or when you were walking through Donnybrook at 3 a.m. looking for a taxi. Or if it was a flasher who said it to you. Or two fifteen-year-olds taking the piss. Or when someone told you in a dark laneway and you were on your own. In fact, when you thought about it, there were quite a number of occasions when you could happily live without the compliment.

Still, it was nice that Jake had noticed. Jake had a

nice BMW. It wouldn't look out of place in the drive at Victoria's party. Or her own drive. Not that she had a drive, of course. And the county council had now gone and painted double yellow lines outside her gate.

Anna promised Claire she wouldn't be long.

'I'm going as fast as I can,' she promised before going back upstairs and lighting her first cigarette of the day. It was nice to have a cigarette before you went out. It put you in the mood. As did a little drink. Good idea! She'd have a beer. But to her dismay she found the fridge practically empty. Two out-of-date yoghurts, a very yellow half tub of butter, an egg (God knows how long that had been there!) and one can of beer left over from a party she'd had months back. That would have to do. She snapped it open, gingerly sniffing the contents. It smelled off. It was always hard to tell with beer. She sipped a little. It wasn't horrendous. It wasn't that pleasant either. Then again, if you wanted something pleasant you'd drink coke or orange juice or something, wouldn't you?

Anna reluctantly undressed. It wasn't nice undressing in a place that wasn't room temperature. The flat wasn't sub zero. But it wasn't far off. She brought the beer into the shower and drank a bit more. There, it tasted better already. She turned on the water. Jesus, it was like frigging ice! Then it hit her. She'd forgotten to switch on the bloody immersion. Ah no! She couldn't go out with unwashed hair. She positively stank. Hours of crawling around unclean cardboard boxes in the stockroom hadn't exactly added to her appearance. At least ten creepy-crawlies were planning a soirée in her messy bun.

She caught a glimpse of herself in the tarnished bathroom mirror. Her eyes were like two bullet holes in her sunken face. An angry spot above her left eyebrow was seriously threatening a night out. She felt like collapsing on the bed, finishing the box of cigarettes and getting hammered all by herself. Feck the night out. It was Saturday. That meant queues. Queues for buses. Queues for pubs. Queues for taxis to get from pubs to clubs. Queues for clubs. Queues for cloakrooms. Queues for the bar. Queues for the toilet. For the sink. For the dryer. For the mirror. It meant getting squashed on the dance floor . . . freezing your ass off as you walked home swearing that this would be your last night out until the summer.

The doorbell rang. Oh God, she was still naked. She scrambled into a pair of tracksuit bottoms and pyjama top and pulled on a pair of odd socks.

'Claire,' Anna grinned, 'you look beautiful.'

'Anna, I can't believe you haven't even started to get ready.' Claire looked cross. She'd made a huge effort. Boots, leather mini (to the knee and not at all as tarty as it sounds) and black cashmere jacket. A hint of make-up (God, Anna envied girls who just hinted) and a subtle spray of Miracle. Perfect.

'Sorry, I got held up.' Anna ushered her in. 'Now

tell me honestly, do you think I'd get away without washing my hair?'

'Honestly? Well . . . you'd get away with it but you wouldn't look your best.'

'In other words I'd look like shit.'

Claire said nothing. This was a common Saturday night scenario in Anna's. Nothing new here. Eventually Anna would give her hair a quick splash, add some new make-up to the old and spend the rest of the night wishing she'd made more of an effort.

They abandoned the flat at 10:10 p.m. Not a sound was to be heard from the flat downstairs. The air outside was damp. The front path was covered in wet leaves and faded crisp bags. Anna trod carefully in ridiculously high heels. Her short skirt must have caught the attention of a passing cab. It screeched to a halt outside the front gate. Classic. The girls clambered in.

They decided on a new ultra-trendy club along the quays. Problem was, so did everybody else. The queue was the length of the Liffey. There wasn't a hare's sniff of getting in. Unless you were shagging one or more of the bouncers.

They ordered the taxi man to drive on. He recommended a dodgy-looking place around Clarendon Street and the girls agreed to get out there so as not to hurt his feelings.

'I'd love to go to Burger King,' Anna's stomach was talking to her. She tipped the taxi man.

'Are you mad? We're not going to Burger King dressed like this.'

'You're right,' Anna sniffed. 'Somebody important might see us.'

'We'll go for a drink first and then find somewhere to eat,' Claire suggested.

'Fine.'

They entered a pub at the top of Grafton Street. The place was wall-to-wall jammed with people trying to look cool but failing miserably because of the thermal atmosphere: it was hard to be sophisticated when beads of sweat were bonding on your forehead and two damp patches were propagating at accelerating speed around your armpits.

'See anyone nice?' Claire roared above the crowd.

'Keep your voice down,' Anna hushed, 'I don't want the whole place thinking I'm some kind of desperate eejit.'

'Sorry,' Claire shouted. The jazz band in the corner was obviously playing havoc with her ears. 'What do you want to drink?'

'A beer. Preferably a well-known brand.'

'Right. Crisps?'

'Are you mad? I'm not eating crisps in a place like this.'

'I thought you said you were hungry.'

'Not *that* hungry.'

'Hello, ladies.' Thick east London accent, gold bracelets, very short haircuts, very bad dress sense, very up for it.

'Hello,' Anna replied distantly.

'What are two ladies like you doing in a place like this?' One of them grinned, revealing a gold tooth.

'Just taking it easy,' Claire glanced nervously at Anna.

Gold Tooth offered to pay for the drinks.

'No honestly, thanks,' Anna insisted. 'We'll get our own. But thanks anyway,' she repeated so as not to insult him.

'Have you got a boyfriend?' The one with the sideburns and three earrings slid a scraggy arm around Claire's waist.

'Married.' She held up her left hand. They stared, electrocuted. Unbelievable! It was as if she had waved a magic wand warding off the wicked witches of the west. The three guys disappeared before you could say 'actually I've changed my mind about the drinks'.

'Well, that was weird,' Claire stared after them.

'Yes, very.' Anna tried to catch the barman's attention. 'But don't be waving your ring around – you know, if someone decent shows up.'

Later, at the club, the doorman ushered them in with surprising speed, obviously thinking they were someone else. At the bar a more mature man offered them drinks. A nice start. He was American and thought the girls could be models. Especially Claire. He asked Claire to dance. A friendly dance. Why did men always do that, Anna wondered. Was there such a thing as an unfriendly dance? Claire politely declined, blaming a sore foot. So he asked Anna.

'Go on,' Claire winked at her, 'I'll hold your drink for you.'

Mildly insulted at being only second choice, Anna followed him out on to the dance floor. George Michael's 'Careless Whisper' was playing. Anna hoped he wouldn't whisper anything careless into her ear. Or do anything with her ear.

The American's dancing wasn't great. He shuffled about uneasily after Anna on the crowded dance floor, at one stage colliding heavily with a smooching young couple.

'Sorry,' Anna told the male half.

'Sorry,' he answered her back and held her gaze for longer than necessary. He was taller than average with jet-black hair, long sooty eyelashes and sallow complexion. Probably not Irish. Definitely not unattractive. His partner whisked him away.

The song changed.

'Well thanks for that,' Anna told the American hurriedly. 'I think I'd better get back to Claire.' The hint fell on deaf ears. He followed her back to the bar and bought another round of drinks. Anna scoured the room to see if she could spot that man with the dusky looks again. But to no avail. The place was jammers. Claire and the American were blocking her view. She began to feel hot. On a scale from one to ten, the stuffiness in this place rated eleven. She took a quick note of the exits. Only three were visible. Hopefully the place wouldn't catch fire or anything. Her high heels wouldn't stand a chance. She knocked back her glass of beer and bought the next round. She hadn't eaten she remembered. No wonder the walls felt like they were closing in on her.

The music revved up. The American wanted to boogie. Claire wanted to boogie. Anna didn't.

'I'll be back,' she told them and vanished to the Ladies.

A good twenty-five minutes stood between her and the first toilet. Feck it, she muttered, crossing her legs tightly. Her bladder was about to explode. That was the problem with beer. It ran right through you.

She gave her hair a few half-hearted brushes and injured herself slightly with eyeliner. Tears filled the affected eye.

To say she didn't look her best was an understatement. Maybe you're drunk, she told her reflection. Her next drink would be a coke, she decided. A nice, cool, civilized coke on the rocks.

Claire seemed to be having a whale of a time back at the bar. Lucky divil! Somebody was chatting her up. He looked coincidentally like Simon from the back. Good Jaysus, it *was* Simon. What on earth was he doing here?

'Hello, Anna.' Simon gave her a friendly punch. 'What's the story?'

Anna didn't know. What *was* the story? Claire

gave her a guilty *I can't stop him coming along can I?* look. Anna resigned herself to spending the rest of the evening with a married couple. Great. The American had disappeared. She almost wished he hadn't.

'I'm exhausted,' Claire whispered to Anna eventually, after the three of them (Claire and Simon holding hands) had stood around awkwardly for a while. 'I'm worried about leaving the babysitter, you know . . . it's late.'

'Can you not send Simon home?' Anna was annoyed.

'Ooo-kay . . . I'll say it to him, but . . .'

'No go,' Anna snapped, 'I'll be all right here by myself.'

'Are you sure?' Claire didn't seem to think it was the best idea she'd ever heard. 'I'm not sure I like the idea of you going home on your own.'

'Hopefully I *won't* be going home on my own.'

'Well, if you're positive.' Claire squeezed her hand.

Anna was very sorry her friend was disappearing so early. She could have begged her to stay but was determined not to grovel. So, with a nonchalant shrug, she shed her security blanket. And insisted Claire left without her. Simon gave her a brotherly hug. Claire kissed both her cheeks. They were gone. It all happened so fast.

Right, thought Anna, I think I'll have a bit of a walk around. Simon had bought her another beer (although she'd asked for a coke) before they'd left.

She set off in the direction of the dance floor, pint glass in hand.

Hopefully someone would stop to chat her up. Guys always did that when you walked around on your own, didn't they? Not this time. Anna got around the nightclub's perimeter fairly fast. Well, that walk had proved fairly fruitless. What now? She couldn't do a second lap for at least ten minutes. She lit a fag. And smoked it.

'Have you got a light?' Crikey, it was the dish from the dance floor.

Anna blinked, not quite believing her luck. 'Sure,' she said coolly. Hopefully he wouldn't just light up and leave. She wasn't going to let him just use her like that. She held out the flickering flame and watched him lean forward, catching it in a split second. He inhaled deeply, exhaled slowly.

'So where's your boyfriend?' He raised an eyebrow. He was quietly confident. Mysterious. Well, compared to the usual louts she met in clubs. Very intelligent. Anna guessed he was trying to work her out. She intrigued him somehow. Good. That's what she was there for.

'That oul lad on the dance floor?' she giggled. 'He's not my boyfriend.'

'Right.' He blew a perfectly formed smoke ring. Anna watched it drift towards the ceiling.

'Where's your girlfriend?' Anna decided to play him at his own game.

'I don't have one,' he said, 'yet.'

She was glad the club was so dark. Dark enough for him not to notice the scarlet rash rapidly disfiguring the side of her neck. The heat was something else.

'Who was the girl on the dance floor, so?' Anna decided to be direct.

'A friend.'

God, he didn't give much away, did he? But to be fair he was neither sleazy nor smarmy, more smouldering and sharp. Anna wasn't smitten. Of course she wasn't. But she could see how other girls could be.

'Listen,' he looked at her levelly, 'I could stand here for half an hour and tell you you're the most beautiful girl in the world and that I'm not like other men and all that crap, right?'

'Right,' said Anna, wondering where on earth this could be leading.

'Or I could be honest.'

Honest. It was a word Anna liked. Although admittedly she wasn't too familiar with it.

'Yes?' she emitted faintly.

'Look, I like you. Or at least I think I do. I saw you on the dance floor. I thought, "Hey, not bad!" Now here I am. I'd like your number. If you don't want to give it to me, I'll give you mine.'

'No, I'll give you mine,' Anna said. 'I don't ring men,' she added untruthfully. Well, it wasn't a *complete* lie. She did try very hard not to ring men. Especially those who quite obviously never rang back. But she was learning. These days when a guy failed to ring, she'd try them maybe only . . . say, three times (an improvement on bygone days!) just to be one hundred per cent sure that they were sure they never wanted to see her again.

He asked the barman for a pen and scribbled her number on the back of his hand.

'Thanks,' he surprised her with a quick peck on the cheek, 'I'll be in touch.'

'But . . . where are you *going*?' Anna was alarmed. He had to see her home. He *had* to. She couldn't be seen leaving the club alone. There was nothing more humiliating than leaving a club on your own.

'It's my er . . . friend. She's had a lot to drink and is in a bad way. I can't leave her on her own.'

'Well, we could drop her off and go on somewhere,' Anna said in a little voice and nearly bit her own tongue off. What was she like? God, she might as well stand on top of one of the speakers and scream DESPERATE! Stay cool, she told herself. 'Actually,' she resumed her cool exterior, 'on second thoughts, you'd better go. My friends would kill me if I just left without saying goodbye.'

'Where are they?' He looked round expectantly as if a group of screaming girls might suddenly jump out at him from behind the DJ's box.

'Oh, they're over at the other bar,' Anna said, quick as lightning. 'The queues are something else.'

'Right.' He gave her a quick peck again. 'I'll be in touch.'

He was gone!

So much for a night of fun and frolic. Anna examined her chipped Revlon red nails under the flashing disco lights. She now knew the profound meaning of loneliness in a crowd. She had to get out of there. A single girl had no business staying in a nightclub alone until the early hours of Sunday morning. But she couldn't leave yet, of course. Like a prisoner she felt trapped behind the nightclub's imaginary bars. It was sad, she knew, but if she bumped into that guy and his *friend* on her way out her cover would be blown. God, she didn't even know his name. She fished out the shoddy piece of paper from her bag. Rick. His name was scrawled above his mobile number. He shouldn't have bothered giving her his number too. As if she was going to ring him! Jesus, he'd better be worth all this hassle.

Anna wandered unhappily around the club aiming for nowhere in particular. Her head was like a fairground complete with roller coasters and a big wheel. Everything was spinning around fast and furiously, and then something just suddenly snapped. She'd had enough. Her safe little flat in Ranelagh seemed very appealing right now. Wouldn't it be great to be like Dorothy in *The Wizard of Oz*, click your fingers and simply say 'Home Sweet Home' or whatever the hell she had said.

'Safe home now,' the bouncer said as she braced herself for the freezing night air.

'Thank you.' She gave him a watery smile. That's exactly where she wanted to be. Safe. Home. Now. She wished she'd worn a comfortable pair of boots. These heels were a killer. She tottered up to the traffic lights. And waited. Nothing. She decided to keep walking to prevent her feet from freezing into two blocks of ice. She looked around desperately for a glowing yellow taxi sign. A couple of occupied cabs seemed to be hurrying in the opposite direction, the occupants staring sadistically out of the windows.

None stopped for poor Anna.

Chapter Eight

'I hope Anna's okay.' Claire was full of concern as her husband drove them home to the comfort of their three-bed semi, minutes from Ranelagh village.

'Anna's fine,' Simon said matter-of-factly. 'She's a big girl now – well able to look after herself.'

'I hate leaving her alone in that place, you know, with all those sleazes.'

'I would have given her a lift if she'd wanted.'

Simon stopped at the red lights, laid a gentle hand on his young wife's knee and gave it a reassuring squeeze. 'Don't worry about her,' he smiled. 'She's probably talking to the man of her dreams this very minute.'

Claire genuinely doubted it. She couldn't remember the last time Anna had met a man who was even vaguely suitable. She did it on purpose, Claire reckoned. She shunned security. Now and again she'd go through phases of claiming to crave love and marriage, yet at the mere mention of kids, Anna's eyes would glaze over as she suppressed yawn after yawn.

Simon pulled up slowly outside the front door. It wasn't even two a.m. yet and they were safely home. *Mr And Mrs Married*. Claire gave a short laugh. Anna wouldn't want this for the world.

Fiona, the eighteen-year-old babysitter, was relieved to see them.

'I didn't think you'd be home so soon,' she said brightly, gratefully pocketing her twenty quid. 'The other couple I babysit for don't come home till all hours.'

'Ah, sure we don't see the point in staying out half the night.' Simon handed Fiona her coat. 'Come on, I'll walk you home.'

'Speak for yourself,' Claire muttered as her husband closed the front door. She couldn't help but feel slightly peeved at his throwaway remark. What about her? Maybe *she* might have liked to stay out half the night. Simon often had a night out with the lads. God knew, she rarely got the chance. It would have been nice to spend a bit more time with Anna. To have got a little hammered. Maybe carried each other home, unintentionally popping into Abrakebabra for a kebab and chips . . .

Claire climbed the stairs wearily. Those days were well and truly gone now. Simon had seen to that. It was all about responsibility these days. Mortgages and money matters. Promotions not emotions. Stockmarkets and supermarkets. Aiming high and DIY. Computing and commuting. It was all so . . . so . . . like the way her father had lived. Only worse.

Much worse in fact. When her father had joined the bank in the late sixties, he'd simply had to keep his head down and patiently wait for promotion. It would come to him in good time, her mother would remind him as she baked the daily bread.

All that was done away with now. The roar of the Celtic Tiger and all that. No waiting around these days, thank you very much. Except for office colleagues waiting to cut your throat. Or hang you by the balls. Or stab your designer-clad back. It was all so horrible. In a way Claire was glad Simon had talked her out of going back to work. She didn't know if she could cope with all that pressure.

She opened the baby door quietly and smelled the familiar baby smell that filled the tiny blue boxroom. The light flooded in from the hall. Andrew, asleep in his little yellow babygro with the duck on it, was breathing evenly. Fluffy, his favourite teddy, was tucked in beside him, one paw covering half of Andrew's face. Claire tiptoed gently towards his cot and moved Fluffy slightly away. She bent down and kissed the soft warm skin of her baby's cheek. Happiness surged through her.

Nothing, not all the nights out and wild times could ever replace the intense love she felt for her little boy. She heard Simon's footsteps on the stairs. No wonder he was always working hard for his family. He loved Andrew as much as she did. That was why he spent those long laborious hours in the office, bent over his computer. Because of his wife and child. Because he was aware of his responsibilities. Because he was a good Daddy.

Anna woke in a sweat. Somehow her blanket was strewn across her bedroom floor. Sunbeams streamed through a crack in the check curtains.

What time had she finally got a taxi home? Had she even got a taxi in the end? She vaguely remembered having had an argument with *someone* about the shocking lack of taxis around the place at night. But who cared anyway? She'd got home somehow and besides her head was hurting too much to try to figure out what had been dreamed and what hadn't. The whole night had been a bloody nightmare. A complete waste of time. Anna considered spending the whole afternoon in bed feeling sorry for herself, but a deep thirst forced her out of the bed. Her tongue felt like an old piece of carpet.

Never again, she told herself as she sipped from a half tin of flat lemonade. Yuck. Her insides were craving from the lack of food. Her poor bewildered stomach. She wondered if models always felt this bad. God, it was no great shakes being a waif with your tummy screaming at you, accusing you of abuse. How could one live with the guilt? She fired her empty can at the bin in the corner and missed. Feck it, she wasn't going to pick it up now. If she bent down she'd never get up again. She'd pick it up tomorrow. In fact she'd do a big clear-out. Tomorrow after work. Jesus, work. Ugh!

Anna slumped herself down on a red-paint-spattered stool and rested the side of her face on the cool kitchen table. The chilly surface was a welcome sensation against her fiery flushed cheek. Thank God it was Sunday.

Chapter Nine

'So, Anna,' Elaine sipped her carrot juice as they sat in a veggie restaurant on George's Street, 'have you written out your application letter yet?'

'For what?' Anna looked surprised.

'Don't you know? Your form for the post of assistant manager has to be in by tomorrow.'

'Oh yeah,' Anna stabbed her veggie burger with her fork. She *had* thought about applying for the post – after all she'd no intention of being a mere department manager all her life. But what in the name of God would she do in a one-horse town where if you sneezed everybody would be talking about it? She didn't fancy packing her bags to go off and move to such a town just to exercise a bit of authority in a two-man shop. No, thank you very much. At least in Dublin she was right in the heart of things. And near Claire, of course. Not that she saw much of *her* these days though. Unfortunately, Claire was too busy being the perfect wife. Then there were her parents to consider. They'd miss her dreadfully. Or would they? Anna forced herself to consider it. *Get real here*, she finally chided herself. They probably wouldn't notice if she was abducted by aliens and whisked off to Timbuktu. Who else was there? Mark? Well, he would just have to find someone else to torment. In fact, when she thought about it, was there anybody who would, like, really *really* mind her going at all? It probably wasn't the best thing in the world to think about.

'I'd love to get it,' Elaine's eyes glittered with emerald eye shadow and enthusiasm. Her whole face lit up when she smiled. She really was a striking-looking woman, Anna thought. It was terrible to think her husband had just skedaddled off like that. For no reason. But there was always a reason, wasn't there, Anna thought darkly. No wonder Elaine was throwing herself into this whole promotion lark. Like someone throwing herself off a burning ship. Women did that sometimes. Got involved in lots of different stuff. To get over men. Ridiculous, when you thought about it really. All that energy. Anna wondered what men did to get over a woman. Moved on to another one, she supposed.

'I'm sure you've got a very good chance,' Anna said kindly. 'You're so enthusiastic.'

'I have very little choice,' Elaine said, her eyes hardening, her mouth set in a straight line. 'It's got nothing to do with enthusiasm.'

'Yes, I know, I know.' Anna dipped her spoon into her dessert, an orangey chocolatey mousse, laden with naughty calories. 'Listen,' she said, eager to change the subject, 'how about next Friday, you and me head out on the town? You know, go on the complete rip.'

'Sure.' Elaine's face softened. Anna meant well. Always looking out for other people. It was such a pity she lacked such direction in her own life. Anna's answer to everything could be found in a bottle of something. Or a cream cake. Still, she wouldn't say no to a night out. They might even meet a few men! Not that she'd ever seriously consider getting involved with anyone ever again. No, she'd never ever do that again.

They decided to have their after-dinner coffee somewhere else. Somewhere more sociable. As in a pub.

'So, Elaine,' Anna glanced around the pub to see if she could spot anyone interesting, 'where do you reckon we'll go on our night out? The Sugar Club? The River Club?'

'What was that I heard about a night out?'

Elaine looked up in surprise. The owner of the deep masculine voice stood behind Anna. Tall and well built, he exuded an unmistakable air of affluence. He had the most mischievous and merry green eyes she'd ever encountered. Anna swung around, her face turning a crimson colour. 'Mark,' she said, with a sharp intake of breath. Elaine laughed. It was unlike her colleague to be at a loss for words.

*   *   *

'Thanks for sticking up for me in there,' Anna whispered to Elaine as they walked back to Lolta's twenty minutes later. 'Mark's always slagging me and I'm sick of it.'

'But what exactly *did* happen last weekend?' Elaine was bursting with curiosity, ''Cos you sure weren't with me.'

'I went to my parents,' Anna admitted, feeling absolutely ridiculous.

'That's hysterical,' Elaine laughed. 'Thank God I copped on in there and said we'd had a great night.'

'Yeah cheers,' Anna answered sheepishly.

'So do you fancy him then or what?'

'No!' Anna practically barked. 'Mark is not my type *at all*.'

'Really? I thought a guy like that would be anyone's type. He's absolutely gorgeous.'

'And he knows it,' Anna was emphatic. 'There's nothing quite as tragic as a man who thinks he's God's gift.'

'Well, let me have him then,' Elaine pleaded.

'Have him if you like,' Anna tossed her hair defiantly over her shoulder and hoped Elaine was joking. 'Sally won't mind, I'm sure. She's probably used to it by now.'

Anna escaped work early for a change. It had been a busy day with endless boxes of the Spring Collection being delivered and deposited any old way in the stockroom.

She left the store just after six and started the forty-minute walk home. In the evening it was quicker to walk than to bus it. The rain had abated and dangerous pools of water lurked alongside the footpath. She steered well clear of them. She wondered if Claudine had gone home to Paris yet. The terrible twosome had been nowhere to be seen for the rest of the weekend, thank God! Steve would be sitting alone in his flat with his alternative music. He'd be feeling lonely. Well let him, Anna thought. There was nothing she could do for him now.

The entire house was in darkness. She pushed the front door open and fumbled for the light switch. As the hall lit up the phone rang.

'Hello?' Anna said, expecting it to be for one of the others.

'Ann?'

'Anna, you mean?'

'Oh right. Something spilled on my hand. I couldn't make it out.'

'Who is this?' Anna was baffled.

'Rich.'

'Who?'

'From the other night, remember?'

'You mean Rick?'

'No Rich, short for Richard.'

'Oh hi!' She certainly hadn't expected to hear from him. God, this was . . . well, a pleasant surprise really. When you met men in nightclubs you didn't *automatically* expect them to ring. She wondered what he'd seen in her. She'd been fairly langers when they'd stumbled into each other. Not an amazing start. She'd probably looked like a tart gone wrong. In fact, oh God, it was all coming together now . . . she hadn't even bothered to wash her hair!

'How are you keeping?' He had a throaty voice. A neutral accent. He was Irish most definitely but she couldn't figure out from which part exactly.

'Fine.' Anna tried to keep her voice level. She didn't want him to think she was excited about the phone call or anything. *As if he was the only man who ever called*.

'What are you up to?'

'Nothing,' she said, immediately regretting it. How could she let herself down like that? She was supposed to be a woman with a jam-packed calendar.

'Can I call round?'

God, he wasn't a bit shy in coming forward, was he? What could she say? She'd just gone and admitted to having no plans made. 'Where do you live?' he pushed.

She told him. She felt she had no choice.

It took Anna exactly fifteen minutes to scramble speedily around the flat, shoving lone shoes and socks under the bed, grabbing air freshener from the bathroom and drenching the air with it. She emptied the overflowing ashtray, cleaned two coffee cups and checked to make sure the packet of Jaffa cakes was still intact in the press.

What else? Oh yes, she grabbed three visible books, *Mars and Venus on a Date*, *Mr Maybe* and *Amanda's Wedding* and threw them in a nearby press. No point giving him any daft ideas. There. She was ready. She took a quick glance in the mirror. Christ! This wouldn't do at all. She slapped a generous scoop of Flawless Finish on her face, painted a pink mouth somewhere near her lips and sprayed herself liberally with Miracle. The doorbell rang.

A shocking thought suddenly struck her. This guy was a stranger. What if he was a murderer or a raving nut head? Or an addict? A sex addict maybe, oh God. The bell rang again. She couldn't let him in. She couldn't. How would she possibly be able to explain it all later to the police as they took fingerprints from her battered body and examined her fingernails for traces of broken skin? The door from the upstairs flat opened and suddenly someone was running down the stairs, Grainne! Thank God. At least it looked like her behind the facemask.

'Are you answering the door or what?' Grainne looked exasperated.

'Yes . . . well . . . Would you ever do me a huge favour?'

She explained her predicament. Grainne listened, gobsmacked.

'So you see, if you could just check in on us in about fifteen minutes, say,' Anna whispered excitedly.

'Fifteen minutes might be too late.' Grainne's eyes widened dramatically.

'Right, ten. Thanks, Grainne.'

Anna shot downstairs and threw the door open. 'Sorry I didn't hear the door,' she said breathlessly, 'I had the TV on.'

He stood in the middle of the porch, combat-clad legs slightly apart, hands stuck deep in his pockets. He wore a navy fleece and a black cap. His eyes were an earthy grey, his bone structure was even. Anna thought he looked even better than he had in the nightclub, which was good. Usually it was the other way round.

'Well? Can I come in?' he looked slightly bemused.

'Sure.' Anna was quite pleased he'd come. Another contestant for Victoria's party! Perhaps he'd fare better than the last one.

They went upstairs. 'Sorry about the mess,' Anna said, thinking it was lucky he hadn't called fifteen minutes earlier.

'It's fine,' he said nonchalantly, throwing himself on the sofa and putting his feet up on her foot stool.

'Tea?'

'Sure, milk and two. Got any biccies?'

'Yep.' Anna proudly handed him the Jaffa cakes.

'Anything on the telly?' Rich bent down and picked up the remote.

'I dunno,' Anna said doubtfully, 'I don't really watch it.'

'Don't you?' Rich was amazed. He patted the cushion beside him. 'Sit down. Hey, tell you what, gotta beer instead of the tea?'

'Wouldn't you prefer to do something else . . . like go out, say?'

'Nah, Monday nights in Dublin are crap.'

'Right.'

'So, what kind of beer do you have?'

'Bud or Bud.'

'I'll have a Bud so,' Rich laughed.

Anna laughed too although she wasn't quite sure why.

There was a loud rap on the door. Grainne was bang on time. She barged into the room, immediately clamping her eyes on Rich.

'You're . . .' she blurted and stopped suddenly. 'I know you.'

'I don't think so.' Rich gave a coy smile.

To give him credit, he stood up like a gentleman to shake her hand.

'Will you join us for a Bud?' he offered.

'Why not?' Grainne plonked herself down on the sofa beside him. 'I'm always game for a Bud.'

Anna reluctantly retrieved three from the fridge. She opened a bag of nuts too.

'I know I know you from somewhere,' Grainne was adamant. 'I never forget a face, D'ya ever go to Copperface Jack's?'

'Nope.' Rich was grinning almost abnormally.

'Are you a friend of Sandra's?'

Rich shook his head.

'Marion's?'

'No.'

'I give up so,' Grainne admitted defeat. 'What's on TV then?'

'Nothing much,' Rich was beginning to show signs of restlessness.

'We could watch *Mr Motivator*.' Grainne gave Anna an obvious wink. The joke was lost on Rich. Thankfully.

'I've *Reservoir Dogs* upstairs,' Grainne said suddenly.

'Deadly.' Rich's eyes lit up. 'Go get it.'

Grainne put her beer on the floor and bounced out of the room like a woman on a serious mission. Anna sat down beside Rich.

'What'll we do?'

'About what?' Rich looked genuinely surprised.

'You don't seriously want to watch *Reservoir Dogs*, do you? We can just tell her we've changed our minds when she comes back down.'

'Why? What else would we be doing?'

Anna opened her mouth as if to say something and shut it again.

'Besides, Tarrantino is a genius,' he added, as if that made sense of everything.

Grainne was back. She popped the video in, squeezed herself in between Anna and Rich and retrieved her beer. 'Sandra might pop down later,' she said happily. 'She says she's doing nothing else.'

Great, Anna thought as she felt herself being pushed against the armrest. Why don't we ask the lads downstairs while we're at it? This was ridiculous. It wasn't a date at all. Did she not look attractive? She should have worn something sexier. She glanced down at her plain navy suit. Horrifyingly unsexy. Shoot! He probably thought she dressed like this *all* the time. And now that Grainne was here there was no chance to change.

You're a disaster, Anna Allstone, she told herself. A complete and utter hazard. There should be warning signs sent out about you. No wonder men don't stick around very long.

The three of them sat in silence. In fact, the only audible sound (besides the actors in the video) was of Rich and Grainne slurping their cans of beer. Anna felt like reading the evening paper she'd bought on the way home from work. And why wouldn't she? It wasn't as if the others would even notice. Suddenly Rich picked up the remote and pressed *pause*.

'Where's the loo?'

'Just off the bedroom.' Anna nodded in the right direction.

'Back in a sec.' He disappeared.

'He's a bit of an all right,' Grainne commented when he was gone.

'Do you think so?' Anna wasn't so convinced.

'Sure. I've met him somewhere before though. His face is awful familiar.'

'Maybe he shifted one of your friends.'

'That must be it,' Grainne said cheerfully. 'By the way . . . you don't mind me being here do you?'

'Not at all,' Anna said and nearly bit her tongue off. Of *course* she minded. But what could she say? That she and Rich had some catching up to do? That they needed to spend some quality time together? What a joke! Grainne knew the score. She'd be here for the night.

Rich reappeared. The video started up again. The beer drinking resumed.

Another knock on the door.

Sandra's inquisitive face sprang from behind it. 'I heard there's Bud going around here.'

'You'll have to sit on the floor,' Grainne ordered.

'Have my seat,' Anna stood up without knowing why.

'Not at all,' Sandra walked purposefully towards the sofa. 'Push over everybody.'

Another beer was fetched for Sandra. She made herself comfy on the armrest. Whatever Sandra thought, though, there was clearly not enough room for them all.

'I'm Rich,' Rich said.

'I wish I was,' Sandra giggled and shook his hand flirtatiously. 'Jesus! I know you.' She gave a sudden scream.

Everybody jumped. Grainne kicked over her beer. Anna rolled her eyes to the ceiling. What now?

'You're the fella from the cough medicine ad,' Sandra squealed.

'Oh yes!' Grainne's eyes widened as she rubbed the spilled beer into the carpet with the sole of her shoe. 'I knew you had a famous face.'

Anna screwed up her face to suppress a smirk. Famous? Whatever next? Soon he'd be signing autographs for them. He probably felt like the fifth Beatle sitting in her flat. A slow satisfied smile was spreading across his face. The video rolled on unwatched.

'So,' Sandra settled herself well into the sofa, 'what else have you done?'

'This and that.'

'Tell us. Go on,' Grainne urged.

Rich didn't need that much encouragement. 'I was in *The Bill*,' he said.

'Which one?' Sandra asked. 'I've seen nearly all of them.'

'The one with the big train crash.'

'Really? What part did you play?'

'I was a paramedic. I said, "Pass me the oxygen."'

'Cool,' Sandra and Grainne answered in unison.

'I was also in *When Brendan Met Trudy*. Just a "blink and you'll miss me" part.'

'Still,' Sandra said encouragingly, 'it's a start.'

'Don't forget us when you're rich and famous,' Grainne said.

'He's already Rich,' Anna said dryly.

The other three collapsed into convulsions of laughter. For a moment Anna had a sudden urge to be somewhere else. A thought crossed her mind. She could run across the road and invite Mark over. Then they'd only be one guy short. She eyed Rich and his two new-found friends disdainfully. Three girls and one guy was a bit unfair. Then again, it was Monday. Mark would be working late. Or getting ready for bed. He'd think she was insane inviting him over to meet this lot. And besides . . . she was on a *date*! How could she have possibly forgotten?

'Have you met any stars?' Grainne snapped open a second beer and tucked her feet in under her.

Rich took a cigarette from Sandra's outstretched hand and contemplated the many celebrities he'd rubbed shoulders with over the years.

'I met Guy Ritchie once.' Rich blew a jagged line of smoke towards the ceiling. 'Madonna wasn't with him at the time though.'

'Did you?' Anna was genuinely impressed. But regretted showing it as she watched Rich's chest practically explode with pride.

'What did he say?' Grainne sat up straight.

'Oh nothing to me,' Rich swallowed, 'but he asked my friend the time. We were all so busy filming we didn't have time for chit-chat.'

'I see,' Anna cracked open a beer for herself while there was still some left. No one seemed to be going anywhere. In fact she was the only one who had to be up in the morning.

'I've met the whole cast of *Fair City* of course,' Rich added.

'Of course,' Sandra giggled.

Grainne shot her a warning look. 'So tell us about the ad? Was that fun? What was the girl like? She's very pretty, isn't she?'

Rich made a face. 'She's very big-headed really. Not at all friendly. Like she wouldn't go out with you unless you drove a big car and threw money at her . . .'

'. . . which you didn't,' Sandra finished the sentence for him.

'Er . . . no.'

They turned back to the film in silence.

'So can I see you again?' Rich seemed reluctant to disappear without arranging a return visit. The girls had rapidly retired during the film credits. Anna was gobsmacked. She hadn't exchanged five sentences with him all evening. And now he was looking for more! Perhaps he was lonely. Yeah, that must be it. Maybe all his friends had emigrated to Australia at the same time. Possibly he had a thing for nurses. What else? Because surely, *surely* he hadn't considered the 'date' a success.

'Give me a ring,' Anna bid adieu soberly.

'Sure.' He looked for a split second like he was going to lean over and kiss her. But he didn't. 'Goodnight.' He gave her a curious wink and disappeared into the darkness.

Chapter Ten

'So what age is he?' Elaine stubbed out one cigarette and lit another.

'I don't know,' Anna sighed and rubbed her eye with the back of her hand. 'Same age as me, I suppose.'

'And you didn't go out at all?' Elaine frowned.

'No, Dublin's crap on Monday nights.'

'I see,' Elaine looked as if she didn't see at all.

'Anyway, it's nice to sit in now and again,' Anna said defensively.

'Now and again, but not on a first date.'

'Mmm.' Anna didn't have much interest in pursuing the conversation.

'So did you hand in your application?'

'No, I'll do it tonight.'

Their fifteen-minute break was soon up. Time to go back to work. Another two hours till lunch. Perhaps she'd go to McDonald's. Mmm . . . a nice creamy chocolate milkshake . . . mmm . . . and fries . . .

The rest of the day dragged on unmercifully. Anna

typed out her letter of application and formally handed it to Evans, the store manager.

'Good luck,' he said kindly.

'Thanks,' she answered automatically.

She wondered briefly when Rich would call again. As far as she knew he wasn't working. He was between jobs as they called it in the acting world. He was attractive all right though, Anna thought as she straightened a clothes rail absent-mindedly. But he wasn't exactly Mr Perfect for the Party. God, Victoria would have a field day with someone like that. It didn't bear thinking about. Cough medicine ad indeed!

The bus sat in a steady stream of traffic the entire journey home. Mobile phones were going off at a great rate, people answering calls at the top of their voices with 'Hi, yeah I'm on the bus now. D'ya want me to pick you up a sandwich or anything on my way home? . . . No it's no trouble at all . . . Ham? No? . . . Oh right, cheese . . . Oh yeah there was a lot of trouble about that. Yeah . . . major shit, like, you know . . . anyway I'll tell you about it when I get home . . . yeah . . . about fifteen minutes . . . yeah . . . crawling along . . . okay . . . yeah, just cheese . . . okay . . . yeah bye . . . yeah . . . right . . . bye . . . oh hang on . . . hello? . . . hello? . . . hell . . . ah . . . ffffffff . . .'

A grey-haired drunk was yelling at people who suddenly found themselves engrossed in their evening papers.

'That's right,' he yelled. 'Don't answer me back. It's the age of technology and all that crap but one day you'll be dead and all the computers in the world won't be able to save you. Good luck.'

Anna stared out of the window terrified that he might catch her eye. Thankfully she was sitting too far behind for him to harass her. Instead he directed his heated statements towards a scarlet-faced, acne-covered youth. Poor man, Anna thought soberly. Imagine if he was your dad or your brother. He was *someone's* relative. It was sad when you came across someone like that. It kind of put your own life into perspective.

The old man got off the bus just before it turned into Ranelagh village. She looked back out of the window and saw him continue his argument with the bus stop. Life was cruel, she thought shaking her head sadly. He was definitely someone the Celtic Tiger seemed to have forgotten about.

She found the house in complete darkness. Briefly she wondered where Steve was. Did he ever think about her? Or did he just see her as the desperate old tart upstairs? Hopefully not. It wouldn't be nice for anyone to think about her in that way. Maybe she'd bump into him again and they could be friends. She hadn't seen him since Friday. Tonight was Tuesday night, wasn't it? She wondered if he'd be having another mad party. Or would he be writing *chansons d'amour* to Claudine?

The phone was ringing as she pushed open the

front door. She threw her bag down and lunged for it.

'Hello?'

'Anna?'

A male voice. Hurrah! But who was it? One male voice sounded much the same as another.

'Hi,' she pretended to know who it was, 'how are you?'

'It's me.'

'I know,' she said. *Who the hell was it?*

'How do you know?'

She was confused. The voice was undeterred by her brusqueness. This wasn't Mark. And it wasn't Rich unless he was acting. But she wasn't going to back down now.

'Because your voice is always the same,' she played along.

'It's Jake,' the voice said.

Silence followed. Who the hell was Jake? Stunned silence followed that. Oh sh . . . sugar! Jake was the fella she'd met at Claire's. The plant and all that. Yikes, he'd think she was mad. What was *he* ringing her for? Janey Mack, she'd two fellas ringing her now. Well two was better than none, she supposed. It was a rare occurrence and deserved to be celebrated.

'Who did you think it was?' Jake asked testily.

'My dad,' Anna answered dryly.

The laughter that followed nearly burst her eardrum. It continued for five minutes. Well maybe not that long, but it certainly felt like it. 'Anna, ha ah hanna ha ha ha, you're . . . ha ha . . . hilarious.'

Jesus, he must be on drugs, Anna eyed the phone suspiciously as she held it a safe distance from her ear. What on earth did he want? Had Claire put him up to this? She'd kill her, she really would. She tried to remember what Jake looked like. As far as she recalled he wasn't bad. Respectable looking. Not as nice looking as Mark, of course, but as nice or nicer than Rich.

'Are you there?' Jake sounded miles away.

'Er . . . yes.' With a bang Anna landed back to earth. 'What can I do for you?' *God, she sounded like a sulky sales person.*

'Well . . . as a matter of fact ha ha . . . I was wondering if perhaps you might be interested in er . . . possibly meeting up sometime?'

'Oh,' Anna said because she couldn't think of anything else to say.

'I could pick you up later?'

Crikey, he was keen, wasn't he? This was good. Two dates with two different men in two nights? You couldn't beat that, could you? And Jake had a nice car as far as she could remember. Enough! Stop it! People who thought about money were the lowest of the low. 'I'd love to,' she said suddenly. There! She'd agreed. There was no going back now.

'I'll see you at eight, Jake. Don't be late,' she said. 'Oh and by the way, could you hoot your horn to let me know you're outside?'

Another five minutes of laughter. God, he certainly wasn't the full shilling, Anna decided. What
was so funny about hooting one's horn? She'd better
get off the phone before she changed her mind about
the date. At least she had got in the bit about the
horn, though. Hopefully Steve would look out of
the window, if he was in, and see what a good catch
she'd made. Miaow.

Now. What was she going to wear? Something
conservative would be good.

She flung open her wardrobe doors, taking a
disdainful look at what was hanging there. Besides
her work clothes were six pairs of jeans, an unworn
lime-green mini two sizes too small, a pair of com-
bats with a faulty zip, and the *fuchsia* bridesmaid
dress she'd worn to Claire's wedding. Swiftly she
declared her wardrobe a disaster area. What time
was it? A quarter to eight. Oh God, no! Why oh why
had she agreed to this? Finally she retrieved a pair of
black trousers from the bottom of her dirty basket.
She sniffed them. They stank of stale cigarettes. Oh
well, it was them or the bridesmaid dress. The black
trousers won hands down. She'd better give them
a rapid iron. At times like this she wished she'd a
trouser press. Or a maid. Or a wife. It would be so
handy. She wondered if Claire *did* know anything
about this date. She could give her a quick ring.
Another glance at her watch. Oops! Maybe not.

The front door opened. Someone was wheeling a
bike into the hall. Steve. Oh yes. Brilliant. What

perfect timing. Happy now and with a lightness in her step she danced around the sitting room to Roy Orbison's 'Pretty Woman'. Pretty was exactly how she felt. Pretty chuffed. Pretty excited. And pretty pleased about her new-found sex appeal. All these men. Wasn't it fab? Maybe she could invite a bunch of them to the reunion. Maybe Victoria could build a kind of harem cum marquee out the back for them all. A loud banging on the door put an abrupt end to her fantasies. What the hell . . . ? God, he hadn't wasted much time.

'Just a minute,' she called, the sweat-beads forming furiously across her forehead. She rushed into the bathroom and squeezed a generous blob of minty toothpaste onto her toothbrush. A quick rinse with mouthwash should finish the trick. She sniffed her underarms. Oooh dear, a blast of Sure for Men wouldn't do any harm. The door hammered again. Hang on, that couldn't be him. Sure, who could have let him into the house?

'It's me.' Grainne's big booming voice was unmistakable.

Jesus, that's all she needed, Anna opened the door, her mouth full of Listerine. If Grainne thought she'd be spending another night with Anna and her date, she could forget it.

The other girl barged in.

'Guess who rang?'

Anna ran to the sink and spat out the Listerine. 'Who?'

'Rich.' Her eyes were shining.

'Great,' Anna said, her tone of voice suggesting that it was anything but.

'He's coming over tonight. He's bringing us over the video of *The Bill*, you know the episode he was in, and a pop video he was also in and . . .' Grainne paused for breath as Anna sneaked a nervous look at her watch '. . . and another programme he was in with Elizabeth Hurley before she was famous . . . and anyway it'll be great. We've bought two twelve-packs and loadsa crisps . . . oh, and the lads from downstairs are coming,' she added.

Anna felt her heart shoot up to her mouth. *The lads from downstairs?* She stood rooted to the spot in her black trousers and white bra. 'I can't go,' she said stiffly.

'Why not?' The disappointment showed on Grainne's face. 'Rich probably won't stay if you're not there and he's such good craic . . . and he's promised to introduce us to all his famous friends.'

'I'm really sorry,' Anna said, her head swimming with comical visions of Brad Pitt, Jude Law and Ben Affleck all drinking beer in Grainne and Sandra's flat. 'I've a splitting headache.'

'Why do you look like you're ready to go out so?' Grainne was as sharp as an eagle when she wanted to be.

'Oh okay so, I'll tell you the truth, I'm actually going on a date.'

'Another one?' Grainne practically choked. 'Have you joined a dating agency or what?'

Anna explained. Grainne listened open-mouthed. 'So you see, you have to play along with me.'

'I see,' Grainne nodded. 'Well, don't worry, myself and Sandra will look after Rich.'

Anna had no doubt that they would.

A loud horn hooted outside. Grainne rushed to the curtains. 'Is that him in the navy beamer?'

'Yes,' said Anna, delighted.

'He looks nice,' Grainne squinted to get a better look. 'He's wearing a suit.'

'You'd better go,' Anna suddenly panicked.

'Yeah . . . well, good luck.'

'Thanks,' Anna smiled. Then she thought of something. 'How many people have you invited up there tonight?'

'Oh there's a big gang of us.'

'Don't let any of your friends tempt Steve, do you hear?' Anna threatened playfully and reached for her black cashmere jumper.

Grainne paused at the door, confusion spread across her face. 'Steve? From downstairs? What do you mean?'

'I know how wild those Tuesday nights can get.'

'But Steve's single again. Didn't you hear? He split up with the French bird when she was over here.'

The horn hooted again. Impatiently.

Chapter Eleven

'Simon's not in the office right now,' Shelley's smooth secretarial tones came down the line. 'Can I take a message?'

'Er . . . no, thanks,' Claire said awkwardly, wishing she hadn't called the office at all. Simon's phone was switched off and Shelley didn't seem to know where he was. Unusual for her, Claire thought uneasily. Shelley usually knew everything.

'Is that Claire?' Shelley asked shrilly.

'Of course,' Claire managed to keep her voice even. Who else would it be? She shouldn't have called. She only did it out of boredom. Her fingers had dialled the digits before her brain even clicked what she was doing.

'Can I give him a message?'

'No, thank you,' Claire said wearily and hung up. Images of Shelley in her impossibly short skirts and skyscraper heels flooded her head. What was wrong with her? She'd seen too many immoral soaps recently – that was the problem. When Andrew slept there was precious little else to do. She'd have to get a job. Even a part-time one. Sure there were millions of jobs going now. She'd *walk* into something. Although she loved Andrew more than life itself, she couldn't limit herself to endless bizarre conversations with Damien the Duck and Freddy the Frog.

She was bored. And anxious to get out of the house. Maybe she'd head into town and spend her birthday money on something. Her mother had made her swear she'd spend the money on herself. Not on the kitchen. Not on the garden. Not even on something cute for Andrew.

'It's for *you*.' She'd been emphatic. 'Just because you're a married woman doesn't mean you can let your appearance go. Your husband married an attractive woman. He'll expect to continue to be married to an attractive woman. Sometimes wives who let themselves go find themselves replaced before they know what's hit them,' she'd warned. Claire had laughed. Her mother was always overreacting. But her smile had since vanished. She pictured Shelley's glamorous 'PA to the boss' image, all hair and make-up with matching plum lips and nails, and gave a slight shudder. Maybe her mother hadn't been so off the mark after all.

She'd ring Mrs Murphy next door to see if she wouldn't mind looking after Andrew for a while. Mrs Murphy, a kind grandmotherly type, doted on the baby. She couldn't ring Fiona: Fiona would be at her lectures in Belfield. Or hanging around the

Arts block giving blokes marks out of ten. Claire remembered doing that with Anna. Those really were the days – carefree and man-mad, worrying only about the number of students she'd snogged after ten cans of Ritz at The Suitcase Ball. That was before she met Simon, of course. He was studying commerce and could religiously be found on the third floor of the library, head buried under a ton of books. He was to be Claire's last steady boyfriend.

Andrew's faint whimpering from the bedroom broke her thoughts. She opened the door gingerly. His little face broke into a gurgling smile at the sight of his mummy. She picked him up gently, noticing how warm and soft his body was, wrapped in a blue velour babygro.

'Are you hungry?' she cooed.

Andrew gave a baby chuckle.

'You're smelly, aren't you?' Claire wrinkled her nose and carried him over to his changing board. 'You're a stinky dinky, that's what you are.' She gave her son's soft cheek a tender kiss. He answered by reaching ten little fingers towards her face and giving a curious sort of screech. She laid him on the board beside Danny the Dinosaur to whom he immediately turned his attention. People had often told her that a baby would change her whole perspective on life for ever. But nothing could have prepared her for the intensity of love that she felt for him. He was undoubtedly the most important thing in her life. The product of a deep love shared between two people. Nothing and nobody was ever going to destroy that, she thought determinedly. And certainly not some brazen floozie in a ridiculously short skirt.

On Grafton Street, the bright lights of McDonald's caught Claire's eye. God, when was the last time she'd treated herself? She meandered over and pulled the door open. Before she knew it she was standing in the queue ordering a Big Mac and a strawberry milkshake. Yum!

She brought the tray upstairs and ate in the corner, remembering the many school parties she'd enjoyed there, wearing a silly paper hat and competing with other kids to see who could find the longest chip. It was funny to think that in a few years she'd be organizing some such party for her own kids. That's if she had any more, she thought grimly. Certainly they hadn't discussed it. Andrew had been a mistake, albeit a most welcome one. But Simon had never mentioned the possibility of another one. And never failed to remind Claire to take her pill.

Outside a cloudless sky promised some sunshine. It was unusually bright for early February. Claire walked past Hallmarks, noticing its vivid window display of vibrant red. Oh yes sure, Valentine's was next Monday, wasn't it? She'd have to buy Simon a card even though he thought the whole thing was a cod. Of course it was, Claire agreed. Anyone would be a fool to think otherwise. But it was fun. She gazed longingly at the cute *I Love You* bunnies. There was no harm in it. It was just a bit of craic. Ah well, she crossed the street and strode into the cosmetics section of Brown Thomas. Simon had given her the gift of life commitment and wasn't that better than any amount of dead flowers and tacky heart-shaped balloons?

The beautifully made-up assistant considered Claire's skin carefully before recommending an expensive cream. It came with a free washbag. The girl assured her that positive results would be evident after a few weeks. Good, Claire thought. She wanted to feel beautiful and rejuvenated for Victoria's party. She wasn't going to have that snooty cow look down her nose at a washed-out-looking Claire. Simon, of course, thought she was making a big fuss over nothing.

'Sure it's only a reunion,' he'd said casually one morning over his newspaper as Claire rabbited on about what she was going to wear. 'It's not like some really important do,' he'd added.

Not to Simon, Claire thought. But he'd no idea how much that girl had taunted Claire and Anna in school. Claire shuddered as she remembered the time she'd been in hospital getting her tonsils removed. Victoria had spread rumours about her being treated for anorexia. Half her friends had innocently come to visit bringing boxes of chocolates and doughnuts in an attempt to fatten her up.

But it had been worse for Anna. Victoria once stuck chewing gum to her lovely long hair and she'd had to get it all cut off. Victoria had then called her a lesbian for weeks after that and although nobody had even known what lesbian meant, they presumed it wasn't very nice.

Everyone in the year had a story about Victoria Reilly. One girl had even been taken away by her parents after Victoria had emptied a bin over her head then made her pick up all the rubbish. It was baffling how Victoria had never been expelled. But later it came out that her parents had donated a substantial amount of money towards the upkeep of the school sports grounds. And therefore she stayed. A bit like politics really. School politics.

The assistant placed the anti-wrinkle cream in the traditional black and white Brown Thomas bag. Claire thanked her and made her way up the escalator. She was looking forward to viewing the new Spring Collections. Being a weekday, there were no crowds in the store. It was pleasant walking around. She made for the designer wear and fingered some of the soft new fabrics. Then glanced at the prices. Uh oh, maybe she should purchase a lottery ticket before the day was out.

'Claire Fiscon, I don't believe it!'

Claire jumped. She swung around and blinked hard, unfolding her brain into reality. She didn't recognize the slender blonde dressed in a classic cream suit.

'It's Victoria!' The girl smiled, revealing snow-white teeth behind blood-red lips.

Jesus, Mary and Joseph! The colour drained from Claire's face. The two women stood on either side of the clothing rail, facing each other. 'Hi,' Claire flashed a wary smile, 'what a . . . a nice surprise.'

'Thank you.'

'You, er . . . look . . . great. Love the scarf. Er . . . where did you get it?'

'Paris.' Victoria smiled triumphantly.

'Oh I love Paris . . . in fact I love many parts of France.'

'Yes,' Victoria said.

Claire could feel the colour rush back into her cheeks. It was ridiculous the way this other girl was affecting her. She'd better regain some self-control before she made a complete fool of herself.

'I'm married now,' she told Victoria. 'I'm not Fiscon any more,' she added.

'Who did you marry?'

'Simon Adamson.'

'Would I know him? What does he do?'

'He's in Finance,' Claire said, wondering if she'd have told the truth if her husband was a binman.

'Oh.' Victoria presented sudden interest. 'Well, I'll look forward to seeing him at the party so. You're both coming, I hope?'

'Absolutely.'

'Are you shopping?'

'I haven't found anything I like yet,' Claire lied,

taking note of Victoria's several shopping bags.

'I know the feeling,' Victoria sighed. 'You really have to go abroad for variety.'

'Yes,' Claire agreed uncomfortably.

'Any plans for kids?'

'Sorry?'

'Do you hear the patter of little feet yet?'

'I have a son,' Claire said proudly and groped in her bag for Andrew's photo. 'That's him.'

Victoria peered at the photo of Andrew sitting up in his cot surrounded by furry friends and looking totally adorable. 'Very nice,' she said unfeelingly.

Claire swiftly placed the photo back in her bag. She was furious. Very nice indeed! You'd describe a car as very nice. Or a garden. Not a child who was as stunningly beautiful as Andrew. She wasn't going to waste a single second more with this cold, condescending woman.

'I'd better be off,' she made a big show of checking her watch, 'Simon will be home looking for his dinner.'

'Oh that's awful.' Victoria heaved a theatrical sigh. 'Vincent and I rarely eat in.'

Claire felt her throat constrict with annoyance. 'Well, you'll find once you've children it won't be so easy to go out any time you feel like it.'

'That's why we're not intending to start straight-away.' Victoria gave a silvery laugh. 'We want some time to enjoy each other before we get tied down. After all, everybody knows once you start having kids your life is practically over.' She paused. 'Well goodbye,' she said eventually. 'It was fantastic bumping into you after all this time.'

'The bitch,' Anna agreed heartily.

'You don't think I'm being paranoid, do you?' Claire demanded over the phone.

'Not at all, Victoria's just jealous,' Anna reassured her. 'Andrew is a divine baby. By the way, did you set me up with Jake?'

'Jake?' Claire sounded amazed. 'Of course I didn't.'

'I went out with him last night.'

Claire nearly dropped her baby in shock. She'd never have put Anna and Jake together. Still, no harm. It'd be nice to hook up with the pair of them on a double date.

'That's great,' she told her friend. 'Will you be seeing him again?'

'Next week,' Anna told her. 'Time enough.'

'You don't sound too enthusiastic.'

'I am, it's just that . . .'

'Ow!'

'Do you want to put Andrew down and get back to me?'

'No . . . Stop it, love . . . He needs his bath, it's late.'

'Right, well it's like this: Jake flatters me and thinks I'm funny and all but . . . I'm not sure he's the one.'

'God, Anna,' Claire sounded exasperated, 'not every man you meet is going to be the one.'

'That's all right for you,' Anna said sulkily. 'You're happily married.'

'Yeah.' Andrew was dribbling onto Claire's silk blouse and pawing her hair with chocolate-covered fingers, 'I forgot, you're so right.'

'Put Simon on to me,' Anna demanded, 'I'm going to kill him for setting me up like this.'

'He's not here,' Claire sounded subdued.

'Right . . . by the way, did Victoria mention me?'

'No.'

'Silly cow.'

'Yeah.' Claire had gone all quiet.

Afterwards she sat in the kitchen, slowly watching Simon's shepherd's pie going cold. She'd spent the last two hours making the kitchen sparkle. The heart-shaped candle she'd bought had practically melted. She blew it out. It was late. She really should go upstairs and take off her make-up. She was looking forward to testing her new cream. Simon showed no signs of coming home. The only messages on the answerphone were from her mother and a neighbour wondering if she was interested in joining the neighbourhood watch scheme.

By midnight there was still no sign of Simon. She dialled his office. The phone rang off unanswered. Claire was beginning to feel sick with worry. All the goodness had gone out of her day, what with bumping into Victoria and her husband's no-show.

She climbed into the big empty double bed and switched on the television to try to take her mind off things, but every time she heard a noise her ears pricked up, expecting to hear the key turn in the front-door lock. Sometime in the early hours of the morning she drifted into a restless sleep.

Chapter Twelve

Anna decided on a plain navy suit. She'd been given a half day to go to the head offices near O'Connell Street for her interview. As she marched past the Molly Malone statue, all high heels and business she asked herself what the hell she was doing.

She wasn't sure if she wanted to be sent to Ballygobackwards for six months and limit herself to nights out in one of two pubs where the local lads would be aged either eighteen or eighty. Okay, she'd be an assistant manager of Lolta's but was that what she really wanted? Surely it would be better to stay in Dublin with all her friends? Hmmm. What friends?

Anna checked her watch and quickened her pace. It wouldn't do to be late. She crossed O'Connell Street thankful her skirt was nun's length. The wind was biting. She passed one of the pound shops and was assaulted by the display of Valentine's Day merchandise. Valentine's! What a horrendous occasion. Yet again she wouldn't be receiving anything. There was a time she'd sent herself cards . . .

but she was too old for that now. Way too old. She bumped into Elaine coming out of the offices looking like death.

'Elaine, how did it go?' Anna was concerned.

'Awful.' Elaine's face was a worrying grey. 'I didn't get a wink of sleep last night worrying about it and, after all that, they didn't ask any of the questions I'd prepared.'

'Oh dear,' Anna was at a loss for words. She couldn't understand for the world why anyone would lose a night's sleep over something like this.

'I desperately need the pay rise,' Elaine wailed.

So do I, Anna thought. But not at that price. 'Listen, I'll ring you later,' she said, 'and we'll go for a drink. I'm sure it went a lot better than you think.'

'Good luck.' Elaine gave her an awkward hug and went off up the street.

Crikey, Anna thought as she touched up her make-up in the Ladies. Some people took life far too seriously by far. Elaine really would need to chill out. Or maybe, an uncomfortable thought suddenly struck her, just maybe Elaine was right. Perhaps Elaine had her priorities all in the right order. Was Anna the eejit here? Someone who just went with the flow? People who went with the flow kept flowing down the river. Right? And drowned at the end of it, she supposed. Not a nice thought at all. She took three deep breaths, strode purposefully out of the Ladies and braced herself for a successful interview.

'Where do you see yourself in five years' time?' Mr Walton the grey man from Personnel barked at her.

In your chair not, she thought. *Hopefully on a beach somewhere in the Bahamas with a handsome husband rubbing oil onto my back, having made my fortune in private retailing.*

'I'd like to see myself reaching my highest potential within the company,' she said, trying not to gag.

Walton drummed his Bic thoughtfully on the desk. He was impressed, she could see. The young colourless woman at his elbow was scribbling like something on Speed. Anna wondered what the hell she was writing.

'Do you see yourself as a leader?'

Anna took a deep breath and frowned as she prepared to consider the question seriously. 'Absolutely,' she said eventually. 'I'd like to motivate my staff so that as a team we make Lolta's grow as a company, encourage business and deliver high customer satisfaction.'

God, if anyone could hear me talking like this I'd die, Anna thought.

Walton lashed out a few more, obvious questions before he gave a fraction of a smile and wrapped up. 'Have you any questions, Fidelma?'

Fidelma did. 'Describe yourself in three words.'

'Cool, calm and calculated,' Anna beamed. That was an easy one.

Fidelma's eyes widened, horrified. Walton's blank stare swiftly became mild alarm. He gave a short cough that seemed to get caught somewhere in the middle of his throat. Anna swallowed in disbelief.

'Sorry . . .' she felt a rush of blood flow to her forehead, '. . . collected, I mean. Cool, calm and collected. That's what I mean.' She smiled helplessly.

'Yes,' Fidelma said awkwardly. 'Well, that's about all,' she added stiffly. Her expression conveyed immeasurable contempt.

Oh you can't let me go now, Anna panicked. Oh God, no, *please don't let me walk out of here like a complete twat*, she begged.

'Thank you, Anna,' Walton took her limp hand in his and gave it a hurried shake. 'We'll let you know on Monday.'

'Yes, great,' Anna said, false gaiety brightening her voice. She slunk from the room, tail between her legs.

In Kiely's pub, Anna added a splash of tonic to her stiff gin. She mixed it round with her straw, then knocked back half. Elaine was nowhere to be seen. A group of rugby lads surrounded the bar, shouting and clapping each other on the backs. Anna scrutinized the small TV screen in the corner and pretended to watch the match of the day. She hoped Elaine would bloody well hurry up. It was unusual for her to be late. Hopefully she hadn't thrown herself under a train or anything. She took another sip of her G&T. There wasn't much left. A studenty-type barperson wiped around her glass with a damp cloth and emptied the two cigarette butts lying in her ashtray. Anna noticed a couple of the rugby lads turning round and sizing her up. She ignored them.

Maybe she was just being paranoid. Sitting alone in a busy, well-known Dublin pub on a Thursday evening had a way of making the most confident person feel uncomfortable. She wished she'd brought a newspaper.

'Hi,' Elaine's voice made her start. 'Sorry I'm late,' She shook her damp hair.

'Is it raining outside?' Anna asked in alarm. She hadn't even thought of bringing an umbrella with her.

'No, I had a quick shower to try to wash away all my worries. So,' she settled back into the comfy cushioned seat, 'tell us all.'

'Oh God, it was a disaster,' Anna scowled. 'A complete and utter fucking nightmare.' Her blood ran hot and cold even thinking about it.

Elaine ordered herself a double brandy and a second G&T for Anna. 'What kind of questions did they ask?'

Oh no, Anna's heart sank. Surely they weren't going to have a post-mortem on today's fiasco. The whole point of going out and getting twisted was to forget today, enjoy the evening and act as if there mightn't be a tomorrow. 'Oh, just the usual,' she answered absently, her eyes glazing over.

Elaine got the message. 'We'll go over it tomorrow.' She raised her glass. 'To the future and all its uncertainty.'

'To the future,' Anna agreed heartily.

They clinked glasses and laughed. Alcohol was amazing the way it altered your outlook on life.

'Oh, wouldn't you kill for a figure like that?' Elaine turned as a tall svelte blonde sauntered past in a clingy black dress.

'I know,' Anna watched enviously as the girl linked arms with a tall well-dressed man. The man turned. Anna froze. She watched Mark hail the barman. He placed his order and glanced casually across the room. Anna picked up the menu and pretended to study it.

'Are you hungry?' Elaine questioned in a loud voice.

'I am a bit,' Anna muttered, determined not to let Mark see that she was on another manless night out. God, why couldn't he have turned up in The Bailey on Tuesday night where he would have seen her sipping cocktails with Jake?

'Oh look, it's Mark,' Elaine shouted. Anna rolled her eyes to the ceiling. It didn't take long for Mark to parade his date across from the bar to meet them.

'This is Sally,' Mark beamed. He looked fantastic, a heavy cashmere coat half hiding one of his customary exquisite suits.

Anna offered a reluctant hand. 'I've heard so much about you,' she forced a smile.

Sally returned a look that said *I haven't heard anything about you*. Anna ignored it. 'This is my colleague, Elaine,' she said, delighted at Sally's distrusting expression.

'Can I get you girls a drink?' Mark enquired.

'That'd be great,' Elaine accepted before Anna got the chance to refuse.

Mark returned to the bar. Sally stood awkwardly clutching her bag.

'Busy day?' Anna asked politely.

'Every day is extremely busy for me. I work very long hours. I'm still studying as well. For my fellowship.'

'Oh.' Elaine looked lost.

'Well, it must be great to get out now and again,' Anna said.

'Yes. Is this a girls' night out?'

'No.' Anna gave a somewhat sarcastic smile. 'You see all those guys at the bar? They're with us.'

Mark was back. He was about to sit down when Sally suddenly spotted a cosy space over on the far side of the pub. 'There's more room over there.' She gave him an endearing smile. 'We don't want to be crowding you girls out,' she addressed Anna and Elaine.

'Have a good night,' Mark looked almost sorry to go, 'don't go too mad.'

'Don't count on it,' Elaine giggled.

'Oh, Anna?' he hesitated.

'Yes?'

'Ring me.'

They disappeared into the crowd.

'Well, what do you think of that?' Anna stared after them indignantly.

'It was very nice of him to buy us the drinks. He's a gentleman.'

'Don't be ridiculous,' Anna snapped. 'Don't you see he was just trying to make us all jealous, Sally included?'

Elaine didn't see at all. 'He's very good looking,' she swooned. 'Sally's lucky.'

'No she's not.' Anna was sticking to her guns. 'Sure you couldn't trust Mark as far as you could throw him.'

'How do you know?' Elaine accused. 'Have you proof?'

'Well . . . no,' Anna began.

'Has he ever tried to shift you?'

'Unless you count ten years ago, no. But that's not the point.'

'You see, you've nothing on him. I think you fancy Mark.'

'That's outrageous,' Anna said. The drink had obviously shot to poor Elaine's head. 'Mark? God, the thought of it!'

'Don't believe you,' Elaine said drunkenly. 'Don't believe you,' she repeated.

They'd turned up the music. People were spilling into the pub. Elaine had cheered up no end. Anna was pleased. Elaine deserved a bit of fun.

After Kiely's a taxi took the girls to Anabel's where they were treated to champagne by a bunch of golfers over from England. Two of the golfers wore wedding rings. Two didn't. Anna directed most of her conversation towards the available ones. They weren't much fun but, hey, the champagne was nice! Elaine was determined to dance. Not on the main dance floor, mind, but on the small one in the members' bar where nobody else was dancing. Despite Anna's gentle protests, she strutted her stuff to the delight of onlookers. God, she's going to regret this in the morning, Anna thought. Elaine's dancing was decidedly uncool. She must have seen *Grease* about sixty times. An odd-looking man in an ill-fitting velvet jacket joined her on the dance floor. He took Elaine's hand and tried twirling her around. She missed her footing and fell. Anna rushed to the dance floor and scooped her up.

'Let's go back to my place for coffee,' She led Elaine to the cloakroom to collect her coat.

'No.' Elaine was belligerent. 'I want to have fun. I never have fun any more. I don't want to go home,' she said adamantly.

'But we can't stay here,' Anna pleaded. 'The club is closed. The lights are on.'

'Are they?' Elaine covered her face with both hands, horrified. 'Ish my make-up all right?'

'It's fine.' Anna guided her towards the front door. 'No one will see it now anyway, we're going home.'

'I'm not going home.' Elaine stood her ground in the car park of the Burlington Hotel.

'Where are you going then?' Anna wanted to know. It was a bitterly cold, early February morning. The wind was biting.

'Leeshon Shtreet.'

'Right.' Impatience rising within her, Anna marched over to the other side of the road and stuck her hand out to flag down a passing cab. 'But we're only staying for half an hour.'

They spent the following forty minutes sipping a bottle of plonk in a deserted Leeson Street club. Four women in cocktail dresses were dancing around their handbags. In a corner a dodgy-looking grey-haired man was lunging at a woman half his age. It was depressing.

'Are you glad you came?' Anna lit her last cigarette.

'To be honest with you, yesh.' Elaine raised her bloodshot eyes. 'I'm shick of feeling shorry for myshelf. From now on, I want to enjoy my life.'

'Well done,' Anna gave her a hug, 'that's the spirit. Hey, how about we call it a night?'

Elaine nodded drunkenly and knocked back the last of the plonk. Oh dear, Anna thought. She wouldn't like to be Elaine's head in the morning.

She saw Elaine home first before falling into her own flat and onto her bed, fully clothed.

Chapter Thirteen

Claire pushed Andrew's pram along Dún Laoighaire pier. The wind was against them but the sea air was fresh and the sound of Ranelagh traffic seemed a million miles away. She'd tried to persuade Simon to join them. She'd thought the walk would do him the world of good. But Simon had refused, choosing to stay home with the PC. Claire was worried about him. His mind was at work even when his body wasn't. Where would it all end, she wondered. Life wasn't supposed to be all about working and making money. She'd confronted him about the nights when he didn't bother coming home. 'It's all about bonding,' he'd explained. 'You can't just shut yourself off from the office crowd, you know. You have to put in appearances, now and again.'

'Now and again, yes,' she'd agreed. 'But you don't have to stay out the whole night. Can't you just take up golf or something like other blokes?'

He'd said he was sorry and would seriously think about joining some kind of sports club. But Claire wasn't holding out too much. In some ways she

wished she were single all over again. Like Anna.
Anna really lived her life. Her world was like that of a
soap opera. Men coming and going like trains. It was
so far removed from Claire's humdrum existence.
She'd always thought having a family would make
her life complete. So where had it all gone wrong?

She thought of her brief meeting with Victoria and
shuddered. Victoria had life all worked out. Had
Claire rushed into commitment without a moment's
consideration? Maybe she should have waited before
diving in at the deep end of motherhood without a
few swimming lessons first. Then again, who the hell
was Victoria to judge anyone or anything?

She parked Andrew's buggy at the end of the
pier and sat on the bench staring across to Howth.
The sun seemed to be shining over there. Not in
Dún Laoighaire, where a thick black cloud threatened rain. It was always the way, wasn't it, she
thought ironically. No matter where you were, the
sun seemed to be shining elsewhere.

Somewhere just out of reach.

She hoped, like any young wife and mother, that it
would all work out fine for them. That she wouldn't
be a statistic on Ireland's new divorce list. Marriage
took a lot of work and she was sensible enough
to realize that. She didn't want to become another
bored housewife, her world revolving around nappies and napkins. A part of her envied Anna's work
schedule and roller-coaster love life. Of course Anna
was always complaining about her lot but it was

a horrible thought to know you weren't *needed* somewhere every day. That nobody was *expecting* you to turn up on Monday morning. That if you lay in bed all day nobody (except of course your family) would particularly care.

She'd have to get a job. No question about it.

Because it was Sunday, a rather larger than usual crowd had gathered at the end of the pier despite the glum weather. Claire moved Andrew's buggy slightly to let people pass. A youngish man clad in a navy wax jacket sat down.

It was time to go but her legs were steadfastly refusing to budge. They often resented being marched for miles. Andrew's cheeks were a healthy pink and he was dribbling onto his blue bunny coat. Claire found a tissue at the bottom of her bag and wiped his mouth.

'What a beautiful baby,' the young man sitting beside her commented in genuine admiration.

'Thank you,' Claire said without looking at him. He was well spoken. In fact his voice had a tinge of familiarity. But she was wary of striking up conversations with men while she was alone with her child.

'What's his name?'

'Andrew.'

She raised her head to get a look at this well-spoken man who had taken such a shine to Andrew.

As soon as she did, mutual recognition set in.

'My God, it's Tom, isn't it?' she exclaimed.

'That's right.' He broke into a smile. 'You're Emma's sister, aren't you?'

'Yeah that's right. You've got a great memory. What are you doing up in Dublin?'

'I live here now. I moved from Galway a couple of years ago . . . So this is your little fella.' He rubbed Andrew's cheek with the back of his hand. 'He's the image of you.'

'Is he?' Claire was delighted. 'People say he has my eyes but Simon's nose.'

'Simon's your . . .'

'. . . husband,' she finished for him.

'And does he not like walking?'

'No,' Claire said unhappily. 'No, he does not.'

'So how is Emma anyway?' Tom swiftly switched subjects. 'Still as mad as ever?'

'Yeah, she's on a world tour at the moment with a bunch of friends. They must be in Australia by now,' she said wistfully, imagining Emma in a bikini on a remote beach somewhere.

'I was in Australia myself a couple of years back, never wanted to come home.'

Claire noticed a sadness in his voice as he spoke. Perhaps he'd left a girlfriend behind on the other side of the world. He'd a kind face, deep brown eyes behind odd-shaped glasses, and a generous mouth.

Without warning, Andrew picked up Derek the Dalmatian and flung him with great force. Claire watched in dismay as Derek bounced down the slippery rocks towards the direction of the sea and landed in a small puddle.

'That's bold, Andrew,' Claire said crossly.

Andrew's little face crumpled. He opened his mouth and began to howl. *Oh Jesus, please don't create a scene here now, Andrew, please.*

Tom looked deeply distressed by the drama of it all.

'I'll get it,' he said chivalrously, standing up.

'No, leave it,' Claire urged. 'The rocks are wet.' God, it wasn't worth risking your life for a £3 toy.

But he was gone. A small crowd watched Tom brave the elements for Derek. When he rescued the sopping-wet doggy from a pile of wet seaweed, a couple clapped comically.

Tom beamed as he wrung Derek's saturated body in an attempt to dry him. 'That's my good deed for today.'

The wind had started up again. Claire decided to head back. They walked together along the pier, Tom taking Andrew's buggy half way to give Claire a break. At the car park, Tom offered to get a couple of ice creams.

'Sure, why not?' Claire laughed. 'I haven't had an ice cream here since I was a child.'

They sat in Claire's Fiat, sticking the pieces of flake deep into the whipped ice cream.

'I feel great after that,' Claire said. 'Walking is hugely therapeutic, I find.'

'That's how I feel about it.' Tom gazed through

the windscreen at the angry Irish sky. Wherever he was, Claire decided, it was a million miles from Dún Laoighaire pier.

'I try to come out every Saturday and Sunday,' she said quietly.

'That's funny, so do I,' he snapped back into the present. 'I've never seen you walking here before.'

'Well, I haven't been out much recently due to the dreary weather.'

'Yeah, roll on the summer, this winter has been the longest in history. Well . . .' he seemed to hesitate '. . . thanks for the chat.' He opened the passenger door slowly. 'Give my love to Emma when you're next talking to her.'

'Will do.'

'And you, young man,' he grinned at Andrew strapped into his baby seat, 'you take care of your mother, do you hear?'

'Ahhh,' Andrew answered back joyfully.

He was gone.

What a lovely man, Claire thought. A gentleman. And nice looking too. She wondered what age he was. Probably the same as Emma – they'd been in the same class in UCG. Sure, what's it to you? she asked herself, reversing out of the car park. Chances are you'll never lay eyes on him again.

Chapter Fourteen

'What do you mean, you don't know how the interview went?' Anna's mother frowned at the pan of sausages and turned down the ring.

'You never can tell,' Anna said, playing with her knife and fork, feeling like a child again. Her mother was using the exact tone of voice she'd used when asking about the leaving certificate exams. *What do you mean you don't know how Maths went? Maths is very straightforward. You either know the answers or you don't.*

'I think it went fine,' Anna said to shut her up.

'So you're in with a good chance then?' Mrs Allstone cracked one egg after another and splashed them onto the pan, making a hissing sound.

'Oh I suppose,' Anna made a face.

'You're not getting any younger, you know.'

'I know, sure don't you remind me every time I'm over?'

She really didn't know why she bothered calling at all. Their dear son didn't bother his barney phoning, never mind calling round.

Yet, they'd watched joyfully as Roger swotted for his first-class degree and secured a job in a prestigious Dublin firm before being headhunted by an international London-based company. His salary was six figures, his bonus probably twice that.

Anna had lacked the natural academic ability of her brother and her parents had never let her forget it. Neighbours were filled with stories of Roger's substantial success, but stories concerning Anna were swiftly skimmed over. What they conveniently failed to admit though, Anna thought wryly, was the fact that Roger was living with a divorcee ten years his senior. And her two kids by two different fathers. Roger hadn't even come home for Christmas last year so intent was he on avoiding his mother's disapproving stare. Life wasn't always what it seemed in the Allstones' sunny Stillorgan residence.

'So what does this boy do with himself?' Her mother was referring to Jake, who was on his way to her parents' house. Anyone under forty was a boy according to her.

'Stockbroking.'

'I see.' Her mother gave a faint smile. Stockbroking was respectable, obviously. Not as stable as law or medicine of course, but it would do. 'I wish you wouldn't ask strange men to barge in on your father and me when we're not expecting them. The kitchen's a mess. I've left your father's underwear on some of the radiators and there's a stink in the hall. Someone must have let the dog in.'

'He's not coming to meet you,' Anna snapped. 'He's collecting me and we're going out for a drink.'

'He's not drinking and driving, is he?' Her father looked up from his unappetizing-looking fry.

'No,' Anna said. 'And he's not coming in either.'

'I don't trust a man who doesn't want to meet a girl's parents. You'd wonder what he had to hide,' Mrs Allstone sniffed.

The doorbell rang. Anna made a dash for her bag and coat, kissed her parents goodnight and fled.

As she fastened her seatbelt in the passenger seat of Jake's car, she looked up and saw her mother peeping out of one of the bedroom windows. She half expected her to call out, 'Be home by ten or else.'

'You look smashing.' Jake was, as usual, forthcoming with the compliments. 'Nice time with your folks?'

'Very nice,' Anna lied. She wasn't about to go into her whole family history with a stranger. She'd done it before only to find the stranger suddenly got abducted in the middle of the night. 'My parents were in great form.'

'I can't wait to meet them.' Jake started up the engine.

'I'm sure they'd be delighted to meet you, too.' *Not.*

'Any siblings?'

'Just a brother. Roger.'

'Fantastic.'

'Yes.' *Whatever.*

'Is he as funny as you?'

'No.'

Jake screamed with laughter. Anna stared at him in mild horror. She wasn't sure if she liked being thought of as hilarious. It put pressure on you to try to make people laugh all the time. Tonight she felt like being serious. Something to do with meeting her parents perhaps.

They whizzed along the dual carriageway. Jake put his foot down and they sped into town.

Jake held open the door of Elgon's bistro for her. A young girl took her chocolate-coloured scarf and coat, then they were led to a table for two.

Anna glanced around the room to see if she recognized anybody. She spotted a friend of her brother deep in conversation with a glamorous brunette. Uh oh, she grimaced. As far as she knew his wife was definitely a redhead. A group of well-known politicians were laughing loudly in one corner, a well-known actor was sipping champagne with his second wife – or was it his third? Anna graciously accepted her menu. Ah yes, this was the life she was meant to lead. Being driven around town in a fancy car, by a nicely dressed man who thought she was as beautiful as a supermodel and as funny as a comedian. It was the BIZ!

Anna opted for the vegetarian bake and Jake chose the salmon. He ordered the second most expensive wine on the list. She smiled at him. He had class. Yes, he was the one. Not for the rest of her life, mind. *God, no!* But he'd be great at Victoria's party. Jake was up there with the best of them.

Jake made a toast to the most stunning girl in the room. Anna looked around tentatively to see who it might be. 'It's you, silly,' Jake whispered. Anna immediately softened. She felt anything but stunning. But she wasn't about to chide Jake for flattery. Flattery was everything.

'Thank you for a wonderful evening,' she said between mouthfuls of chocolate mud pie.

'The pleasure is all mine,' his eyes twinkled, 'but the evening isn't over yet, is it?'

'Well . . . no,' Anna replied hesitantly. She wondered what he was thinking. He couldn't come back to her place, that was for sure. And she didn't particularly want to go back to his place either. Sure she hardly knew him. 'We could go dancing?' she suggested.

'We could go to Lillies?'

'Great,' she said before excusing herself to go to the Ladies.

When she came back the bill had been paid. *Naturellement.*

Lillies was jammed and Jake ushered her into the VIP area. It was a bit quieter in there. Jake found a seat and disappeared off to get the drinks. Anna looked around with interest. The place was dotted with glamorous blondes and men who looked like they *might* be vaguely famous. Some well-known sports celebrities were having a drinking competition in one of the booths, in another Anna recognized the 'stars' of a naff Irish soap. One of them seemed to be waving at Anna. She squinted to see who it was. Then, horror of horrors, recognition set in. Rich. She smiled weakly. He stood up and edged his way out of his circle of friends.

'Hi,' he said, standing next to her, hands deep in his pockets. He seemed genuinely pleased to see her. 'What are you doing here?'

'I'm here with a . . . friend.' Anna shifted uneasily in her seat. She glanced at the bar where Jake was paying for the drinks. 'And yourself?'

'I'm here with . . .' he rattled off a list of marginally famous actors.

'Wow,' Anna said.

'You weren't at Grainne and Sandra's party. I was disappointed.'

Jake was back.

Anna introduced the two men.

They shook hands. An awkward silence followed. Suddenly Jake spoke. 'Your face is very familiar. Did you study commerce at UCD?'

'No.'

'Are you in stockbroking?'

Rich shook his head.

'That's funny,' Jake looked puzzled, 'I know I know your face.'

Rich said something about needing to get back to his friends. He added a comment about being pleased to see her again.

He was gone.

'Who was that?' Jake took a sip of sparkling water. He'd decided not to drink any more for fear of being stopped on the way home.

'Oh, he's a pal of the nurses upstairs.' Well, it was *partly* true.

'Is he?' Jake didn't sound too convinced. 'He seemed pretty taken with you.'

'Ah no,' Anna tried to hide her delight, 'he's just a friend.'

Jake appeared to accept that and spent the rest of the night cracking jokes and making small talk. Anna laughed her head off. Not because the jokes were funny but because she knew Rich was staring at them. At the end of the night, when Jake went to collect their jackets, he sidled over, his eyes slightly bloodshot, his tie undone around his neck.

'Can I give you a ring sometime?'

'Sure. A diamond would be nice.'

'Seriously though. Can I call you?'

'If you want,' Anna shrugged. What did she have to lose? It wasn't as if she was married to Jake or anything. She belonged to no one and nobody belonged to her.

It was a quick walk to Jake's BMW. It was very nice to be getting into a warm comfortable car with soft leather seats, rather than having to scour town for a taxi along with a million other people.

Jake turned on the radio. David Gray's voice was

smooth and seductive. Anna was glad she was going home though. She was feeling incredibly sleepy.

They were home.

Jake jammed on the brakes and turned off the engine. 'Well goodnight.' Impulsively Anna leaned over and kissed Jake's lips. Unfortunately he took this as an invitation to come in. He unfastened his seatbelt as she unfastened hers.

'Jake?' Anna hesitated. She didn't want to hurt his feelings.

'Yes?'

'Listen, Jake, I've had a truly wonderful evening, but I'm afraid I'm going to have to call it a night now.'

Jake cleared his throat uncomfortably. 'Er ... that's perfectly fine, Anna, I don't want to pressurize you into anything, you know. You're amazing company and it was an absolute pleasure to take you out.'

God, this is all very formal, Anna thought. She almost felt guilty for scarpering off. Mind you, he'd paid for her company and nothing else. She shouldn't feel the slightest bit of guilt. She leaned towards him, wrapped her arms around his neck and indulged in an impossibly long snog, the car gears sticking uncomfortably in her side. He wasn't a bad kisser after all. Anna wondered what else he was good at.

'Goodnight,' she said eventually, disentangling from him before she was tempted to change her mind.

'Goodnight,' he said dolefully, and reluctantly refastened his seatbelt.

Anna gave him a slight wave from her doorstep. Why did he look like a wounded puppy? Why did she feel like she'd done him a terrible injustice? She wasn't for sale. He couldn't buy her affections. They'd had a wonderful evening. End of story.

She pushed the heavy front door open. The hall was dark and gloomy. She turned back to wave one more time, half tempted to run out, tell him she'd changed her mind and invite him in after all.

But she didn't.

She just wasn't that type of girl!

She'd barely one foot on the stairs when the door of the downstairs flat opened. Light flooded the hallway. Steve stood in the doorway, naked except for a towel covering his modesty. His skin was sallow against the contrasting white. His hair was damp as if he'd just emerged from the shower. Tiny drops of water glistened on his neck and shoulders. She could see he was smiling. She stared back in silence. Her head urged her to keep mounting the stairs. Her heart begged her not to.

'Hi there,' he said eventually.

Her head and heart were at war with each other. Her head was winning the first round but her heart threw the final punch and the referee counted to five. The bell sounded. The crowd cheered.

'Hi,' she smiled and walked towards him.

Chapter Fifteen

'It's the mad one for you,' Simon handed the phone to his wife.

'Anna?' Claire answered the call.

'Yeah, oh God, Claire I've done something terrible. I . . . Claire are you there?'

'Uh huh.'

'I snogged Steve.'

'Steve?' It took Claire a few seconds to register. 'Oh, Steve as in the student?'

'Yes, and I swear to God it was just so amazing – he's divine – but you see, the thing is, right, I snogged Jake earlier on and remember Rich?'

'Rich? . . . Er, I think so.'

'Well he phoned this morning to invite me to a premiere he's got tickets to. He's got a small part in it apparently.'

'So what's the problem?'

'It's just I feel like such a bitch. I mean, I like all three of them but I feel bad for leading them all on.'

'Men do it all the time,' Claire retorted crisply and noticed that Simon flinched at his computer.

'Yeah and we hate them for it,' Anna argued.

'How long have you been single, Anna?'

'Practically all my life.'

'Well, what are you complaining about? Men are like buses. They arrive in threes. If you miss them you've to wait a decade for another one. Enjoy.'

'I suppose you're right.'

'You've got three options for Valentine's – that's a bonus if anything,' Claire said loudly enough for her husband to take note.

'Yeah, but Steve's cooking and he's the best kisser so I'm sticking with him.'

'Remember last time he dropped you like a hot cinder?'

'Yeah.' Anna didn't particularly care to be reminded. 'Anyway my plan is that if Jake rings you I've the flu or something. I'm recovering at my aunt's and you don't know the address, right?'

'Right.' Claire didn't sound too convinced.

'How's Andrew?'

'Great,' Claire brightened. 'I took him for a lovely long . . .'

'Claire, I've just remembered I've a tart in the oven, see you soon.'

She cut off.

'What was Anna saying?' Simon asked casually as he swung his rotating chair around to face his wife.

'This and that. You know Anna, everything's always a crisis.' Claire was wary about saying too much to Simon. He didn't appreciate his friends being slagged off. It was all right for him to do it, of course. But that was different. Simon would be livid if he thought Anna was giving Jake the run-around.

'Is she still seeing Jake?' he wanted to know.

'Kind of,' Claire admitted. How much did her husband know? Had Jake confided in him? Why was Simon so secretive? Why did men never communicate?

'Has Jake said anything?' Claire tried not to appear too interested.

'He thinks she's attractive.' Simon turned to his computer. Claire gave his back a look of dismay. Her husband thought speculating on other people's relationships was a complete waste of time.

'Did he say anything else?' She was careful to tread carefully.

'Of course not,' Simon scoffed. 'He's a bloke. He wouldn't have the time or the patience to analyse things that trivial.'

Andrew started to wail in his playpen.

Simon showed no signs of budging.

As usual it was his mother who picked him up.

Chapter Sixteen

'For you.' Elaine handed her the phone at the customer service desk.

'Who is it?' Anna was barely able to speak. Jesus, that bottle of wine she and Steve had drunk the night before must have been one of those 99p bottles. Never again. No really. It just wasn't worth it.

'Hello?'

'Anna?'

'Yes?'

'Mr Walton here, head office.'

'Yes?' Anna felt the walls closing in on her.

'I'm pleased to inform you that your first interview was a success and we'd like to invite you for a second and final one next week. If you would like to arrange with Personnel for a time that suits . . .'

Anna barely heard the rest. She couldn't believe it! A second interview? What was going on? She'd done a crap interview.

'Thank you, Mr Walton . . . Yes, delighted . . . Yes, thank you very much.'

'What did he say?' Elaine was beside her with a face that was devoid of any colour whatsoever.

'He . . . Oh God, Elaine . . .' Anna's stomach gave a violent rumble and she fled the shop floor.

Clinging onto the toilet bowl, tears running down her cheeks, Anna cursed the day she ever hooked up with Steve. It was all right for him to get pissed out of his mind any day of the week. But she was too old for this kind of carry on. Far too old.

She heard a pair of high heels click clicketing along the corridor. Oh God, she really didn't want one of the shop girls to hear her retching.

Eventually she came out of the cubicle. June was at the mirror spraying cheap perfume onto her giraffe-like neck. The powerful stink made Anna want to vomit again.

'Well, I must say you've surprised us all by your interview skills,' the older woman almost spat.

Interview skills? Sure, it was the quick blow job I gave Walton when Fidelma wasn't looking that did the trick.

Anna grimaced and said nothing.

'But don't think you've got the job yet,' June added spitefully. 'There's still plenty to be done around here. I want a full sales report for last week on my desk before you leave here this evening.'

The bloody bitch, Anna thought as June sashayed out of the door. Just because *she* didn't have anybody taking her out tonight.

It didn't feel like Valentine's at all, Anna thought

as she sat in the bus with the fogged-up windows and the disgusting smell of wet clothes drying. Mind you, what was Valentine's *supposed* to feel like? Were you supposed to wake up with a loving feeling? Oh God, no.

Anna was tired and feeling unbelievably unromantic. Thank God Steve was cooking and she didn't have to go out to a restaurant and compete with lots of other couples in a *who looks the most in love?* contest.

She pushed open the door of the flat. A strong smell of curry came from downstairs making her stomach rumble. She absolutely adored curry!

She'd better slip upstairs to make herself look presentable. There was no way she was arriving in his flat still dressed in her work clothes. In her cubby hole she found a big white envelope. She brought it upstairs and tore it open. It was a card with a big gaudy gold and pink rose on it. She opened it up.

> *To my Valentine,*
> *You're beautiful and clever and I still can't*
>   *believe you're mine.*
> *Love, Jake*

Very romantic not. Anna tossed the card across the kitchen counter. The cheek of him writing a message like that! Who did he think he was?

And by the way, where the hell was Rich's card?

Anna slumped down on a chair. Valentine's day was depressing.

She began to get ready.

She hadn't even shaved her legs and it was almost eight o'clock.

An unexpected knock on the door made her jump.

She opened it slightly, aware that only one leg was shaved, the other resembling a small forest. Surreptitiously she moved the forest behind the door.

It was Steve. He was carrying the most enormous bunch of roses she'd ever laid eyes on.

Anna was so overwhelmed her eyes filled with tears.

'Steve,' she sighed, 'you shouldn't have.'

'I didn't.' He looked uncomfortable. 'They're not from me. Someone delivered them earlier on but you weren't here so I offered to take them in for you.'

Who are they from, Anna wondered as she struggled to find a vase for the roses that seemed to have taken on a mind of their own. Rich. They must be from him. How sweet!

'Anyway, dinner's ready. Are you?'

'Just a minute.' Anna winked. She had to shave the other leg and make sure the iron was unplugged and the heater was switched off.

After all, she had absolutely no intention of coming back to this flat tonight.

Chapter Seventeen

Elaine was busy, busy, busy. No time for chit-chat.

'What are you doing for lunch?' Anna asked her eventually, cornering her in the stockroom.

'I'm meeting a friend,' Elaine said coldly.

'Who?'

'Nobody you know.'

'Is there something bothering you?'

'Why did you lie to me?' Elaine was blunt.

'What do you mean?'

'I think you know exactly what I mean.' Elaine's eyes danced dangerously in her head. 'You lied to me about your interview.'

'What!'

'Anna, come off it. You said you made a balls of it.'

'I did,' Anna raised her voice higher than she intended. 'I honestly did.'

'Well, they obviously didn't think so in head office, did they?' Elaine's voice was brittle.

'I don't know what happened. You know as well

as I do that I didn't even particularly want the friggin' job. If it was up to me I'd give it to you.'

'Thanks.' Elaine looked at her with steady contempt. 'Now, if you'll excuse me, I've work to be done,' she snapped before turning on her heel.

Anna ate lunch alone.

But the food lay practically untouched on the plate in front of her.

What was Elaine's problem? You'd swear she'd just gone and got herself a top government position the way Elaine was carrying on.

After lunch, she wandered around Grafton Street killing time. She was in no hurry to get back to Lolta's. A fresh breeze danced with her hair and lifted her spirits slightly. Why was she so afraid of the promotion anyway? Was it the change? But didn't they say a change was as good as a rest?

After all, once Steve finished his finals he'd probably vanish from her life. Anna wasn't a complete fool. She knew Steve wasn't the kind of guy to hang around a rented flat in Ranelagh for the rest of his days. And anyway the promotion wouldn't do her bank balance any harm. Best of all, she wouldn't have June at her throat like a ravenous Rottweiler.

Anna paced up Grafton Street thinking hard. Yes, it would definitely be worth it. Even if it meant living in a field in Ballydehob, she was going to take this promotion very seriously. Imagine the look on her ex-classmates' faces when she, Anna Allstone, announced she was an assistant manager. That'd give them something to put in their pipes.

The atmosphere in Lolta's was fraught with tension. Elaine was buzzing around the store as if a wasp was stuck to her ear. Anna continued to work mechanically. The sooner she got out of this place the better, she conceded, redirecting queues at the checkouts. Why had she ever considered staying in the first place?

She was home early. An Indian takeaway flyer was pinned to her door. On it was scrawled a message.

Rich rang from London. Says he's a speaking part in Casualty. *What's the story? Grainne.*

Anna whipped it down and shoved it into her bag. She knocked on Steve's door. No answer. Of course, she suddenly remembered, he was studying late tonight. He wouldn't be home till at least ten. No harm, Anna thought. She quite fancied a night in for a change. The last few nights had been seriously hectic. She dragged herself into her flat. A damp, depressing, early evening mist had found its way into the flat and hung gloomily in the air. Anna made a beeline for the electric heater, whipped the curtains closed and switched on the kettle. She sat on the sofa and removed the RTÉ Guide from her briefcase.

The place was eerily quiet. She turned up the volume on the telly and hoped the nurses weren't trying to sleep. She'd soon know if they were, of course – Grainne and Sandra weren't shy about hammering on the ceiling.

The kettle gave a brief whistle and snapped itself off. Anna tore herself away from the comfort of the sofa and poured herself a cuppa. She pushed the sofa nearer the telly, grabbed a blanket from the bedroom and a box of Pringles from the press. Now she was all set. What was on the box at all? *Coronation Street* was wrapping up. Damn. She hadn't seen *Corrie* for ages. Now she wouldn't have a clue what the girls in the canteen were yapping on about. She flicked channels. RTÉ news was on. Sure she might as well watch that. Keep herself up to date on current affairs. She yawned lazily as some politician droned on and on about something irrelevant. Well, irrelevant to Anna anyway. It was funny to watch people in the background pretending to be interested. One man stood beside the politician, frowning as the rain fogged up his glasses. He probably wasn't listening at all but was acutely aware that people at home might see him. It was a gas. Two young inner-city type boys were jumping up and down madly. A couple hurried past under a big umbrella. The man's arm was wrapped protectively around his wife's waist. He looked a bit like Jake. Jesus flipping Christ, it was Jake! Anna knocked over her tea, scalding her lap. She screamed. The *prick*! Jake was supposed to be out of town. That's what he'd told *her* anyway. But according to RTÉ he was very much in town. Outside Dáil Éireann to be precise. The two-timing rat!

Raging, she rummaged through her little black

book. She wasn't going to let him get away with this. She found his number and, fired up with anger, she stomped down the stairs not quite knowing what she was going to say to him.

She let her fingers fumble for the digits.

He answered. She let two twenty-pence pieces fall into the slot. This was very uncool, she decided. It was time to get one of those rotten little mobiles.

'Hi, it's me,' she said, which was ridiculous really because she knew full well her number was flashing on his phone.

'It's ... er you,' he answered foolishly. Anna gritted her teeth to stop herself from screaming at him. She could hear loud traffic. They must have been heading towards Stephen's Green.

'Thanks for your card.' She stuck in a fifty and another twenty. Jesus, calls to mobiles ate money.

'You're welcome,' he said, his voice filling with alarm. 'Listen, can I ring you back?'

'Oh no,' Anna explained dangerously, 'I *miss* you. I want to hear your voice.' She was enjoying this. 'Can you come over?'

'No,' he gave an odd-sounding screech, 'I can't, I'm just outside Dundalk,' A blatant lie. 'It'll take me a while to get over.'

'Right,' Anna played along, 'because I'm in bed and I'm bored.'

'I can come over later though,' Jake explained eagerly.

'Oh, that'll be too late,' Anna gave a mock sigh.

'But tell you what, if you get home before the late edition of the RTÉ news be sure to tune in. If not, get your mother to video it.'

'Why?'

'Oh you'll see,' Anna said sharply. 'Goodnight and good luck.'

She cut him off. Dead.

Chapter Eighteen

'You did not. I don't believe it.' Claire nearly dropped the phone.

'Too right I did,' Anna began to chuckle. She couldn't help it. She tried to picture Jake's face confronted with his five minutes of fame.

'You know, I never really trusted Jake,' Claire admitted. She'd always thought Simon's colleague was too smooth for his own good. Well, Anna was well rid of him now.

'Thanks for telling me,' Anna said huffily.

'Well, it's not like I shoved you into his arms,' Claire retorted. 'Anyway, in a way you've a bit of a cheek being angry with him. Aren't you supposed to be going out with thingumajig?'

'Rich?'

'No, the student.'

'Steve?'

'Yeah.'

'That's different,' Anna said defensively.

Claire giggled. She couldn't help it. Anna was so unbelievably self-righteous. She blamed men for everything yet was just as bad as them. Worse even. Oh well, she was right, wasn't she? Pity there weren't more women like Anna about. Men like Jake needed a kick up the ass. Soon Claire was laughing loudly down the phone.

'Fair play to you, Anna.'

'Thanks. I'm well rid of that eejit. Besides I've still two more options for the party,' she said wickedly.

'In the form of Rich and Steve?'

'Yeah . . . thing is, I don't think either of them is particularly suitable for Victoria's party.'

'So we're back to square one,' Claire said dryly.

'I'm afraid so.'

Something occurred to Claire as soon as she put the phone down. Did Simon know about Jake's other woman? And if he did, why hadn't he said anything? Did he think it was better for Anna not to know? Or did he think 'Good on ya, Jake, it's well for some'? She'd have to ask him when he got home. If he *did* come home of course.

She rang his mobile and cursed the voice that said, 'Your call has been diverted. Please hold.' What was the point in having a mobile if you didn't keep it switched on? His office line was worth a try.

It rang out.

Well, feck him anyway.

He could starve tonight.

Sleep didn't come easily. Andrew started to cry and Claire rushed to the baby room to soothe him back to sleep. She was wide awake after that. Her throat was dry She tiptoed downstairs to the kitchen, opened the fridge door and removed a two-litre bottle of 7-Up. A half litre of vodka sat in the middle of the fridge. It seemed to be pleading *drink me please*. Nah, Claire banged the door shut. Only alcos drank alone. She thought of Simon getting pissed somewhere with Jake. Who else was with them? Perhaps Jake's floozie had a friend? God, it didn't bear thinking about. She opened the fridge door again and snatched the vodka. Sure, one drink never killed anyone.

She poured a tiny bit. Added six cubes of ice, then drowned the vodka with 7-Up. She brought the glass to her lips. No, no good. She couldn't even smell the alcohol. She poured another bit. This measure was more generous. She gulped some down and winced as the fluid burned her throat. Heaven. She ambled round the kitchen, drank some more vodka and tried Simon's mobile once again. *Your call has been . . .* 'Fuck off,' she yelled, then rebuked herself for shouting while her son slept upstairs.

She switched on the radio and danced angrily to JJ72. When JJ72 switched to Steps she pulled out the radio plug in disgust. As if she could dance to something as cheesy as Steps. She found an old ABBA tape lurking at the bottom of the CD holder. That would do.

Her drink was finished, she noticed glumly. She'd promised herself just the one. Oh well, promises were meant to be broken. What would Anna think? Anna always said Claire was as solid as a rock. But rocks eroded over the years. She'd learned that in Geography. She pictured her old Geography teacher's beady eyes, poodle perm and pursed lips, and gave an involuntary shudder.

The phone rang, making her jump. She picked it up slowly. 'Hello?'

'Claire?'

'Simon?'

'Claire, listen I tried to call you earlier but the phone was engaged. I'm out with clients.'

'Lucky them,' Claire said dully.

'It's gone on longer than I expected, so it's better that I stay at Jake's.'

'I thought Jake already had company.'

'Sorry? Are you still there, Claire? The line's pretty bad. Catch you later, okay honey?'

Claire hung up. He was drunk. He only ever called her 'honey' when he was drunk. Why was he still out drinking? He hadn't always carried on like this. Somebody must be influencing him. There was no other reason. But who?

Claire poured herself another measure. Her head was feeling deliciously dizzy now. What would her mother make of all of this? 'Be careful of men who've never lived,' she'd once said. 'Because one day they'll snap and wonder what they've missed out on.'

That was it, Claire gave a strangled cackle. Simon was trying to catch up. He'd spent all his twenties studying, going on courses and attending interviews.

He'd only had sex with one other girl, his other long-term girlfriend. He'd rarely got out-of-his-face-scuttered drunk and had never smoked (cigarettes or otherwise). He'd never jetted off to Tenerife on a bad lads' holiday – in fact, it suddenly dawned on Claire, the only time he'd ever gone anyway mad was when his exam results had come out. It all made sense now. Simon hadn't ever really *lived*. No wonder he was showing the beginnings of a mid-life crisis.

Chapter Nineteen

Anna woke at ten on Thursday morning. She stretched lazily like a cat in the bed, and then fell back against the mound of pillows.

Having a weekday off was one of the advantages of being in the retail business. It meant you could browse around town without the Saturday afternoon crowds jostling you out of the way.

Anna wasn't exactly what you'd call a shopaholic. Two shopping trips a year sufficed – one in the autumn and one in the spring. She couldn't bear crammed dressing rooms with unforgiving bright mirrors and nauseating air-conditioning. It was horrible the way cheeky teenage shop assistants would yell, 'Are you all right in there?' as she fought to fasten the zip on the hipster jeans that hadn't seemed so tiny on the hanger. Most of all she hated it when the assistants offered to fetch a *large* or an *extra large* just to be sure.

With a slap of foundation and a few tugs of the oul wig she was ready to face town. She grabbed her bag, ran down the stairs and danced down the path of the house. An angry black cloud stared at her. She was about to glare back but decided against it. If she were to pick a fight with the cloud, the cloud would win hands down. And Anna didn't feel like getting soaked. A passing car threw a beep. The nerve! Anna fumed. It wasn't as if she was dressed like a tart or anything. In fact in her green wax jacket and sensible cords she looked more like a farmer. 'Pervert', she muttered. The car jolted to a halt a few yards down the road. It was one of those new Saabs. A black one. She slowed her pace. Her heart began to beat faster. Suppose the owner of the car was trying to abduct her? Should she turn and run now while there was still time? A male head appeared out of the window.

'Anna,' it yelled, 'would you ever hurry up and stop making me look like a bloody kerb-crawler?'

Relieved, Anna ran towards the car. Mark leaned over and opened the passenger door for her. He looked cute in a cream polo and chinos.

'Why aren't you at work? *Nice* car, by the way.'

'I'm on two weeks' leave. So you like her? Our eyes met across the showroom floor. She begged me to take her home.'

'And as usual you couldn't say no,' Anna checked her reflection in the side mirror. 'Mind you I can't understand how anybody who lives in this city could spend money on a fast car. The traffic is hell.'

'I see you've been back to those charm classes again. Really, I think you should take a break. You're in danger of becoming too nice.'

'Sorry,' Anna smiled, 'she really is a beauty. I'm just jealous. By the way I thought you were going away?'

'I'm visiting a friend in London next week.'

'A girlfriend?'

'A friend who's a girl, that's right,' he said cheekily.

'And she doesn't mind putting you up for a few nights, does she?'

'She doesn't have a problem with that, no.'

'Fantastic,' Anna said airily. 'I suppose Sally's too busy to mind.'

'She doesn't know.'

'See? I always knew you were a bastard.'

'It's so unfair to call me that. It's actually all off between Sally and myself.'

Anna sighed. Men like Mark were impossible.

'Why the sigh?' he pressed on. 'Don't you believe that somebody finally found the strength to give me the boot? Am I that irresistible?'

'Piss off,' she laughed.

'Day off?'

'Uh huh.'

'Lunch?'

'Um . . .'

'Stop trying to think of a reason why you shouldn't.'

'I've had my lunch.'

'A drink then?'

'At this hour? Do you think I'm an alco or what?'

'Tell you what, we'll go for a walk.'

'Nah, too cold.'

'Cinema?'

Anna considered it. The idea kind of appealed to her. 'You're on' she agreed.

Mark sighed with exaggeration. 'You're a tough one to please,' he chuckled. 'No wonder the student ran a mile.'

'He's back,' Anna blurted out defensively.

'Great,' he indicated in a tone that wasn't so great at all. 'I'm pleased for you, Anna. Don't forget to invite me to the wedding.'

'I'm pleased for me too,' she replied tartly. 'But don't rush out buying me a wedding present. It's not that serious. Yet.'

They drove in silence out to the Ormonde complex.

'How about *Bridget Jones's Diary*?'

'I'm easy,' Anna shrugged.

Because it was afternoon, the cinema was half empty. They sat in the middle halfway up. Anna made herself comfortable. It was hard to imagine, Anna thought as they sat in the darkness, that it was the middle of the day. During the film she was very aware of Mark's bare arm brushing against her own. She made no attempt to move away. And she was almost sorry when the credits rolled, telling people it was time to move on. Now there were no more excuses for accidentally catching Mark's fingers as they both reached for the popcorn. The lights brightened, urging punters to leave and get on with their own mundane Irish lives. Anna sighed.

'I don't feel like going home now,' Mark said

suddenly, echoing her thoughts. 'How about a drink in town?'

'Too noisy,' Anna proclaimed. 'I'm too tired to stand in a crowded pub with a load of suits.'

'Johnny Fox's?'

'Ah why not?' Anna brightened. She hadn't been up to that place in years. The highest pub in Ireland. If you couldn't get away from it all up there, well there was no hope for you.

Mark started the engine. They zoomed off.

In Johnny Fox's they settled in a cosy seat beside one of the log fires. A true gentleman, Mark took her jacket and hung it on the back of a chair. 'What'll you have?'

'A Heineken will do me just fine.' Anna pulled her chair closer to the warmth of the fire.

He came back with two pints, a Heineken and a pint of the black stuff for himself. 'Well, this is nice.' He sat down. 'You're impossible to nab for a drink.'

'I just need a good bit of notice,' Anna insisted. 'I'm a busy woman, you know.'

'I've learned my lesson you'll be glad to hear. Next time I'll give you plenty of notice.'

'Well, I'll need it. I'm going to be up to my eyes from now on . . . and Steve's very possessive,' she added just to annoy him.

But the look on his face didn't give her much satisfaction and she felt guilty almost immediately. Why be nasty to those who were nicest to you?

What had Mark ever done wrong except flirt with her occasionally? It was hardly a crime. Yet for some bizarre reason she felt she had to keep up this 'treat 'em mean, keep 'em keen' attitude whenever he was around. He deserved it, though. He was a man after all. And an extremely good-looking one at that. She almost hated him for it.

'So how is work going?' He lifted his Guinness to his lips and sampled it thoughtfully.

'Great,' Anna tried to say cheerfully but Mark's eyes seemed to question her. 'Actually,' she took a climb down, 'things are pretty terrible.'

After some further probing, Anna gave in and admitted the whole nightmare situation with Elaine over the promotion. He listened carefully and gently squeezed her hand as she told him about the breakdown in communication between herself and Elaine.

'That's a pity, she seemed like a nice girl,' Mark commiserated.

'She is,' Anna gratefully accepted his man-size Kleenex, 'that's the whole point.'

'Success has its price,' he continued thoughtfully. 'Take for example the lads I used to hang around with in UCD – you remember most of the lads, don't you?'

Anna nodded. How could she forget? Herself and Claire had snogged most of them.

'Anyway, I thought we were like this huge inseparable gang bonded by a love of rugby, women and booze. In college we were all pretty much the same

– you know, busy sending off vanloads of CVs and turning up to open days in suits. Some of us thought this was all hilarious, spinning around on the merry-go-milkround. But some people took it all very seriously.' His face clouded.

Anna eyed him over the rim of her beer glass and pretended to herself that she didn't know how good looking he was.

'Everything changed after college.' He paused and drained his Guinness. 'I saw my friends turn from fun-loving party animals into competitive freaks. I reckon some of my office colleagues would happily bring their sleeping bags into the office if they thought there was a promotion in it for them.' He shrugged. 'The Celtic Tiger for you, eh?'

'Unbelievable.' Anna shook her head and wondered if she should order another drink in case he decided to suddenly call it a night.

'Same again?' He beat her to it.

'Yeah, thanks,' she answered almost shyly.

She watched him order the second round at the bar, unable to steal her eyes away from his thick rugby neck, broad rugby back, broad muscular shoulders and a bottom that just begged to be pinched.

Jesus, what was she at? She scolded herself for harbouring such sinful thoughts. Mark was her friend. A *friend*. Like Claire was her friend. She didn't fantasize about pinching *her* bottom or making sure her legs touched Claire's as they sat side by side having a drink in the Merrion Inn on a Friday night. *Stop it*, she reprimanded herself. You've gone mad altogether. Surreptitiously, as if to make a point, she moved her chair slightly away from Mark's. If he noticed any change when he returned from the bar, he didn't comment. He simply placed the drinks on the table and smiled.

'Thanks for listening to me,' she returned the smile. 'I know I sound like a wet weekend.'

'I don't mind listening. That's what friends are for.'

'Yes,' she agreed in a high thin voice that sounded nothing like her own. She resented the way Mark constantly referred to their 'friendship'. 'Friends are extremely important. And I'm here for you too.'

He looked at her puzzled.

'I'm here to listen,' she continued and patted his knee like a mother would a small child. 'Now what about this break up with Sally? Are you upset about it?'

'I . . .'

'Well, there's plenty more fish in the sea,' she continued like a robot. 'I hope everything works out with your one in London. She seems very nice.'

'How do you know? I haven't said anything about her.' He began to laugh at her poker face.

Anna opened her mouth to say something but shut it just in time.

'Her name's Jane,' he said finally. 'She used to go out with my brother.'

'Super,' said Anna. 'So she's already met the family.'

'It's not like that. Anyway, Anna, since when have you been interested in my love life?'

'God Almighty, is it that late? Steve will be out of his mind with worry,' Anna said knowing he'd be nothing of the sort. He'd be up there studying in the UCD library until the bell sounded, telling students to sod off back to flatland.

'It is late, time flies when you're having fun.' Mark held her jacket open for her. 'Thanks for your company.'

'No, thank *you*,' she answered guiltily.

He parked his new Saab outside his front gate. 'I'll walk you home,' he offered.

'Ha ha very funny.' She sneaked a quick glance across the road. Darkness enveloped Steve's downstairs flat. She hoped Mark wouldn't notice.

'I'd invite you in for a nightcap but I don't want Steve hammering on my door with a battleaxe,' Mark said.

'Of course.' Anna looked mortified. She knew that *he* knew there was no chance of Steve going near anyone with a battleaxe. A deep colour crept into her cheeks but she wasn't prepared to take another climb down. 'Goodnight,' she said awkwardly.

'Goodnight,' he replied and retreated to his bachelor house. Alone.

Chapter Twenty

'I like niva iva wanna come hoime.'

Claire listened politely as her sister Emma rattled on and on about how wonderful Oz was. Apparently the place she lived in was just like *Home and Away*. Trouble was, since Emma had gone Away she now didn't seem to be planning to come Home. She'd adopted an irritating Australian accent, the result of hooking up with some surf dude named Brad no doubt. Claire's parents were freaking out at the prospect of Emma settling on the other side of the world. Dublin was bad enough, they thought, but at least Claire could get to Limerick in three hours in a crisis.

'Guess who I met the other day?' Claire tried to keep her voice as neutral as possible.

'Who?'

'Tom.'

'*Who?*'

'Tom from Galway.'

'Oh that Tom, how's he coping?' Emma sounded all serious all of a sudden.

'What do you mean?'

'Tom's fiancée was killed in a car accident last year,' Emma continued in a morbid voice. 'We all thought he'd go off the rails. She was so perfect for him. Shocking tragedy so it was.'

'That's terrible.'

'I know.'

'Tell him I was asking after him if you see him again.'

'I will,' Claire said soberly.

'How's Simon? Still stuck to his computer?' Claire's sister had never considered Simon to be the world's most exciting man.

'Oh great,' Claire said with a cheerfulness she didn't feel. 'And Andrew's got so big you wouldn't recognize him.'

'Send us a recent photo, won't you?'

'Sure . . . listen, sis, this is costing me a fortune. Talk to you again.'

'Love ya.'

'You too.' Claire hung up. Talking to her little sister usually lifted her spirits no end. Not this time. Poor Tom, she thought. Some people had it very tough. She wished she could help him somehow. But she wouldn't know where to begin. Besides she didn't even know where he lived or worked. He might think she was a prying old busybody or worse, somebody pretending to help, just to make herself feel better. An involuntary shudder shot down her spine. Maybe that's what she was trying to do. Feign concern about other people's misfortunes when her own shoddy life was crumbling all around her. She met her eyes in the hall mirror. You freak, she told herself, you miserable freak.

Simon arrived home in good spirits. The market was strong, he told his wife as he nabbed a beer from the fridge. In all it had been a good week's trading so far. In fact, he added like a bombshell, it was so good, the office was going out celebrating.

Claire's face fell. Not another night alone with the TV and a sleeping baby. She just couldn't face it. She was supposed to be a young wife for God's sake, not the merry frigging widow! 'No you're not,' she said deliberately, stopping just short of stamping her foot.

Simon had been about to switch on the box in order to catch up on the sports news but suddenly thought better of it. The look on his wife's face was thunderous. What was the story? What the hell was wrong now?

'Fire ahead,' he pretended to be contrite, 'what have I done? Left the lid off the toothpaste again? Silly me.'

'You're not going out again, I'm sick of it.'

'What do you mean you're sick of it? I'm the one bloody well working my ass off all day long. I'm entitled to the odd night out!'

'Odd?' Claire gave a high-pitched squeal. 'If you go out again tonight, that'll be the third night in ten days.'

'Oh my God, she's counting,' Simon sighed. 'She's keeping tabs on me already. This is why they tell you not to get married.'

'They? Who's *they*, may I ask? Jake?'

'Listen, don't throw that at me.' Simon could feel his blood pressure beginning to rise. 'I was dead against Jake and Anna pairing off from the start.'

A fraught tension hung between them.

'Come out with us,' Simon finally suggested. 'Why don't you?'

'Who'll mind Andrew?'

Simon concentrated on the remote control as if it could somehow provide the answer. 'Fiona?' he suggested limply.

'Fiona can't baby sit on weeknights till after her exams. You know that, Simon.'

'What about Mrs Murphy?'

'It's too late to be asking her.'

'Have you any suggestions then?'

Claire saw a flicker of impatience cross the face that had been smiling barely ten minutes ago. 'What about your mother?' she said suddenly.

'My mother!' Simon couldn't have acted more surprised if she'd suggested The Cookie Monster. 'That's out of the question.'

'Why?' Claire placed her hands defiantly on her hips. 'Why is it so out of the question?'

'My mother's too old,' he said tonelessly.

'And what about mine? She's the same age but

Mum didn't mind taking Andrew for a whole week after Christmas.'

'You mother was glad of the company.'

'Bullshit,' Claire's eyes bulged with rage. 'She did it to give us a break. But some women are too selfish to give a hand.'

The look on Simon's face was one of sheer disbelief. 'Are you referring to my mother?'

Claire shrugged. 'Well,' she spoke deliberately, 'she certainly did a very good job of raising a self-centred son.'

Minutes later the front door slammed. 'And fuck you too,' Claire muttered, her face dissolving into a river of tears. She flung open the fridge door, grabbed a bottle of white wine, filled a teacup and swallowed it all in one go, wincing as the alcohol stung the back of her throat. Immediately she refilled her cup. God where had it all gone wrong? What had happened to her dreams? Cosy nights in with her handsome husband? Adoring baby sitting in between them? A roaring fire and good home cooking? How had her husband gone from finding her the sexiest siren that ever lived, to the most boring woman in Ireland? She drank some more. Why did everyone pretend marriage was the be and end all of life? Simon had been mad about her for years. He hadn't stopped grinning the night of their wedding. He hadn't let her sleep a wink in their big double bed. And then Andrew had arrived and changed everything.

Claire sat on the chocolate-coloured leather arm-chair, her hands choking the neck of the wine bottle. She switched on the TV and promptly turned it off again. She took another long slug of wine and began to feel more optimistic. Things would have to change around here. It was simply a matter of working things out. But she would have to play her part too. No more unwaxed legs, unplucked eyebrows, chipped nails, unwashed hair and flaky skin. These days Claire rarely bothered to brush her hair unless it was for a dinner party or something. Madness. No wonder Simon preferred a night out with a bunch of slappers than a dull evening in with his plain Jane wife. Maybe one of those slappers would end up getting her wicked way with Simon. Claire frowned at the bottle. According to Anna, the women around town had very low morals and would sink their false fingernails into your man before you knew what hit you. Apparently the ratio in Dublin was two women to every man. There weren't enough single men to go round.

It was unnerving to think that someone could take Simon if they desperately wanted him. A man's willpower wasn't as strong as a woman's. If Claire was silly enough to drive her husband away with her moaning and moping, she was her own worst enemy. She drank a little more and started to cheer up. Everything was in her hands. She was going to make this the happiest marriage ever. Herself and Simon would be the ideal *Hello!* couple. Victoria

Reddin would be *envious* when she turned up on her doorstep with her adoring husband. She wouldn't turn up her nose and say '*very nice*' then.

It was late. She'd go to bed. She'd put on her sexiest nightie instead of the old tracksuit she'd got used to sleeping in. Maybe Simon would want to make mad passionate love to her when he got home. She was his wife. She was young. She was pretty. Still. And they said women hit their sexual peak sometime in their thirties. This was not the time to let herself go.

She popped into the baby room. Andrew was breathing softly. Claire smiled. It was a miracle that herself and Simon had produced this incredible little being. She had to make this marriage work for Andrew's sake. She shut the door quietly.

Slipping on a flimsy nightie, Claire sank onto the huge bed with feather pillows and sumptuous duvet. She remembered buying this bed. The marital bed. She'd felt so grown up in the furniture shop discussing the different types of beds with the salesman. The mattress couldn't be too soft because Simon's back wasn't the best. And the bed with the shelves underneath would probably be the best-buy. Nothing too fancy or too fashionable. Because they didn't intend replacing it every couple of years. And nothing too ridiculous either, like a four-poster, say.

They'd had a lot of fun in that bed, Claire gave a little smile. Of course, these days it was used for sleeping and not much else. Andrew's arrival had made sure of that.

It was funny, the baby had dominated every waking hour of his first few months in the world. Claire's unobtainable dream had been an uninterrupted night's sleep. Now she longed for something else. A bit of passion. Some spice. She remembered an article she'd read in the dentist's waiting room. It was all about jazzing up your sex life. It wasn't the type of thing you'd like people to see you reading. Some of the tips were bizarre. Like dressing up as a maid. Claire knew that that was out of the question. Sure if Simon saw her in an apron and a frilly white hat, he'd presume she was doing a massive spring clean. If she messed around with chocolate sauce, Simon would be furious for soiling the bed clothes. There'd been a number that you could ring to order a catalogue. But suppose they delivered it to Mrs Murphy next door by mistake?

Anyway, surely the tips were for people married a long time? Or weird people. Not for a normal healthy young couple. No, there had to be a better solution than resorting to shameful sex toys. Suppose they had a fire that burned everything except the glow-in-the-dark dildo? Or suppose Anna called over one night when they were away to feed Blackie and stumbled across a box of canary-coloured condoms. After all people couldn't help having a little snoop around. Even though they'd rather die than admit it.

Claire had to start re-igniting the flames of passion. Simon would then see her as a woman once more. Not just the mother of his son. She'd have to stop talking about nappies et cetera. 'There's nothing as dull as a woman who can talk about nothing other than her offspring,' her mother had once said. She'd been right.

Claire awoke in the darkness to the sound of rain thundering on the roof. She sat bolt upright in the bed. Where was Simon? A wave of cold perspiration engulfed her. Her mind was racing. What had happened to him? Why hadn't he come home? She leapt from the bed and tore into the spare room. The neatly made single bed hadn't been touched. She ran to the window and pulled back the curtains. The car was gone. Oh God, suppose he'd crashed? Suppose he was lying in a ditch somewhere covered in blood? Caught in a whirlwind of panic she thought about ringing the police. But they might laugh at her paranoia. They probably knew about husbands who stayed away for the night. She returned to the main bedroom and tried Simon's mobile. 'The customer you are calling is unavailable. Please try again.'

Chapter Twenty-one

Anna was single again.

Steve had sat up in the bed on Saturday morning and decided the relationship was affecting his studies. Anna also sat up and lit a cigarette. A spring dawn was creeping through the curtains making the room look yellow. She inhaled the smoke deeply and wondered how she could leave the room with her dignity still intact.

A little something in Anna had died, as it did when any man suddenly decided he didn't want to share his life with her any more. It was an ego thing. It bruised her. She knew the whole 'studying' thing was rubbish. Women weren't as naïve as men thought. But thankfully she wasn't *that* cut up. Perhaps the fact that Steve had given her the boot before made it easier. At least she didn't have that terrible sense of despair she'd felt in the past — that she'd never ever again find someone else to love. Realistically she knew she didn't love Steve.

He was a nice guy, a nice young guy who simply had neither the time, the money nor the interest to take her out.

Life went on. She'd learned that much over the years. She was mature now. No more bombarding her ex-loves with frantic phone calls, telling them she thought they were different, as if guilt could somehow make them come back. No more slamming down phones hysterically, mourning for days and then going out and repeating the process all over again.

She was all grown up now, or so she liked to think. She wouldn't be twenty again for anything. How had she walked around with so little self-respect? God, it seemed like yesterday. Those days spent hanging around student bars throwing herself at guys who showed zero interest. Guys who'd eventually got off with her because they were so drunk and she'd just happened to be there. A horrible thought struck her. If twenty seemed like yesterday, then forty was like . . . like tomorrow. Oh God. Oh God. Oh God.

'I agree with you,' she told Steve, reaching for an empty coke can to deposit her cigarette butt.

'If you don't start slogging now, you've a lousy life ahead of you.'

Steve didn't seem too delighted by her enthusiasm. 'You sound like you wanted this too,' he said.

'You're right.' Anna reached for her T-shirt and yanked it over her head. Her smile was practically

sellotaped on. 'I've kind of moved on . . . met someone else . . . someone older,' she grinned plastically,
knowing how much that would hurt.

'Right,' said Steve.

'Right,' said Anna. 'Now where are my socks?'

Chapter Twenty-two

Like a warrior bracing for battle Claire pushed Andrew's buggy down Dún Laoighaire pier. She didn't see the young couples strolling arm in arm alongside her. Didn't notice the kids racing in circles around her or the excited dogs barking joyfully, delighted with their weekly dose of fresh air. She saw only the pale Irish sky and bleak uncertainty ahead. She hadn't slept at all last night. Simon had arrived home this morning. At seven.

He'd showered wordlessly and left again. No explanations.

She'd thrown his shirt, tinged with cigarette smoke and beer stains in the wash along with Andrew's soiled bibs. How in the world could their marriage survive this kind of carry on?

Reaching the end of the pier, she settled herself on one of the benches and resumed normal breathing. The wind was playing havoc with her hair and she punished it by trapping it in a scrunchie. As usual the sun was dancing over the hills at Howth. Why didn't she just go and live there, she thought wearily.

'Still here?' A hand on her shoulder made her start.

'Tom!' Her face broke into a smile upon recognizing him. 'How's it going? It's nice to see you again.'

'Ditto,' he laughed and patted Andrew's curly head.

She hadn't honestly expected to bump into him again so soon. Though she had to admit, the meeting wasn't totally unexpected. He'd told her he walked the pier regularly.

He sat down beside her.

'Guess what? I spoke to Emma yesterday. She's made it to Australia and is loving it.'

'Great.' His face lit up. 'I'm delighted for her.'

'Yeah, it makes me feel jealous. I should have taken the plunge and done it myself.'

'Oz is great. I think the climate has a lot to do with it. The sun puts people in a great mood.'

'Well, I don't suppose I'll ever get there now.' Claire twiddled her ponytail. 'I'm too old.'

'Would you go away out of that? Sure, you're only a young thing,' Tom said generously.

'Thanks. The fresh air out here makes me feel young.'

'It certainly does blow away those work cobwebs.'

'Where do you work?'

'I'm a computer analyst.'

'God. No wonder you spend half your life here.'

'Well it pays the bills. But it's far from fascinating. Ideally I'd like to paint full time. I'm mad about art . . . but that won't keep the wolf from the door. What do you do yourself?'

'I'm a housewife.' Claire felt herself go crimson. Christ, she felt so old-fashioned. Like she'd suddenly arrived from another era. The word 'housewife' was horrible. It sounded like you were married to your house or something.

'Goo ga goo . . .' Andrew interrupted as if on cue. They both laughed.

'I think that's great,' Tom said diplomatically. 'If I'd . . . if I'd ever got married,' he continued very quietly, 'I'd have liked to support my wife.'

'That's what you think,' Claire said tonelessly, 'but what would have happened when the glamorous woman you fell in love with turned into a dowdy frump who talked about nothing but the price of Pampers?'

Tom turned to her, startled. With horror Claire realized her massive blunder. God, how could she be so senseless? Tom had lost the woman he'd wanted to marry. *Of course* he'd never thought of her as a frump. For the rest of his life he'd remember her as she was – young, vibrant and in love with life. For a moment Claire felt strangely jealous of the dead woman. She'd never grow old. He'd never get the chance to get sick of her.

'I'm so sorry, I really didn't mean what I said,' the words stumbled out awkwardly. She rose unsteadily.

He extended a hand and pulled her down again. His eyes searched hers. 'You surely don't think . . . you don't think of yourself as a . . . ?'

'No.' Claire stared at the concrete beneath her feet.

'Because—' he said and stopped.

'What?'

'Because . . . oh God, I don't know if it's my place to say it but you're one of the most attractive girls I've ever met.'

And he turned away quickly before he could see her face.

Chapter Twenty-three

Outside head office, Anna plucked a few fair hairs off her black business-like suit. Trembling, she tried to light a cigarette. The wind would simply not allow it. Damn. This wouldn't do at all. Her nerves were in bits. Glancing at her watch, she realized she'd fifteen minutes to kill. Sitting in the reception area like a spare tool was not an option. Refuge was sought in a nearby café.

She ordered a black coffee, which burnt her tongue. She set the cup down again and managed to successfully light her cigarette. Why was she so bloody excited? A few weeks ago she hadn't given a hoot. But a lot had happened since then – Elaine's hostility, June's perpetual *I know you're going to fail, loser* smirk, Steve and Jake's rapid disappearance. She had to get this job. If only for her self-esteem. She *had* to.

Anna noticed to her dismay that the tiny inconspicuous hole in her barely black tights had suddenly expanded and a ladder was subsequently riding up her thigh. Oh Christ, why? She pulled down her knee-length skirt as far as it would go. Not a hell of a lot else could be done now.

'What are the individual qualities you feel you could bring to the new position?' Mr Walton pushed his glasses back onto his nose.

Anna took a deep breath before she answered.

'Professionalism, dedication . . .'

'Dedication, hmmm.' Mr Walton wrote something down. His assistant was not with him today. Was she on leave? Had she resigned? What did it matter? Anna chided herself. Why was she contemplating such ridiculous trivialities during what was probably the most important interview of her life.

She sat rigidly in her seat under the scrutinizing gaze of her interviewer, whose forbears, she imagined, could have sat on the Spanish Inquisition. His questioning was thorough.

'We have over fifty internal applicants for this position, Miss Allstone. Tell me why we should choose you over all these highly competent applicants?'

Fifty applicants! Jesus, she didn't have a hope. 'Because I badly want it, Mr Walton.' Anna strove to put into her voice the professionalism and enthusiasm that she knew were called for. 'Because I assure you I'm the best person for the job and if you give me this position I won't let you down.'

Mr Walton looked vaguely satisfied by this response. He adjusted his spectacles once more, leaned back and carefully contemplated his interviewee.

'How do you feel about relocating?' he threw at her.

'I'd welcome the change,' Anna replied levelly. 'It would broaden my horizons and give me a chance to discover a different side of Lolta's. I'm willing to learn all that I can.'

'Do you believe you can sufficiently cope with the enormity of this particular challenge?' he asked as if he were sizing her up for the position of chief executive.

'I've never been more sure of anything in my life,' said Anna and prayed hard that this man would believe her.

Ten minutes later found her shivering at the bus stop, willing the number 13 to arrive. She *thought* the interview had gone okay, but she couldn't tell for sure. After all, the last one had felt pretty disastrous and she'd got it. Mr Walton said they'd be in touch before the end of the week. But his face had remained blank. She buttoned up her coat. An unforgiving wind whipped her ears. God, it was cold. A bus with a sign saying *Out of Service* raised false hopes.

Eventually Anna reached the empty house. Wearily she pushed the door open, glad that Steve was studying so hard that she wouldn't have to bump into him. What was it with her and men? What did she do to push them away? If she were thinner would it make a difference? Not that she was particularly large or anything but thin girls weren't used and then discarded like empty beer cans. Thin ruled.

Anna sat alone in front of the TV seeing nothing. She poured herself a well-deserved glass of wine and opened a box of sour cream and onion Pringles. She popped one and then another. It was true what they said about popping and not stopping. She lit a cigarette. Puffing away, she pondered her luck with men. Or ill luck rather. Claire was lucky. She'd never really had any problems with men, didn't know what it was like to pine for someone, didn't know what it was like to lie awake all night praying for some man to notice her. Anna knew all about that. She knew what it was like to be choked with pain when men failed to reciprocate your feelings, and to know that although the ones you desperately wanted, would court you, snog you, sleep with you even, the woman they'd ultimately choose as their steady girlfriend/wife, would be a lot more sophisticated, more self-assured and perhaps a lot prettier than you.

Of course Claire *had* been dumped. And regularly. But the reasons had usually been because she'd absolutely refused to sleep with them. Not because they thought she was unattractive in any way.

At least Anna couldn't ring Steve and beg for a second ... *sorry* ... third shot at making their 'relationship' work. Not unless she went out to a payphone to do it. Ah well, she wasn't going to waste any more time thinking about him. She had her possible promotion to think about. That was some compensation. If she got a transfer she wouldn't have to bump into the likes of Steve, Jake or Elaine for a very long time. It was a very comforting thought.

The front door bell rang, making her start. Who could it be? Perhaps Grainne or Sandra had locked themselves out. Or Steve. Well, he could bloody stay out! It rang again. A long ring this time.

'Mark, you're back.' Anna couldn't help breaking into a smile.

'London was too busy,' he grinned. 'Too many people.'

'Right.' Anna wasn't fooled. 'Whatsername must have kicked you out.'

'Absolutely not,' Mark protested. 'Anyway you've got that all wrong as I told you before.'

'Come in,' Anna widened the door.

'Actually –' he paused '– would you mind coming over to me? My fridge is crammed with food . . . too much for one man to eat alone.'

'Uh . . .' Anna started.

'Unless you're doing something with that young lad of yours.'

'No,' Anna retorted. 'I'm not doing anything with him . . . tonight.'

'Good. Right. You ready?'

'Sure.'

She followed him across the road, delighted with the prospect of some company. Sitting all alone for one more night was not something she'd been looking forward to.

Mark's house was as always a pleasure to walk into. Thick carpets and a roaring – or was it a fake? – fire in the sitting room. Anna removed her jacket and let him hang it up. No seriously, this place was cool with abstract art stuff which she couldn't make head or tail of, and oriental-looking rugs. She should be living in a place like this at her age. She was too old to be living in a crap place. She should be living in a nice three-bedroomed house with a Labrador and maybe a husband. To rent a place anyway half decent on your own in Dublin cost a bloody fortune. Mark was so *so* lucky he'd bought before property prices had gone through the through the roof.

'Sit down and relax.'

It was exactly what Anna intended to do. She installed herself on the purple-and-white-striped sofa. There was an ambient pleasure about the front room, a certain pride in it. Not to show off or impress, but for its own sake.

Mark was back with the wine. 'Vino?' he offered.

'I'd murder a glass.'

He poured. She drank. Immediately Anna began to relax. This was far *far* better than sitting in her own flat or in Steve's for that matter. No wonder women fell for Mark. It was probably the house that did it.

He removed his own jacket, revealing the outline of his shoulders and slim waist. Again Anna could see why women might fall for Mark.

This time it had nothing to do with the house.

She really should invite him to the dreaded party. Mark would pass the strictest Victoria Reddin test.

'What are you thinking about?' he asked suddenly.

'Nothing,' Anna sighed, 'it's been a long day, that's all.'

She told him about the interview.

'When will they let you know?' he enquired.

'Dunno,' she answered glumly. 'The sooner the better really.'

'Why the sad face? I'd say you've nothing to worry about.' He placed a hand around hers and gave it a squeeze. 'They're lucky to have someone like you working for them.'

He disappeared into the kitchen to grab the food, returning with two plates containing something delicious.

'What is it?'

'Wild mushroom risotto.'

'Hey, I didn't know you could cook.'

'You'd be surprised at what I can do.' His eyes met hers. She looked away first. He'd better be careful and remember this wasn't a date. If Mark thought he could suddenly win her over with a bottle of wine and some grub, he'd better think again. The food did live up to its smell, however. Home cooking beat a ready-to-go-meal-for-one any day. And the company lived up to usual expectations. Anna sipped her wine and studied her companion, congratulating herself on being able to sustain a platonic relationship with such an attractive man. Weaker women would have snapped under the strain of it all. She was proud of herself. After all it was easy to be friends with a dog. Most women had at least one male friend with a 'lovely' personality. Mark was Anna's male friend, though some doubted the friendship. Namely Claire. Then again what would Claire know about anything? The only men she knew were those idiot friends of Simon.

'Let me take your plate,' Mark said after a while. 'Are you full or could you manage a piece of Black Forest gateau?'

'I could, yeah. Have you been baking all morning or what?'

'As if.'

'Who made it so?'

'A lovely man in a lovely deli.'

'I give up,' Anna laughed.

'So how's the love life?' Mark asked suddenly as she dug her fork into the cake.

'Great,' Anna replied nonchalantly and wondered why he always brought up this silly topic, over and over again. 'Not a bother,' she added with a plastic grin.

'Are you in love?'

'I might be.'

'No, you're not,' he contradicted. 'You don't have that glow about you.'

'Glow?'

'Yeah . . . you know, when you're in love and you

don't need to eat or drink and you forget to sleep and forget to ring your mates. And it doesn't matter if it's raining outside because your own world is full of sunshine . . .'

'Jesus, you're some poet.'

'Thanks.' Mark's eyes twinkled with merriment.

'I'm perfectly happy,' Anna insisted.

Mark put down his dessert spoon. He seemed to suddenly drift into space. Then he was back again as Anna began to speak. 'I don't know if I've ever truly been in love,' she said. 'I mean at the time I think I am but once it's all off then I think I definitely wasn't. Does that make sense?'

'Does to me. When I was in first year college I was in love with three girls all at the same time. I remember wondering how I'd ever be able to choose. In second year I didn't fancy any of them.'

'You heartbreaker, you,' Anna giggled.

'Do you think we'll ever get married?'

Anna nearly choked.

Mark resumed eating like he'd said nothing out of the ordinary. Just like that. As if he'd casually mentioned that it might rain later. Or asked if she'd any holidays booked for this year. Anna searched his face for traces of sarcasm but found none. She stopped toying with her piece of cake. She had suddenly lost her appetite. 'Excuse me?' she asked in a puzzled voice.

'Well, just out of interest like, have you thought about it?'

'Marrying you?' Anna was shocked.

'Me?' Mark looked equally shocked. 'God no not me ha ha ha you and me ha ha could you imagine!'

It's not that fucking funny, Anna silently fumed. What was going on here? Did he think this was some idea of a joke? 'What's wrong with you?' she snapped.

'Nothing.' He looked apologetic. 'Sorry.'

They sat for about a minute in silence.

'What I meant was . . .' he began again. *Christ, couldn't he just drop it?* 'What I meant was, do you think either of us will ever tie the knot . . . like with anyone?'

'It's not something I've really ever thought about,' Anna replied coolly.

'But you're thirty.'

'So?' She glowered at him.

'And everybody else is doing it.'

'Mark,' she sighed, 'if everybody else was running down Dún Laoighaire pier in a bid to throw themselves off the end, do you think I would be running along in the middle of them? I don't want to be like everybody else. And to be quite honest I think a lot of people get married just 'cos they're bored. Their jobs are boring, their nights out are boring, their twice-weekly trip to the gym and Sunday drives aren't enough to keep them going. So whey hey they get engaged. Now they've a wedding to plan. It's something to do, you know?'

'God, you're cynical.'

Anna shrugged. 'I think I'm just being realistic. There's no way I'd walk up the aisle looking like a meringue in front of a bunch of relatives I don't know just because everybody else is doing it.'

'What about your biological clock? Is that not ticking?'

'No,' Anna remarked dryly, 'I think the batteries must have fallen out.'

Mark laughed. 'So you're serious, you don't want to get hitched, have a family and that?'

Anna stared at him. 'If I were a man I'd probably want seven kids, but I certainly don't want to be pregnant like for ever. Mind you, I wouldn't mind one, you know, for the experience. It could look after me in my old age. Anyway if I was planning on getting married any time in the near future, do you not think I'd be going out with someone a bit older than Steve? Someone with prospects,' she added cheekily.

'A suit?' He grinned.

'A suit with a three-bedroomed house.'

'Ah well, that's me out of the picture so.' Mark stood up to reheat the kettle. 'This place has only two bedrooms.'

'So, Claire, what do you think he meant by all of that?'

'Dunno.'

'I mean, it's pretty odd for blokes to start talking about marriage out of the blue.'

'Yeah.'

'Claire, I don't think you're listening to me.'

'I am, I am. Now stop it, Andrew, stop that. Good boy.'

'Do you think I'm reading in to it too much?'

'Well, kind of. But you know what I think. I think you fancy each other like hell. You really should think about having a relationship with someone at this stage. A proper relationship like. Not one of those silly flings that you've been having recently. With all those unsuitable people.'

'Do you know who you sound like?' Anna laughed, 'Your mother.'

'Oh no, do I?'

'Don't worry, we all turn into our mothers some day.'

'That's what I'm afraid of,' Claire said doubtfully. 'I'm beginning to think Simon sees me as some old mother hen these days.'

'Ah nonsense, your imagination is in overdrive,' Anna said dismissively.

Claire decided not to divulge any information regarding her husband's late nights. Nor mention the planned trip to the National Art Gallery with Tom. Anna would only get the wrong idea. It was better to tell nobody her business. Then they couldn't be jumping to ridiculous conclusions. Anyway it was obvious Anna had a lot on her plate at the moment. The pressure of this interview and all this sudden daft talk about marriage . . .

'Claire, are you still there?'

'Sure. Listen, Anna, that's Andrew crying. I'm going to go and put him down. Talk to you soon.'

She was gone.

Anna headed back up to her room. Claire had it so wrong about herself and Mark. She didn't fancy Mark. And even if she did she'd never ever let him know. Men like Mark would run a mile if they thought you were seriously interested. Men were hunters. That's why Mark (between short intervals) was always single. Hadn't she already made one mistake with Anthony Lorcan? Remember him? She gave an involuntary shudder. Would she ever forget?

She sat alone in her sitting room thinking it was very small after Mark's place. It was cold too, and cheerless.

Anthony Lorcan, eh? He had chased her. Ran around UCD after her. Waited outside her lectures for her. Stared at her constantly in the library. She hadn't really fancied him at all. At first. But she was flattered. Flattered that someone who didn't look like a complete pig actually fancied her. Imagine someone decent fancying her – Anna Allstone! Flattery of course though was her big downfall. She began to take notice of this Anthony fella. She began to feel disappointed the days she didn't see him hanging around. Then she took it upon *herself* to hang around his lectures. To catch him coming out. Not that she let on of course. Oh no! She'd make a point of turning her back once he'd spotted her. This drove him wild. Anna was delighted. It was so much nicer for someone to be mad about you than the other way around.

He wasn't a Brad Pitt or anything. But he was cute. Even Claire admitted she wouldn't say no. That gave Anna an enormous sense of power. A friend of *his* had told a friend of *hers* he had the hots for her. Only he thought she was too hard to get. This made Anna determined to live up to this wonderful illusion.

Nobody had ever thought Anna hard to get.

It was fun.

The game had started.

Anna was going to play it for all it was worth.

She started to make serious eye contact with him in the UCD bar in the afternoons, over the pool tables. His sandy-coloured hair would flop into his green eyes and she'd catch him flicking it and looking over far more than was necessary.

But she always left the bar first. Even if she was having a whale of a time and desperately wanted to stay on.

She always left the bar first.

And then one day for some reason she didn't leave. She stayed on in the bar with a crowd from her philosophy class and got drunk. Plastered. Wasted. In fact she became so twisted that she didn't recognize herself in the Ladies' mirror.

When she stumbled out Anthony was standing

beside the door. She fell. He caught her. They snogged for half an hour.

And then she did something she'd never done before. Without a word she disentangled herself from Anthony's golden arms and made a beeline for Mark. Told him she was so sick she was going to die. And made him escort her from the bar.

What Anthony Lorcan saw leaving the UCD bar that evening was the most blasé woman he'd ever met in his life. Nobody had ever walked out on him like that. On the arm of another bloke too!

Instead of being insulted, Anthony was intrigued. The girl must have tons of confidence to be able to take or leave guys as she pleased. In Anthony's short nineteen years he'd never met a girl who carried on like that. The lads did it all the time and it was usually hilarious. But now the lads were taking the piss out of him and wondering where his bird had disappeared. Nobody treated Anthony Lorcan like that, he decided. Nobody. As though his life depended on it he was determined to get Anna Allstone.

What Anthony Lorcan did not see, however, was the unobtainable woman of his dreams, puking her guts out into a pretty bed of flowers. Less than a hundred yards from the bar, Mark Landon was holding Anna's shoulder-length hair within safe reach of it getting saturated with sick. But Anthony was spared the unpleasant sight.

He didn't hear Anna wail, 'Oh my God, what have

I DONE!' before bursting into hysterical drunken tears and collapsing under a tree, convinced that she could never ever face Anthony Lorcan again.

But face him again she did. And although (due to tremendous willpower) she turned him down again twice, eventually she succumbed under the strain of his relentless pursuit.

You see somebody had spotted him over in the canteen. Chatting to Victoria Reilly. And that had put the fear of God into her. Because Victoria wouldn't be bothered playing hard to get with a guy like Anthony. Victoria got whatever she wanted with an irritating toss of her bleached blonde bob. And so, after a couple of sleepless nights, Anna decided she was going to say yes to Anthony.

The following day when Anthony yet again approached her after one of her lectures for a date, she said yes.

Though she desperately wanted to say no.

Because by saying yes she also knew she was saying GAME OVER.

Of course, it didn't finish the following evening over dinner. Or during the week when they snogged all the way through a boring film despite violent kicks to their seatbacks by two teenage boys. It lasted, say . . . about three weeks. And then one afternoon he failed to meet her at the 'blob' on the Arts concourse. She thought she must have got the time wrong and rang him. And he sounded distant, saying he'd forgotten. She only half believed him.

The next day she tried to get him to talk. It was a complete disaster. She'd never forget his panic-stricken face when she tried to discuss their 'future'.

'It's best if we take things slowly,' he said, fidgeting furiously with his beer mat in Madigan's pub one Tuesday night.

'Do you think I'm rushing things?'

'A bit.' He stared at the ceiling as if Michelangelo himself had painted it. 'We've only been seeing each other three weeks.'

'Yeah I know but . . . but you've never once told me how you *feel* about me.'

He said nothing. God he was infuriating!

'Sometimes I think you don't even like me,' she continued. It was true. Anthony, on the few occasions he wasn't trying to rip her clothes off, usually looked like he'd rather be with anyone in the world other than her.

'Look, I wouldn't be here if I didn't like you,' he sighed resignedly.

'Maybe we should split up,' she suggested, not meaning a word of it. She'd no intention of parting company with him. But the idea of losing her might shake him up a bit, she thought craftily.

'Actually I was kind of thinking along those lines myself,' he said.

Anna couldn't have been more surprised if he had slapped her face. She was flabbergasted! This wasn't what she wanted at all. Not at all!

What was she going to do? She couldn't very well

just turn around now and say, 'Ah no I was only messing.'

So she said nothing.

All words escaped her.

She was miserable.

'But we can be friends,' he squeezed her thigh. 'I'd like that.'

God, she'd never get over the embarrassment.

So that's why Claire had no business giving her advice about men. Anna had already learned her lesson.

The hard way.

Chapter Twenty-four

Claire got ready as soon as Simon left the house. Fortunately Fiona had agreed to babysit. Andrew had reached the stage where one eye looking over him was an eye too short. Pulling phone wires and reaching for creepy-crawlies were great fun. Thank God for *Rugrats*!

Fiona arrived and settled herself and her books in the kitchen with a cup of coffee and a clubmilk.

A golden opportunity for a bath, Claire thought as she relaxed in a mountain of bubbles. She couldn't wait to catch up with Tom. It was always nice to meet a friend. Friend. Hmmm. Could she really call Tom a friend? Sure she barely knew him. Ah, hang on, what harm was it? They were only looking at paintings, for God's sake!

She swiped a bath towel off the boiling radiator and wrapped it around her damp, fresh-smelling skin.

It was going to be a great day.

She slipped out without Andrew noticing. Tears were avoided that way. The sun was high and the

bright light stung her eyes. Donning a pair of sunglasses solved that problem.

At the gallery Tom looked pretty anxious.

'Sorry I'm late,' she said breathlessly. 'Parking's a
nightmare in this city and those bloody clampers are
everywhere.'

'Tell me about it. Why do you think I work night
shifts?'

He looked well. But she didn't tell him this. *Obviously*. After all it wasn't a date or anything.

The morning passed pleasantly. Tom was a bit of
an expert in art history and through his extensive
knowledge was somehow able to bring the paintings to life.

Afterwards over coffee and carrot cake Claire
discovered she'd a lot in common with Tom and
they chatted easily for hours. Just before twelve Tom
apologetically announced that he had really better
get going. Where had the time flown, Claire wondered. Reluctantly she stood up, not sure what she
could do with herself for the rest of the afternoon.
There was no point going home when Fiona had
been booked for the entire day. Suddenly an idea hit
her. If she called into Simon's office now she might
catch him for an early lunch. And sure why not? She
was all dressed up with nowhere in particular to go.

Claire strode into Simon's office unannounced.
She flinched at the sight of Simon and Shelley, their
heads bent earnestly over some documents on his
desk. Her long sleek mane of hair hung over her

right shoulder. Her short suede skirt revealed far more than was necessary for work on a Monday morning, and her tight-fitting cashmere cardigan strained against her ample bust.

'Hello, Simon.' Claire tried her best to sound bright and breezy but her voice sounded more like a squeak.

'Claire.' The expression on Simon's face was a mixture of surprise and alarm. 'Is everything okay?'

'Sure,' Claire was determined not to waver under Shelley's menacing stare, 'I've come to treat my hubby to a slap-up lunch. Hello, Shelley.' She nodded curtly to the other woman.

'God, this is a surprise,' Simon sounded both pleased and relieved. 'The only thing is . . . we're fairly snowed under at the mo—'

'Don't you worry about a thing,' Shelley interrupted, patting Simon's arm. 'You go off and enjoy your lunch,' she cooed and Claire felt a resentment she had not thought was possible.

'You're a star,' Simon called over his shoulder as they left the large office with its futuristic pieces of furniture, potted plants in abundance and secretary sitting moodily on the enormous mahogany desk, biting her manicured talons.

They ate lunch in Milano's on Dawson Street. Claire ordered pasta and found it difficult to eat after the huge slice of carrot cake. But she decided not to tell Simon the real reason for the trip into town. There was no point.

Arriving home later that evening with a couple of large Mothercare bags and a couple of Bewley's cakes, Claire pushed open the front door. It had been a great day altogether and she was looking forward to putting her feet up and enjoying a nice relaxing evening with her family.

Fiona stood in the hallway looking completely worn out. Andrew was lying on the floor having the mother of all tantrums, flinging toys all around the place.

'Simon rang a second ago,' Fiona told Claire. 'He says not to leave out any dinner for him 'cos he won't be home.'

'He won't be home,' Claire echoed parrot-like, 'I see.'

Chapter Twenty-five

June poked Anna's shoulder blade roughly. 'Did you not hear me calling for you? There's someone on the phone.'

'Who?' Anna was up to her ears in dust trying to sort out boxes of ladies stockings from the men's briefs. All the numbers on the boxes were higgledy-piggledy and they were three staff down, Elaine was on holiday and the computer system had just crashed. Again. In all a typical day at Lolta's.

'Head office.' June's beady eyes bore through her.

'Good news?' Anna asked and then immediately regretted it.

'I don't know,' June snapped, 'news from head office is confidential information.'

Dazed, Anna made her way to the phone in Mr Evans's office. 'Anna Allstone speaking,' she said with a brightness she definitely didn't feel. Then, as if in a distant dream, she heard Mr Walton's voice congratulating her on her new position. She'd be starting the following Monday, he said. Anna, half hugging the receiver, thanked him politely before handing it back to a vicious-looking June. She watched the older woman put the phone down and utter a strangled 'Congratulations'.

'Thank you very much,' Anna said with saccharine sweetness. 'I know you wanted this for me almost as much as I did myself.'

The rest of the week passed in a blur. A multitude of things had to be organized. Her landlord had to be given notice, her new company car had to be collected and her parents had to be called with the good news. Oh and God, yes, she had to find somewhere new to live!

She didn't contact Mark. She just avoided it. Probably because she wasn't sure what to say to him. In a way, she was afraid he might make her change her mind or something. And she was determined not to let anyone do that. She'd give him a call when she was settled in Galway. That's what she'd do. Invite him up to visit her some weekend. And she was relieved Elaine was out of the country so she wouldn't have to say goodbye to her either. Her parents were, not over the moon maybe, but somewhere up there with the stars anyway. Claire had cried on the phone, her reaction somewhat over the top, Anna thought. She was going to Galway, for God's sake, not the other side of the fecking world!

She hooked up with Rich for a boozy night of celebrations in Lillies. He swore blindly that he'd miss her, ordered a bottle of champagne and then remembered that he'd forgotten his credit card. Anna happily paid for it and for the subsequent taxi fare back to her place. She felt sorry for Rich tied up in the badly paid world of acting while she, Anna Allstone, was heading for a major career in retailing. Sure wasn't it only fair of her to foot the bill?

Stumbling out of the taxi as he gallantly held the door open for her, she tried to recall if there ever had been a time he actually *had* paid for *anything*. But her mind was blank. Too much champagne and all that. Then suddenly she remembered. Of course! He'd sent her that magnificent bunch of flowers on Valentine's, hadn't he? How could she have forgotten that? Had she ever got round to thanking him?

She tried to remind him and thank him in the bedroom as he unbuttoned the front of her shirt and showered her neck with butterfly kisses. He didn't respond so she tried again.

'Sorry?' It suddenly dawned on him that she was trying to tell him something. 'What flowers?'

She withdrew from his embrace and eyed him suspiciously.

'You don't know what I'm talking about, do you?' she asked coldly.

'Nope.' He shrugged and went to unbutton his jeans.

'I think you'd better go,' she said icily.

'Why?' he asked foolishly, his fly halfway down. 'What's the matter, hon?'

'Hon is sick,' she answered sarcastically. *Sick of being taken for a ride by deadbeats like you.* 'Now please go.'

'I've no money to get home,' he said sulkily, dressing himself reluctantly.

'No mon, no fun . . . hon.'

'What's the matter with all you women?' he spouted angrily. 'You all turn out the same in the end. You're all users.'

'Really?' Anna showed him the door. 'That's very interesting. Though what exactly we use you for I certainly cannot imagine.'

He stormed out, slamming the door behind him. She heard him go downstairs. Another door slammed. Good. Good riddance!

It all made sense now. Mark had obviously sent the flowers. Of course he had. Sure God, why hadn't she seen it? Why had she credited Rich with the gesture – Rich who never did anything but watch other people's TV while drinking their beer. She was a silly girl for not giving him the boot long ago.

The car wouldn't be ready for another three weeks, Mr Walton's secretary apologized but she was to hang on to any travelling expenses. The Dublin– Galway train was only half full. Anna settled herself into an empty booth and flicked aimlessly through the *Irish Times*. After a while she was sorry she hadn't bought *Marie Claire* or some trashy novel. The *Irish Times* was a bit too heavy this morning

– she couldn't even manage the simplex crossword!

As the train rushed towards the West, the clouds got darker and the drizzle started. Oh good. That must be a sign they were near Galway.

Nobody was meeting Anna at the train station so, with the detached curiosity of a tourist stumbling on unfamiliar territory, she followed the other passengers who seemed to be heading towards town.

On Shop Street she asked a pedestrian for directions to Lolta's. He confused her with so many instructions that she reckoned she'd be better off just figuring it out for herself.

Eventually, after much traipsing around on tired feet, she stumbled across Lolta's Galway. It was a large grey building casting a shadow over its optimistically vast car park. *A building with eyes*, Anna thought uneasily.

Her heavy bag weighing on her right shoulder, she wandered through the main door and approached a rather colourless woman in a fading grey suit. This must be Miss Browne, she reckoned and introduced herself.

Miss Browne shook Anna's hand firmly and welcomed her to the store as the shop assistants checked out their new assistant manager with interest.

'I hope you'll be very happy here,' she said in a tone that seemed to say 'I actually think you'll hate it'.

Anna was marched around the large store being introduced to staff who cautiously sized her up. They were well used to managers coming and going – it was part and parcel of retailing. But while some managers could be right walkovers, others could be weapons. They reckoned this well-dressed girl with the pretty face and fair hair tied in a high ponytail would be somewhere in between.

The strange thing about moving store was that, no matter how competent and confident you were, you still felt like a new schoolgirl on your first day trying to find out where on earth the toilets were.

Fortunately Grainne had given her the number of her sister Aoife, a final year student in UCG who happened to be looking for a flatmate at the moment. Anna was currently staying in a B&B where Lolta's were putting her up for three nights.

She dialled Aoife's number later from the foyer of the B&B. She was dubious enough about sharing with any relative of Grainne's. Would Aoife be as mad in the head as her sister?

'Hello?' the warm voice came through the line.

'Hi . . . it's er Anna, I'm . . .'

'Anna! I've been expecting your call. Listen, where exactly are you? I'll come and collect you if you like.'

'Yeah, well that's very nice of you.' God, she was enthusiastic. Maybe she was a raving loony. Suppose her last flatmate had vanished in the middle of the night? 'I'm in *The Seaside Inn*.'

'Oh yeah, that's in Salthill, isn't it? I'm not far

from there. The flat's in Rahoon. I'll be about ten minutes?'

'Sure. Thanks a lot.'

Anna waited on the windy steps, facing the rough Atlantic sea and feeling severe bouts of indecision. Rahoon was a good bit out from the centre, wasn't it? She wasn't too sure about living that far out. Mind you, she didn't want to be too near work either. Then your days off wouldn't really feel like days off, would they? And she didn't want to be ringing up people advertising flat shares in the news-papers. You heard so many horror stories, didn't you? Better the devil you know, eh?

A battered green Renault 5 screeched to a halt outside the B&B. A fresh-faced, auburn-haired girl stuck her head out of the window.

'Anna?'

'Yes, that's me.' Anna smiled, prised open the rusty passenger door and climbed in.

Aoife shook her hand vigorously. 'Welcome to Galway,' she enthused. 'How was your first day in the new job?'

'Fine, fine.' Anna hoped Aoife wasn't someone who would want her to talk about work all day long. 'You don't look a bit like Grainne,' she said in an effort to change subjects.

'That's what everyone says,' Aoife laughed. 'Mammy must've kept herself busy,' she winked.

Anna felt herself relax almost immediately. Aoife's high hedonistic spirits were contagious. The apartment

was fine. Included all the basics. And it wasn't far
from the shopping centre – an essential for hangover
and couldn't-possibly-get-into-the-car-and-drive-to-
the-shop days.

'The rent is pretty reasonable,' Aoife explained.
'And it's not too far from the prom – great for
exercising,' she continued hopefully.

Anna drank in her surroundings – clean wooden
floors, cream-painted walls, a modern-looking fireplace she wasn't crazy about – but hey, you can't
have everything!

There was a double bed in her room. 'You're welcome to have guests of course,' Aoife said hurriedly.
Guests? Ha ha!

'Great,' Anna said non-committally.

'Listen, do you want to go away and think about
it?' Aoife wondered. 'You might want to take a look
at a few more places and . . .'

'No, I'll take it,' Anna answered straightaway. 'I
kind of want to settle in as soon as possible, you
know?'

'Great,' Aoife sounded genuinely thrilled. 'Grainne
said she'd a feeling the two of us would hit it off. By
the way, she said some fella was round at the flat
asking for you earlier on. Does the name Mark ring
a bell?'

Chapter Twenty-six

Victoria Reddin sat upstairs in the bar of the Westbury Hotel and sucked on a Marlboro Light. Where the hell had Olive Lexon got to? This was *not* the place to be seen all on your own. The silly cow for making her wait around like this. Five more minutes and she was out of there.

She'd a lot on her plate at the moment what with caterers messing her about and that unreliable DJ cancelling at the last minute because his daughter had gone and got herself involved in a road accident. What had happened to honest-to-God workers? People just weren't grateful for a bit of work any more. There were now foreigners and all kinds of riff-raff running around causing havoc! Not that she'd ever really consider doing the odd day's work herself mind. No *thank* you, she just wasn't into it at all. She didn't agree with these ambitious women you met sometimes who boasted about all the hours they worked as if that was something to be proud of! Bloody fools, Victoria thought, privately. *Let the men do the work!*

Olive arrived eventually, apologetic and out of breath. 'I'm desperately sorry,' she pecked the air near Victoria's left ear. 'Forgiven?'

'What kept you?' Victoria asked crossly. 'I've been waiting fifteen minutes.'

'Sorry,' Olive looked sufficiently upset. 'Wow, what a coat!'

'Thanks,' Victoria fingered the leather collar. 'Don't ask how much it cost.'

Olive hadn't intended asking. She didn't want to be depressed for the rest of the week. 'So how are all the party preparations going?'

'Nightmare.' Victoria killed her cigarette. She hailed a passing waiter. 'My friend here is looking for a drink.'

'Has everyone RSVP'd?'

'Are you mad? About half of them haven't. Ignorant feckers.'

'So who hasn't replied?'

'Well, Valerie in Australia.'

'Well, that's fair enough, her reply is probably on the way.'

'I suppose, but you know with e-mail and all that nobody really has any excuse. And Margaret hasn't got back to me either. She's a funny one. You know she's separated, don't you? Apparently her husband was giving her more than the odd slap. Imagine! I dunno if she'll show up at the party at all.'

'Poor Margaret.' Olive looked sad.

'Oh, she's not the only one to have fallen on hard times,' Victoria continued. 'A number of our ex-classmates are in a bad way. Not everyone is as lucky as you and I, Olive.'

She gave Olive a triumphant little smile even though secretly she didn't think Olive had done particularly well at all. She worked in the civil-yawn-service and had married her boss, a dull dreary-looking man with the personality of a double-glazed window. They lived in an estate where rotten little locals played ball on the road and sat on her front wall. Ugh.

But apparently all of the women in Olive's office had had a kind of a thing for him – so Olive in her own way thought she'd got a bit of a catch. Ha! The office stud! Ha!

'What about Carmen?' Olive asked.

'Carmen's coming,' Victoria brightened. 'With her boyfriend. Lovely lovely guy – one of the Stohans – property and racing, you've heard of the family, I'm sure. Mind you, he isn't showing any signs of committing to poor old Carmen. And I mean it's not like he's not in a position to tie the knot, you know – from a financial point of view. I wonder what's holding him back?'

'Maybe she's holding back?'

'Ah rubbish, sure why would *she* hold back? You're very naïve, Olive.'

'But they're living together so the relationship must be quite serious.'

'It's not the same thing,' Victoria scoffed. 'That is not the same thing at all.'

'Is Anna Allstone coming?'

Victoria lit another cigarette. 'Who?'

'Anna Allstone.'

'I don't remember her at all.' Victoria frowned.

'You must. She was . . . I dunno . . . blonde with kind of chubby cheeks . . . nice girl though . . . quiet.'

'I've no idea who you're talking about. Who did she pal around with?'

'A girl called Claire, she was . . .'

'Oh yes, I remember now, ha ha. Little and Large. Ha ha ha ha . . . No, I don't suppose she's coming, I haven't heard from her yet. Pity really. She might have provided us with a good giggle.'

Chapter Twenty-seven

Outside The Barge in Ranelagh, Claire sat in her car listening to great big heavy drops of rain pound the windscreen. With big baby blue eyes Andrew watched his mother from where he was strapped into the back seat. She stifled a yawn. She'd been waiting nearly two hours now.

The pub was beginning to empty out. Suddenly she felt terribly lonely and silly. What in the name of God did she think she'd achieve by spying on her husband in the middle of the night? It wasn't normal. None of this was.

Andrew began to whimper. It was way past his bedtime.

'Don't cry, pet,' she pleaded softly. 'Mummy's going to bring you home soon.' She switched on the headlights, turned on the engine and put the gear in reverse. Suddenly she froze as her world seemed to come to a halt. There they were. God. Simon and Shelley. Together. She was in her little black-leather mini, sheltering under Simon's big black umbrella. He had his arm around her shoulder. They were laughing.

Laughing.

And Andrew was in the back crying.

Claire felt sick. Andrew's whimpering became louder and louder. Claire was panicking. Should she get óut now or just drive home and decide what to do from there?

Then something made her blood run cold.

Shelley had reached up and kissed her husband full smack on the lips.

Right, that was IT!

She jumped out of the car and slammed the door. Walking boldly towards them, she didn't notice the rain saturating her head and neck.

'Simon,' she screeched.

Her husband froze. So did Shelley.

'Simon,' she was a lot closer now, 'get into the car.'

'Wh . . . what's the matter?'

'GET INTO THE CAR, DO YOU HEAR?'

'Go on, Simon,' Shelley urged.

'But what about you? Will you be okay to get home?'

'She'll be fine,' Claire roared at him. 'If she's able to go around stealing other people's men, she's well able to get her little ass home to whatever hole she crawled out of.'

'How dare you speak to me like that,' Shelley's eyes hardened. 'As if I'm after your husband. You really need to get yourself a life.'

'A life like yours? I don't think so,' Claire said

acidly. 'Come on, Simon, we'll carry on this conversation at home.'

In stony silence they walked to the car.

'Why did you bring Andrew with you?' Simon seemed astounded to see his son in the back seat.

'Well, I was hardly going to leave him home alone while his mother was out spying on his father chasing whores.'

'Chasing whores? What on earth is up with you?'

'I saw you kiss that stupid bitch.'

'She kissed me. That's Shelley's thing. She kisses everybody.' Simon shrugged, 'It's just her thing. I'm sorry it bothered you so much. It won't happen again.'

'Well, I won't be around to witness it if it does.'

'What do you mean?'

'You'll see,' Claire said quietly. 'You'll see.'

Chapter Twenty-eight

'Dad? Hi, it's me.'

'Deirdre? Is that you calling from America? Don't you be wasting your money now.'

'No, Dad, it's me, Claire.'

'Oh it's you.' Her father paused. 'Well, there's nobody here.'

Claire hated the way he always said that. She was tempted to say 'Actually, Dad, it's you I wanted to talk to. How's life? Seen anything on TV recently? Any new spuds in the garden?'

But she didn't.

'When will Mum be back?' she asked instead.

'I don't know,' he sounded irritable. 'She's out with your Nan.'

'I was thinking of coming down to see you,' she tried to sound cheerful.

'Well, you'll have to let yourself in. I can't be here waiting for you.'

'That's no problem.'

She heard the phone go dead.

'Bye bye, Dad,' she muttered. He was probably

rushing out to buy a few balloons, she thought sarcastically. Oh well, she'd made up her mind now. She was leaving. Andrew was coming with her. Simon would survive. Of course he would. With a VBF like Shelley who needed a wife? Let Simon wonder what the hell she was up to now. Let him see how much fun it was.

She scribbled her goodbyes on the back of an envelope.

> *Gone to Mum's. Don't know when I'll be back. Claire*
> *P.S. Don't forget to feed Blackie.*

She propped it up on the kitchen table against a bunch of dying flowers. There, that should make him stew.

Poor Blackie seemed upset to see her pack the car boot. It was as if he knew being left at home with Simon wouldn't exactly be a bundle of laughs.

She was all set. Andrew, dressed in a fluffy yellow cardigan, was strapped into the back seat.

Three and a half hours later she arrived in Limerick.

Her mother was in a tizzy because the spare room wasn't made up. Every window in the place was open to let the air circulate. Claire shivered. It was freezing.

Her sister Aileen was lying on the sitting-room floor munching Taytos, a big green towel wrapped around her head. 'Claire!' Her big chubby face broke into a smile when she saw her sister. 'Andrew, coo chi coo angel baby. It's your Auntie Aileen. Yes it is. Oh yes it is.'

'Aileen, would you ever get dressed, you big lazy lump,' Claire's mother barked. 'Honestly, Claire, you arrived at a really bad time. I can't have you disrupting everyone like this. Aileen's supposed to be studying for her finals and that brother of yours is hoping to pass his leaving.'

Aileen made a face behind her mother's back. 'Talk to you later,' she said. 'I dunno why you bother coming to visit. Once I leave home I'll never put foot in this house ever again.'

It was funny, Claire thought, when you were away from home you lived with this kind of misconception that you missed your family and they missed you. But in reality they'd probably never even noticed you'd left in the first place.

Mrs Fiscon pinched Andrew's cheek and frowned. 'He's very thin.'

'He's not thin,' Claire scowled. 'He's just normal.'

'Are you feeding him the right food?'

'Of course I am.'

'You don't want to be giving him too much sugar,' her mother insisted. 'I made that mistake with Aileen and look at her now. She's huge.'

'She's studying,' Claire countered.

'Well, she's down here every five minutes with her

head stuck in the fridge. Both of them have me driven demented.'

'Poor Mum. You're worn out.'

'I notice you're looking a bit worn out yourself.' She picked up one of her father's white shirts and draped it across the ironing board. 'When was the last time you got your hair done?'

'Mum, I've been up to my eyes looking after Andrew and . . .'

'I raised five children and never missed my weekly hairdressing appointment.' Her mother patted her coiffed auburn bob. 'What about that money I gave you? Have you bought something nice yet?'

'No,' Claire admitted guiltily.

'You'll have to pull up your socks, Claire. You're thirty going on fifty. You'll just have to cop yourself on.'

Claire's father trudged in from the cold and threw his hat and coat onto the kitchen table. 'Claire,' he acknowledged his eldest daughter.

'Dad,' she returned the acknowledgement. The Fiscon household was not one where you'd throw your arms around someone and give them a big hug.

Claire suddenly thought of Anna's home and all its walls plastered in photos of the family. The pictures on these walls were of cows and sheep and tearful-looking members of God's family.

'He's the image of me.' Mr Fiscon picked his only grandchild up and threw him in the air. Claire was about to object but didn't when she heard Andrew squeal with laughter. 'He'll be a fine rugby player.'

Claire's father had played rugby for Ireland and was somewhat of a rugby hero in the area. His son Mickey was a bitter disappointment to him. He didn't see why grown men would run around a field after a ball. He was more into poetry and jazz and stuff that meant something.

'George, hang up your coat, dinner's ready.'

Her husband obediently cleared the table. Aileen was called down. Mickey was nowhere to be found. As usual. He thought family dinners were naff.

'Did you make sure to leave plenty of food in the house for Simon?' her mother asked between mouthfuls of Shepherd's pie.

'Of course I did,' Claire lied. Of course she didn't. The whole point of going away was to make Simon suffer. If she'd left him any food he wouldn't notice she was missing.

'He's a fine lad, Simon.' Mr Fiscon spoke with his mouth full. He adored the fact that his son-in-law could talk for hours about rugby.

'That's right, he's a super guy,' his wife agreed.

'Why didn't he come down with you?' Aileen reached for a second helping of mashed potatoes.

'Simon's too busy. All work and no play.'

'No harm,' her mother said matter-of-factly. 'Sure, wouldn't it be worse to have him under your feet all day?'

Andrew, determined not to be ignored, gave a surprised shout from his baby chair.

'Oh he's so adorable,' Aileen gushed. 'I can't wait to have a baby of my own.'

'You'll have to wait till you're married first,' her mother said firmly.

'And where would I find a husband? There's nothing but eejits around here. I wouldn't touch them with a barge pole.'

'Ah Aileen, you've plenty of time yet,' Claire said kindly.

'Not really,' her mother sniffed. 'You were Aileen's age when you met Simon.'

Feeling her pulse rising, Aileen made a swift exit from the room. Her father disappeared into the good room to watch the news. Claire and her mother tackled the washing-up.

'My biggest mistake was not sending Aileen and Mickey to boarding school.' Her mother scrubbed one of the big saucepans fiercely.

'But I hated boarding school,' Claire argued, 'I was so lonely.'

'Well, look how well you've done. You met all the right people and moved in the best circles. And I mean I have to say you married one of the best catches around.'

'I dunno about that.' Claire gave a plate a half-hearted wipe. 'Simon is out a lot with his friends.'

'George did that too at first. But look how settled he became. I turned a blind eye to it all. Just made sure I kept myself slim and attractive.'

Claire sighed. This conversation was getting her

absolutely nowhere. Not a negative word was allowed to be heard about super Simon.

She'd have to go back to Dublin in the morning and try to sort things out herself.

Chapter Twenty-nine

Back at home, Claire found it hard to be civil to her husband. Although on the outside she put up a semblance of normality, inside she seemed to be constantly crying. At night she found it increasingly hard to sleep and spent most of the time staring vacantly out of the kitchen window where darkness stretched into infinity.

She felt trapped. She didn't know what to do. One moment she was Claire and everything was normal and then she'd remember Shelley kissing her husband and her world would spin out of control again. She had to do something. But what?

Her own head did not have the answers. Anna had moved on to her new job in Galway. Nobody was around. Nobody seemed to be there for her. That's why when Tom rang to innocently arrange another trip to the gallery, she broke down. It was as if all the torturous anxieties and strangled emotions she had been bottling up over the past few weeks had finally tumbled forth.

Concerned, he invited her to his apartment for

tea the following Saturday. She accepted without hesitation.

Simon didn't dare refuse to babysit, as his wife got herself ready in stony silence and left the house.

As she nervously took the lift to Tom's Dalkey apartment, overlooking the sea, Claire felt an inexplicable wave of guilt sweep over her. But she dismissed it just as fast. After all it wasn't like she was planning anything terrible. Everything was above board. She pressed the doorbell and Tom let her in.

His apartment was simply furnished with white cotton rugs, and flanking the fireplace was a pair of ornate mirrors, designed to give the impression of spaciousness.

Claire was drawn to the view from the bay window. The sea was sparkling like a thousand million diamonds. Magnificent.

'Wow, this is hugely therapeutic,' Claire murmured. 'No wonder you're always in a good mood.'

'Not always.' Tom joined her at the window and slipped a strong arm around her tiny waist. 'Not always I'm afraid.'

'Emma told me about the tragedy,' Claire said softly. 'I . . . I don't know what to say.'

'It's not always easy to find the right words,' Tom said delicately. 'Sometimes it's just best not to say anything.'

When she moved closer to him and felt the warmth of his body against hers it felt like the most natural thing in the world.

They stood in companionable silence, gazing at the breathtaking view. It had such a calming effect. She wondered what was going through his mind. Did he simply feel protective towards her or was it more than that?

She moved slightly towards him. He didn't move away. But that's where the physical contact ended and for some reason Claire was glad of it. Of course it wasn't out of loyalty for Simon. No, definitely not. It's just that somewhere deep deep down, Claire knew that two wrongs would never make a right.

Chapter Thirty

'So what are the fellas like up in Dublin?' Aoife was dying to know. 'Grainne says they're all rides.'

'Oh, I don't know about that.' Anna sipped a cool beer on the bright new yellow sofa. 'I suppose city men make a bit more of an effort with their appearance. But there's more choice in Dublin.'

'More clothes shops?'

'And more men.'

'So are you going to contact that fella who was asking after you?'

'You mean Mark?'

'Yeah, that's the one.'

'Ah no, he's just a friend.' Anna lit a cigarette. Aoife wasn't a smoker but insisted she didn't mind other people smoking, which was great. There wasn't anything much worse than a flatmate who was constantly opening windows to shoo away the smoke.

Aoife was really easy going and Anna just knew she was going to enjoy living with her.

Work was going well too. It was great not having

June breathing down her neck like a demented dragon. She wondered how Elaine was getting on. She'd be back from her holidays by now.

Dublin seemed a million miles away with its constant stream of traffic and pollution. She loved the soft west-of-Ireland air and the fact that the Galwegians didn't seem to suffer the same stress that Dubliners did. Nothing could beat walking the pier in Salthill in the evenings with the fierce Atlantic wind against your face. Living near the sea did one's complexion no harm, that was for sure.

But she did miss Claire and Mark and sometimes in work, though she tried hard to concentrate on her sales figures, images of Mark's smiling face floated past.

The following morning at work, one of the girls handed her a handwritten envelope. Anna was intrigued. It was always great to get something in the post other than company mail. She opened the envelope tentatively.

Inside was a card with a cute cartoon kitten on the front.

Best of luck in your new role, Elaine

Anna smiled. That was big of Elaine. Anna knew how much her colleague had wanted the job. Fair play to her for sending the card.

She was busy busy busy. Being an assistant manager was a huge responsibility. Miss Browne was often out of town, leaving the day-to-day running of the store to Anna. The new position had given her enormous confidence, however, and looking back Anna often questioned how she'd ever doubted taking on the role.

But it left little free time.

For men or anything else.

Often Anna barely had the energy to take off her make-up in the evenings before flopping into bed.

The date of the dreaded party was looming and the thought of it just would not go away.

Who the hell was she going to bring?

She didn't know if she could face going alone.

No matter how successful she'd become those silly twits would still look down on her because she hadn't nabbed a man for herself.

Aoife was very good to her. Insisted on dragging her to Central Park on a Friday night when Anna would have killed just to fall into bed instead. Aoife wouldn't hear of it. She was Grainne's sister after all. The nights were admittedly great craic and the music in Central Park was always brilliant but unfortunately most of the guys who chatted Anna up were younger than her and she wasn't prepared to go down that road again. Oh God, what was she going to do about this blasted party? She couldn't wait for it all to be over.

And then she met Darren.

Totally out of the blue.

A last-minute meeting in Dublin meant that she had to take the early morning flight to the capital. A heavy fog meant a late departure. Anna sat in the airport and stared out of the window waiting for the incoming plane to land.

It felt like it was still the middle of the night.

At first she didn't notice the tall, handsome man take a seat opposite her.

'Is this Terminal One?' he asked.

'Excuse me?' She looked up and locked eyes with him. He was good looking. Very good looking, in fact, with striking blue eyes and razor-sharp cheekbones. He showed her his ticket. Terminal One was clearly written on it.

They both laughed.

'I presume you're in the right place,' she chuckled. Galway airport was tiny, definitely not enough room for a second terminal.

'Must be a mistake then.' He grinned, revealing film-star teeth. 'So where are you off to? Is it business or pleasure?'

'Business,' Anna said firmly. 'Sure what is pleasurable about getting up in the middle of the night?'

'I know what you mean. I'm actually on my way to Manchester.'

'Very good.'

'You don't sound terribly impressed.'

'It's hard to be impressed at this time of the morning,' she laughed. 'If you were going to Bermuda maybe . . .'

'Are you from Dublin?'

'Yeah.'

'Me too.'

Because they were delayed and there was nothing else to do, the conversation lasted quite a while.

By take-off Anna had decided he was the one.

They chatted easily as the plane whizzed across Ireland.

She could barely steal her eyes away from him.

She was sorry after only forty minutes when the plane landed at Dublin airport.

They said goodbye.

Anna wondered if she'd ever see him again.

She did.

At the baggage reclaim.

'Sorry for bothering you again,' he suddenly appeared at her side, 'but I was wondering if by any chance you . . . ?'

'Ye . . . es?'

'Are you in Dublin tonight?'

'Er . . .' she hesitated.

'Listen, if I'm annoying you I'll bugger off. Honestly.'

'No you're not er . . . annoying me at all.' *Far from it!*

'So would you be on for meeting up and doing something maybe?'

'Sure,' she said easily. Why wouldn't she? He was divine. An opportunity like this knocked just once in a lifetime. If ever.

Although a city centre hotel had been booked for her she hadn't had any intention of staying there anyway. She'd actually been planning on spending a bit of time at home with her folks. Now the room seemed like a much better idea.

The family could wait.

'I'll give you my mobile number just in case you change your mind . . .'

'Good idea,' Anna said quickly, knowing there'd need to be a bloody good reason to make her change her mind. 'Well, see you later then.'

He was gone.

Was that a dream?

Anna made her way through the sliding doors and past the crowd of onlookers staring at her hopefully with their cardboard signs. She always felt almost guilty for not being the person they were looking to meet.

She queued at the taxi rank, no longer feeling the slightest bit tired. Sure wasn't it great to be chatted up by such a god-like creature. Anna was totally flattered. What a change from the geeks who normally took a shine to her. She wondered what the hell his bloody name was? Wasn't that just typical of her to get a number and no name.

The meeting droned on endlessly. Anna stared at the flip chart nodding every now and again, pretending to be interested. She took a look around the room at the haggard retail managers. God, they were a miserable-looking bunch, she concluded. Did nobody with decent looks choose retailing as a career? Oh well, it didn't matter really. She was going to ring her sexy stranger once she escaped this dreary old meeting.

Six o'clock couldn't come fast enough.

In the middle of O'Connell Street she dialled his number from a payphone. He should be back from Manchester by now.

'Hello?' came the vibrant voice at the other end of the line.

'Guess who this is?' Anna teased.

'Jennifer Lopez.'

'Try again.'

'The stunner off the plane.'

'Absolutely.'

'You don't know my name, right?'

'And you don't know mine either, smartarse,' Anna laughed.

'It's Darren.'

'My name's Anna.'

'Where are you, Anna?'

'O'Connell Street.'

'Why don't I meet you in the Gresham?'

'Perfect.'

Anna retouched her make-up in the bathroom of the Gresham Hotel, congratulating herself on having managed to stay awake the whole day. She couldn't believe she was actually going on a date now. God worked in mysterious ways. She was convinced of that.

He was bang on time. *He was keen.*

'Hi,' Anna said casually as Darren, all six-foot-three of him, pulled up a chair.

'Hi.' He held her gaze and she felt a butterfly or two flutter from one side of her stomach to the other. 'I needn't tell you you look great 'cos I'm sure you already know that.'

'No you needn't,' Anna pulled at her hair self-consciously, 'because I look like shit.'

'You're obviously not a night owl, are you?'

'You're wrong. I'm very much a night owl. But those red-eye flights are a killer.'

'You're right, they are.' Darren leaned forward, his eyes boring into her. 'I'm wrecked myself. Let's go to bed.'

'I presume you're joking.'

'Of course.' He gave her arm a friendly punch.

'Ow.'

'Sorry, would you like a kiss instead?'

She stared at him blankly not quite knowing how to respond. Was this guy for real?

'Kiss me then,' she teased.

He leaned forward and placed a warm hand on her upper thigh. Her heart began to thud a lot faster than usual. Surely this was a dream? Any minute now she was going to wake up in her little room in Galway and realize this was all a cruel hoax.

And then she felt his strong lips against hers. She closed her eyes and let her own lips respond. This was the stuff Hollywood dreams were made of.

And this time Anna Allstone was the star.

Eventually, slowly, reluctantly, she withdrew from his embrace. She sneaked a furtive glance around her. It wouldn't do if the crowd from Lolta's had happened to come in for a drink. But nobody was watching, thank God. After all, kissing in public was tacky at the best of times. But this kiss was different. It was like nothing before, warming her heart and every part of her body. Impulsively she leaned forward and kissed him again.

He asked if she was hungry. Hungry? How could he possibly think about food at a time like this?

She shrugged. 'Not really.'

'Well, I'm starving. Tell you what, I'm going to pick up my car in the Ilac car park and I'll come round and pick you up if you just wait inside the door.'

Fifteen minutes later when a shiny black Ferrari braked outside the Gresham and beeped the horn Anna chose to ignore it. She stared anxiously down Dublin's main street and looked at her watch. *Come on, Darren, where are you?*

The Ferrari driver stuck his head out of the window. 'You getting in or what?'

Dazed, Anna moved towards the Ferrari. She slipped into the comfortable leather seat and fastened her seatbelt. 'Sorry, I wasn't expecting a—'

'My mini broke down so I borrowed it,' Darren laughed.

This has to be the one, Anna decided as the

car cruised along the street attracting stares from passers-by. He was the ultimate date for Victoria's party. Just wait until those nasty cows saw this babe machine parked outside Victoria's house. She could imagine their faces contorting as she sashayed in with her handsome hunk. She turned to look at his perfectly sculpted face, high cheekbones and strong jaw. When God had been giving out looks, Darren must have booted all the other Irish blokes off the queue.

It was funny the way things worked out, wasn't it? Just when you thought you were facing a brick wall, somehow it crumbled and you were able to step over it. And it was true what they said about meeting people when you least expected it. She'd spent the last few months searching for Mr Right for the night, and then this morning she'd just met him by chance at an airport of all places!

Now let the fun begin . . .

Dinner was at Patrick Guilbauds. Darren ordered for them both and chose an expensive bottle of champagne. A few famous faces dotted the room including a Hollywood star but Anna decided it would be totally uncool to point him out to Darren. Darren looked like the type of guy who'd been born in a Hollywood studio. But he wasn't an actor. He was in business he'd told Anna, and hadn't cared to elaborate. That suited Anna fine. She couldn't bear people who went on and on about their work.

When he suggested going back to his apartment for a nightcap she didn't object. In fact she was dying to see it. Everything about Darren was impressive so far. And he wasn't just some Flash Harry with a credit card either. He was witty, smart and intriguing, and Anna couldn't believe he hadn't been snapped up before this. He explained that it was hard to meet people when you were working crazy hours and constantly travelling. Anna understood that. *It was extremely hard to meet people these days.*

Darren's place was a luxury penthouse suite in Ballsbridge. From the huge windows were stunning views of the city. Dublin was a blaze of welcoming lights from where she was standing and she felt like some kind of crusader about to embark on a tremendously exciting adventure.

Darren retrieved a bottle of Dom Perignon from the drinks cabinet, a monstrous mirrored affair, complete with ice maker. He gallantly poured the champagne into two Waterford crystal flutes and made a toast. 'To us,' he smiled knowingly as her knees went to jelly. 'Us.'

Anna hardly dared look at him for fear he'd realize her attraction to him. Instead she drank in the surroundings. The place looked barely lived in. Huge white sofas, glass tables and modern art hangings. Anna could get used to a place like this. It would be perfect for a young couple like themselves. Stop it, she scolded herself. Aren't you jumping the gun a bit? You've only just met him and already you're planning on moving in. Relax, Anna Allstone. Play it cool.

She wasn't about to blow *this* one. She'd made enough mistakes this year. But it had all worked out in the end, hadn't it? After all if she *had* stayed with any of her exes then she'd never have met Darren. And then she'd have been stuck going along to this party with one of those headwreckers.

Hopefully Darren hadn't anything else planned for the weekend of the party. She'd have to think of a good excuse to keep him in town that night without telling him exactly why. She didn't want to come across as an eager beaver.

'More champagne?' He slipped into the sofa beside her. His aftershave was strong and sensual. She wanted to pounce on him.

'I'd love some,' she smiled.

The bubbles were shooting straight for her head, making her feel dizzy with desire. Darren must have slipped some kind of love potion into her drink. She was completely unable to concentrate on a word he was saying. She was far too busy concentrating on how his torso might look underneath his white cotton shirt. Discreetly she checked out his long strong legs beneath the soft fabric of his trousers. There was no doubt about it, Darren was the most desirable creature she'd ever laid eyes on.

She wanted him to stop talking. He was going

on about life and how it was full of surprises or
something. She wanted him to stay quiet. He was
unbearably sexy. Her arm reached for the back of
his neck and she drew herself towards him. Her
lips locked hard onto his. He kissed her back, fast
and furiously as he fumbled with the top button
of her shirt. Her head was swimming with shock
and pleasure as her hands tugged at his thick
leather belt.

'You're beautiful,' he cried as he helped her with
his belt, 'you truly are a beautiful woman.'

Feeling desirable and powerful, she leaned back
on the sofa and let his hands roam the top part of
her body. Beautiful? Nobody had ever called her
that before (apart from a bunch of drunk rugby
supporters at the last French international). Pretty?
Yes. Attractive? Absolutely. But beautiful? God,
maybe she was. Maybe people had just forgotten
to tell her.

Suddenly her bra was open and Anna wished
there was some way of turning out the lights
without making a big scene. But she was terrified
of coming across as a prude, so when his fingers
caressed her nipples until they hardened, she said
nothing.

She felt sexy and silly all at once. Sexy because
this was something that had never happened to her
before. Silly because this man was a stranger and
if this night happened to turn into a one-night

stand, she knew she'd feel sordid and disgusted with herself.

Besides she wasn't ready for this night of passion. Her bra was black and her knickers were cream with pink faded roses on them. Her legs hadn't been shaved for a week and her toenails hadn't seen scissors in nearly three.

'Stop now,' she whispered gently and pushed away the sexiest man on earth. 'I have to get back to my hotel.'

She noticed a deep disappointment creep into his face, making her feel an incredible rush of power. This was the part she loved most. When the man was mad about you because he hadn't had you yet. You were still this big mystery to him. And it was driving him crazy.

'Please stay,' he begged. 'I promise *nothing* will happen.'

If Anna had a pound for every time a man had made that promise she reckoned she'd be living in a penthouse just like this one.

'No really I *have* to go,' she insisted, wondering where she was getting the willpower to be so firm. This was the new Anna Allstone. The girl who called the shots. The girl who men were driven wild about, never sure where they stood. Anna liked this new girl. She loved her!

'I'll drive you home.'

'No, you've been drinking.'

'Not much.'

'Too much,' she wagged her finger at him.

'Please stay,' he tried again. Fair play to men but they rarely took no for an answer.

But no was the only answer Darren was getting. She rang for a taxi and left.

Chapter Thirty-one

'Tell me all,' Aoife squealed, 'from beginning to end.'

'Oh God, that's going to take some time,' Anna admitted.

'I'm not going anywhere.'

Anna related the story to her enthusiastic flatmate. It felt like she was talking about somebody else. Things like that didn't happen to people like Anna. She was almost afraid to go to sleep in case she woke up and realized this was all some kind of cruel dream. She was afraid that he might remove the blinkers he was obviously wearing and find out she was nothing special.

Just Anna Allstone.

'So has he rung yet?' asked Aoife wide-eyed.

'No.' Anna looked slightly doubtful.

'And would you not think of giving him a shout?'

'Absolutely not!' Anna was adamant.

The phone rang suddenly making both girls jump. Anna's heart began to pound. What was she going to say to him? She took a deep breath.

'I'll get it,' Aoife offered. 'You relax a sec.'

'Hello? Oh, hi Grainne . . . yeah we're fine, we're all fine . . .'

Anna could feel her heart sinking to the bottom of her stomach. This was madness. She shouldn't be sitting in at her stage of life waiting for a phone to ring. She had to get out. Sure didn't everybody know that the minute you left the house the phone started hopping? She grabbed her coat and scarf, waved Aoife goodbye and set out for a walk. The wind should clear her head. It had to.

She sat on a small bench facing the sea and the magnificent Clare Hills. The hour change meant longer, brighter evenings and thankfully tonight the rain had stayed away.

She felt fifteen again. She'd sat on this bench when she was fifteen. Well maybe not exactly the same bench but one just like it. Fifteen had been a horrible age when she'd hated her mother, resented her father and thought her brother was the biggest bollix in the entire universe.

They'd stayed in a caravan just up the road. It had rained for the week. Everybody had been so pissed off with the weather and Anna had resigned herself to the glum fact that she'd never ever get herself a boyfriend no matter how hard she tried looking for one.

Claire had gone to Florida that year and Victoria had been sent as a paying guest to a family in the south of France.

They'd all been tanned and gorgeous back in school on the first of September. And Anna had been her usual white and unattractive self.

Thank God she'd never be fifteen again.

She wondered if he'd rung yet. Probably not. It was too soon. Maybe he wasn't going to ring at all. Maybe he was a serial dater. And had even met someone else since yesterday. Men were fast movers. At this very minute he could well be giving somebody else the eye. There could be another hopeful girl sitting right now in that fabulous penthouse imagining a bright future as Darren's other half.

Maybe this new girl would go all the way with him and he'd forget the frigid Bridget who'd fled the previous evening like a frightened rabbit. Another one bites the dust, Anna thought mournfully as she kicked the ground with the heel of her boot. Feck him anyway. Feck him and every other man she'd had the misfortune to come in contact with.

Feck them all!

'He rang,' Aoife was almost hyperventilating back in the apartment.

'Did he?' Anna could hardly conceal her joy. 'What did he say?'

'He said to ring straight back.'

'Did he sound disappointed I wasn't in?'

'Not really,' her flatmate admitted.

'Oh . . . maybe then he was just ringing out of politeness.'

'Rubbish. Men never ring just to be polite.'

Anna thought about it. Aoife was right. Men only rang when they wanted something. Well that was good then. It meant that Darren wanted her. He wanted HER!

'So are you going to ring back?' Aoife asked.

'No.'

'What do you mean, no? Have you lost the plot or what?'

'No,' Anna repeated.

'He's waiting for your call though.'

'Let him wait. It's his turn.'

'But he mightn't ring back.'

'He will,' Anna said confidently. 'Men mightn't ring initially. But when they do ring and you're not in, they *always* ring back.'

'I wish I was more like you,' Aoife's voice was full of admiration. 'You're so strong.'

'Believe me, I'm not that strong,' Anna said quietly.

It was a vicious circle. She was dying to ring him. But if she did he might think she was too keen. Desperate even.

She'd have to pace herself. She hoped she was right about him ringing back. She was almost one hundred per cent sure he would. Men hated to think someone else was doing the rejecting. They'd such massive egos. But how was she going to stop herself from lifting that phone and dialling his number? Somebody would have to sellotape her hands behind her back.

She'd ring Claire, that's what she'd do. Claire

would be able to give her tons of advice. She picked up the phone.

'Are you ringing him after all?' Aoife enquired.

'Absolutely not,' Anna shook her head.

Simon answered the phone. He sounded different. His voice was strained.

'She's not here, I'm afraid,' he answered.

'When will she be back?'

'God only knows, Anna. God only knows.'

Chapter Thirty-two

Claire sat nervously outside Tom's apartment in Dalkey. She had no idea what she was planning on doing. But one thing was sure. She'd had enough. Enough of the painful bouts of silence that had become the norm in that place herself and Simon called 'home'.

Her husband didn't love her any more. Well, if he did, he had a very funny way of showing it. Maybe he loved Shelley. Or maybe he was too wrapped up in himself to love anybody. Relationships were hard work. Everybody knew that. But Claire didn't know if she could be bothered handling any more work. There was only so much giving one person could do. She switched off the engine and checked her appearance in the side mirror. Her reflection didn't look bad for someone who was crying inside. She stepped out of the car and locked it. Mechanically she walked towards the entrance of the apartment block.

'Come on up,' Tom sounded genuinely delighted to hear her voice.

Wearing faded denims and a dark grey sweatshirt,

Tom certainly didn't look like he'd any plans to go out. Spontaneously he kissed Claire's flushed cheeks and ushered her into the warm apartment.

'Are you okay?' He looked at her with concern.

Claire opened her mouth to say something but instead, to her horror, she felt her face crumble and a hot tear slid down the side of her cheek.

Mortified, she brushed it away with the side of her hand. But then another one fell. And another one.

'Sit down,' Tom ordered gently. 'Surely it can't be as bad as all that.'

'It's worse,' Claire sniffed. God, she was pathetic. Here she was blabbing on to a virtual stranger about the 'trauma' concerning her dull life as an urban housewife, when he had lost his fiancée in a horrific accident. Who exactly should be the one crying here?

'Simon's having an affair,' she blurted.

'How do you know?' Tom handed her a Kleenex. He was very calm as if there could be a very reasonable explanation for all of this.

'He told me he was going out with one of the lads from work tonight.'

'And?'

'And I asked him if Shelley was one of the lads and he said yes.'

'But that doesn't mean he's having an affair,' Tom said quietly.

'I know, I know. It's just a woman's instinct is pretty strong.'

'So where are they going?'

'They're not going anywhere now,' Claire sniffed. 'I walked out and left him with Andrew.'

'I don't know what to say, Claire,' Tom sighed. 'It's not really right to interfere in other people's relationships.'

'You're so good though,' Claire placed a hand on his. 'One day you'll make some girl extremely happy.'

She noticed he winced at her words. Oh God, what had she just gone and said now? She was an idiot. A total dingbat.

'I'm sorry, I—' she stopped mid-sentence as he drew her close to him and let her head rest on his chest.

'Ssh,' he soothed, 'there's no need to say anything.'

He stroked her hair as she clung to him. Why couldn't Simon be more like Tom? Why did terrible things happen to nice people like him? It wasn't fair. She snuggled in closer. Tom's body was lovely and warm. She hadn't been cuddled by a man in so long.

'Tom?' She looked up at him, aware of how close her face was to his.

He tilted her chin with his forefinger and looked deep into her eyes.

'Claire,' he murmured. And slowly but surely their lips met and they kissed softly, sweetly, cautiously.

She pressed herself against him and let him slip his tongue through her slightly parted lips. Their kissing gradually became more frantic, more urgent. How could this be so wrong, Claire wondered, when it felt so right. She threw any niggling reservations to the wind and ran her fingers through his hair, tasting his soft strong lips, hungry for him. His hands began to gently explore her body. She closed her eyes and concentrated on his every move. She hadn't felt such desire since the birth of her baby. Her baby! Oh God! Andrew was at home with his grumpy father while his mother – the woman he depended on for everything – was behaving like an oversexed slut with a strange man.

'This is all wrong, Claire,' Tom spoke first.

'I know,' she withdrew from him, 'you're right. My life's too messed up to contemplate starting an affair.'

She sat up straight on the sofa and rearranged her clothes. Tom was smiling at her. She smiled back. She felt free. For the first time in a long time, Claire no longer felt trapped.

'Thank you,' her voice was genuine.

'For what?'

'For making me feel like a normal human being again.'

'You don't hate me then?'

'Of course not, I quite fancy you actually . . .'

'Ditto,' he said dreamily.

'I'd still like to be your friend,' she said, 'and

I mean that genuinely. Since Anna has moved to Galway I've been feeling a bit low.'

'Well, I know what you mean. A lot of my friends were friends of both of ours – my fiancée and myself. They feel kind of awkward around me now. I kind of understand where they're coming from . . . I might feel awkward too in the same situation.'

'Do you think you'll ever fall in love again?'

'You never know,' he gave a distant smile. 'Recently I find all the good ones are married.'

They both laughed.

'Don't rush into marriage,' she warned. 'It's not all it's cracked up to be.'

'Simon doesn't sound like such a bad guy.' Tom handed her her coat. 'You two will work this out.'

'Hopefully,' Claire grimaced.

'Will you be okay?' he hugged her.

'Yep,' she tried to smile optimistically. 'I'll be in touch. You'll have to come out with me and my friend Anna – she's mad.'

'Well, I'll look forward to a wild night out with the pair of ye so. Take care, Claire, and remember I'm always at the other end of the phone.'

'Would you mind telling me what the hell is going on?' Simon's face was thunderous.

'I was out.'

'Well, that was *obvious*. Out where?'

'With a friend.'

'Who?'

'A guy called Tom,' Claire said wearily.

'Tom?' Simon's eyes narrowed.

'He's a friend of Emma's.'

'And it was just the two of you, was it?'

'That's right,' Claire snapped.

'You're unbelievable, do you know that, Claire?' Simon went to put on his coat.

'Where are you going?'

'Out.'

'If you go out, don't bother coming back,' Claire threatened.

'Why? What are you planning on doing? Changing the locks?'

'Well, I hadn't thought about it but maybe I will.'

'Tell me now if you are. Because if you are, I'll need to stay with a friend.'

'You could stay with Shelley.' Claire's voice was beginning to shake.

'Indeed I could.'

'GET OUT,' she screamed.

'What is the matter with you?'

'I said get out!'

The door slammed. Quickly she bolted the locks. She didn't care if he never came home.

She rang Anna.

'Oh hi,' Anna sounded exhausted.

'You don't sound too pleased to hear from me,' Claire said irritably.

'Sorry . . . . it's just that I was expecting somebody else.'

'A man?'

'Yes.'

'Emmet? Jake? Steve? Rich?'

'No'

'Mark?'

'No, a guy called Darren.'

'Do you not think you're getting a bit old for this kind of carry on?' Claire asked rather uncharitably.

'I'm sorry, Claire,' her friend retorted, 'that I'm not as happily married as you.'

'Don't mind me, Anna, I know I'm being irritable. I've a lot on my mind that's all.'

'Is it Andrew? Is he sick?'

'No, it's Simon and he *is* sick. Sick in the head.'

'No he's not,' Anna laughed.

'He is. He's having an affair. With Shelley. And I'm leaving him, Anna. I've had enough.'

'Leaving Simon? Are you mad? Simon's so good for you. And he's your husband, remember? Most women would kill to get their hands on someone like him.'

'Exactly,' Claire said grimly. 'Women like Shelley.'

'But where would you go?'

'I don't know.'

'You can't come here.'

'Oh, right.'

'Ah come on, Claire, don't be like that. You couldn't bring Andrew here. Aoife's studying for her finals.'

'I see.'

'No, you don't see at all. In fact you're acting pretty weird at the moment.'

'Of course I'm acting weird. My husband is having an affair and I'm supposed to carry on like everything is normal, am I?'

'You're being ridiculous.'

'I am *not* being ridiculous. But I can't expect you to help me. You've a man in your life now so everything is fine. The whole world can fuck off when there's a man on the scene, right?'

'Jesus, I can't believe you're being such a bitch.'

'I can't turn to anybody else,' Claire sounded distraught. 'Everybody hates me. Even Tom doesn't want to know.'

'Who the hell is Tom?'

'Just a friend.'

'Claire, you don't have any male friends.'

'I do now.'

'Are you trying to tell me something?'

'No.'

'Did you ... you didn't snog this Tom fella, did you?'

Claire didn't answer.

'Jesus Christ, don't tell me you slept with ...'

'Don't be daft,' Claire snapped.

'But you thought about it, didn't you?'

'I might have.'

'Jesus, Claire, there *is* something wrong. Don't do anything stupid until Friday. I'll come up to see you at the weekend.'

'Sure.'

Anna put the phone down. It rang again immediately.

'Claire?'

'I don't think so,' said the bemused male voice. 'Try again.'

'Darren,' she grinned. 'Good to hear from you.'

'I'm taking you to Paris.'

'What?'

'First-class tickets. Friday night.'

'Friday? Oh no, I can't go this Friday.'

'Right,' He sounded disappointed.

'Sorry, it's just that something urgent has come up.'

'Bummer.'

'I know.'

'You can't get out of it?'

'No,' was Anna's firm reply. Difficult as it was to turn him down, friendship had to come first. She wasn't going to give Claire the chance to fault her again. 'I'm sorry, there's no way I can go.'

'Well, I'll catch you again,' he said. 'Bye bye.'

Anna stared at the phone in near disbelief. Had she really just gone and turned down the trip of a lifetime with Ireland's sexiest man in favour of a night in with the moaning Claire? Jesus, she needed her head examined.

All her life she'd waited for Mr Right to whisk her off into the sunset and make her dreams come true. Tonight was the closest she'd ever come to that. And she'd blown it. For Claire. Claire who thought the world owed her a lot and spent most of her life trapped in some kind of bubble. Damn Claire and her silly hallucinations. A guy as solid as Simon didn't just go off and have an affair.

Chapter Thirty-three

'I cancelled the trip to Paris,' Darren was on the phone to Anna first thing the following morning.

'Not on my account, I hope,' Anna replied coyly.

'Paris can wait. But I can't wait . . . to see you. I miss you. I can't get you out of my head.'

'Really?' Anna was flabbergasted.

'Can I meet you Saturday afternoon?'

'Sure,' Anna said coolly while hugging the phone in delight, 'Saturday is fine.'

How the tables have turned for you, Anna Allstone, she thought as she whizzed through Salthill in her newly delivered company car. Only a few weeks ago you were being given the run-around by a bunch of useless eejits. Now look at you. With a guy like Darren practically eating out of your hand.

But back to reality she was seriously worried about Claire. Her friend was obviously suffering from some kind of post-natal depression or something. But in fairness Andrew had been born quite a while ago. Surely that couldn't be it.

Anyway, whatever it was, Anna was sure she could sort it all out.

Anna was particularly good at sorting out other people's problems.

She wondered when would be the best time to invite Darren to the party. It was important not to scare him off with too many invitations. Then again it was just a party, wasn't it? It wasn't like she was dragging him along to meet her parents or anything like that. And it was vital that he kept the weekend free.

Anna parked outside the side door of Lolta's and let herself in.

The store was empty.

She turned on the lights and deactivated the alarm.

The phone was ringing.

'Good morning, Lolta's?'

'Anna, is that you?' a sharp voice barked down the line.

Jesus, it was June bloody Neelane. Was there no escaping that wagon?

'Yes it is.' Anna tried to keep her voice even. 'Slight change of plans I'm afraid, Anna. Miss Browne has been taken to hospital due to illness and I've nobody to man the store this weekend apart from you. I trust you'll do a good job and we'll owe you another day off at a later date.'

'But June, I . . .'

'You'll be more than capable, Anna. This is a good opportunity to prove yourself, remember. I'll be at the other end of the phone as always, of course.'

The bloody bitch! Anna stared at the dead phone, stunned. It was as if June *knew* she'd made plans for the weekend. This was a disaster. Claire would kill her for not meeting her and as for Darren . . . well, she could more or less kiss him goodbye. He wouldn't be sitting in watching TV while she ran around like a headless chicken trying to run a store at the other end of the country.

She rang Claire who was predictably devastated and said something daft like not knowing how she'd get through another weekend on her own.

'On your own?' Anna wasn't terribly sympathetic. 'You've a husband, Claire, and you need to start communicating with him.'

'I'd communicate with him if he was bloody well here.'

'Well, ring the Samaritans so.'

'Thanks.'

'I mean it, Claire, they're brilliant. They'll just listen and you can get everything off your chest.'

'But I'm not suicidal.'

'You don't have to be. Just ring them. I'll talk to you later, okay?'

Anna hung up the phone and sighed. If Claire

worked as a retail manager she'd soon know the true meaning of drama. She rang Darren's mobile but it was switched off.

On Friday, everything that could have gone wrong, did. The computers went completely ballistic and a record eight staff called in sick. A lorry load of goods was delivered and lay scattered around the stockroom waiting for someone to have a serious accident.

But Anna coped.

Somehow.

Back at the flat she poured herself a double G&T and switched on *The Late Late Show*. Her aching stockinged feet deserved a break.

Aoife had gone home for the weekend and the place was strangely quiet. Anna settled into the sofa and listened to some Irish 'lollipop' singer crooning into the microphone. The singing sensation was horribly made up with circles under her eyes. Anna was afraid her ginormous head would topple over any minute. God, there was terrible pressure on women in the public eye to starve, wasn't there?

Come to think of it, Anna hadn't eaten much herself over the last few days. There was nothing like a heavy work schedule to keep the calories at bay.

The singing head left the stage and suddenly Pat Kenny was shaking some politician's hand. Yawn!

Then out of the blue the doorbell rang.

Anna's heart leaped.

The clock said ten-thirty.
Who in the name of God was outside?

Chapter Thirty-four

'Hi, is that Claire?'

'Yes it is.' Claire didn't recognize the voice. 'Er . . . who's this?'

'Alice . . . remember from school?'

'Alice Flinton! How could I forget? Are you back for a break or what?'

'I'm back for good actually, five years of living in the city that never sleeps wears you out eventually.'

'Where did you get my new number?'

'Your mum. She was saying you're well married now with a son and all. I believe he's beautiful.'

'Yes he is,' Claire said proudly. 'You have to come over and see him.'

'I'd love to.'

'Come over tonight, why don't you?'

'I wouldn't be intruding, would I?'

'Ah no,' Claire said lightly. As if!

'I'm dying to meet Simon too,' Alice enthused, 'I heard he's a wild thing.'

Wild? Simon? Ah no. She must be mistaking him

for someone else. 'Er . . . who told you that?' Claire asked hesitantly.

'Oh, it's just that my sister Ellie, her friend works in the same firm. She raves about him so she does.'

'And what's her name?' Claire emitted faintly.

'Shelley, Shelley Riffley, a striking-looking girl I must say . . . tall, long dark hair, long . . .'

'I know her,' Claire cut in. 'And she thinks Simon's great, does she?'

'Says it's a pity there aren't more men like him about. Poor Shelley. Her love life has always been a bit of a disaster. She—'

'Did I hear you got married yourself, Alice?' Claire suddenly felt nauseous and was extremely anxious to change subjects.

'Yes,' Alice instantly became quiet, 'yes I did. I'm separated now though.'

'Oh I'm sorry,' Claire commiserated. 'I really am.'

'Ah well, unfortunately things don't always turn out the way you'd hoped.'

'Yes.' *I know.*

'Well, will I see you this evening then?'

'Great,' said Claire, 'See you.'

Good old Simon, Claire grimaced. Wild, huh? Not with his wife he wasn't. Unless you meant wildly boring. Then again, maybe he really was this mad thing when he went out without her. Maybe he danced on tables and mooned at shocked onlookers. Nah, that was ridiculous. It wasn't in Simon to behave like that. He was still fairly solid at the end of the day. People didn't change *that* drastically.

She ran Andrew's bath and sat on the toilet seat as steam engulfed the room. She missed female company. Adult company. It was great that Alice was calling over to chat about the old days.

Andrew shouted joyfully, throwing gallons of water over the edge of the bath. The carpet underneath was getting saturated. Claire wondered if baths had been as exciting for her when she was young. Children were such simple creatures. It was a pity they had to grow up.

Her son squealed with unconcealed delight as Claire rinsed his dark blond curls with warm water. 'Mama,' he shrieked, 'Mama.'

'Baba,' she cooed back. 'Baba good boy, yes you are, yes you are.'

He grabbed his yellow duck and splashed the bathwater even more. Thankfully he'd no idea that his Mama and Dada were involved in a silent war, Claire thought darkly. No idea that his mother had lusted after another man while he slept innocently in his cot at home. No idea why his father would choose to chase the knickers off the office tart.

Claire secured Andrew into his buggy. His mother had seen a stunning sequined silver number in the window of a chic Ranelagh boutique. Maybe they'd have it in a size ten. It would be absolutely perfect for Victoria's party.

She took a critical look at herself in the hall mirror. Despite wearing full war paint and cherry blusher, she looked worryingly pale. A few sunbed sessions were badly needed. The silver dress wouldn't exactly go with snow-white arms.

She pushed Andrew's colourful buggy down the main street, lost in her own little world. A tall handsome man waylaid her on the pavement.

'Sorry,' she muttered and went to manoeuvre the buggy around him.

'Hey, good looking.'

She stopped and stared up at him, the sun almost blinding her.

'Mark,' she laughed, recognizing him. 'Ever the charmer.'

'My charm doesn't work on everybody sadly.'

'I feel so sorry for you,' Claire said sarcastically.

'So how's Simon? I see him now and then around the I.F.S.C. One of these days I hope to nab him for a drink.'

'I'm sure he'd like that.' *The only person who can't nab him is me.*

'How is the fair lady getting on in Galway?'

'She's very busy as far as I know.'

'One of these days I might drive up and surprise her.'

'I'm sure she'd be delighted to see you,' Claire enthused.

'And how's this little fellow?' He made a face at Andrew who chuckled his little baby laughter.

'Great. Hey, don't tell me you're getting broody.'

'I wouldn't mind a mini Mark.'

'Ah go way out of that, you chauvinist,' Claire belted him playfully with her handbag.

'I suppose a daughter would be nice too,' Mark grinned. 'I'd need to get a wife though.'

'Well, maybe if you stayed with someone for more than two weeks you'd have a better chance of getting one.'

'God, you know,' Mark pretended to contemplate the idea, 'maybe you're right.'

Claire pushed Andrew's buggy through the door of the plush boutique. The well-groomed assistant rushed over to help. Claire asked for the silver dress in a small. She was dying to tell Anna about her chance encounter with Mark. God, if Claire was single again she'd jump at someone like Mark.

The assistant returned with the dress. The fabric felt extraordinarily delicate. God, you wouldn't want to behave like a heifer in a little slip of a thing like this. She sneaked a quick look at the price. Holy God! Still, Simon never begrudged her the price of a piece of clothing. Simon's wife had to wear the right clothes, portray the right image. It wasn't a bad thing. At least he wasn't mean. There was nothing in this world worse than a mean man.

God, would she ever forget Neal Marron, the

stunning-looking medical student she'd dated in college? *Everybody* had thought *he* was a great catch.

Especially her mother who'd had the wedding invitations practically written the first evening she went out with him. They'd gone to the cinema, Claire remembered. How could she forget?

She'd arranged to meet him under Clery's clock. Nervous as anything, she'd sat in a fast-food restaurant across the way and stared at him through the big glass window. She was dying to see how long he'd wait for her before moving off.

After a full twenty minutes he checked his watch and started to walk slowly down the street. Legging it out of the fast-food joint, she caught up with him, apologizing breathlessly for being so late.

When they reached the cinema, Neal immediately excused himself to go to the bathroom.

Rather than hang around like a spare tool, Claire bought the tickets. And why not? Sure they were both students, weren't they?

But when Neal didn't offer to pay for the popcorn and coke Claire was a tiny bit disappointed. However she decided to put it to the back of her mind. She'd so looked forward to the date and after all you couldn't expect men to pay for *everything*.

More to the point he was a fab kisser. Not like some guys who didn't really have a clue.

Afterwards they'd walked home hand-in-hand to Neal's parents' place and raided the fridge. They'd 'got to know' each other on the family sofa while listening to some funky songs Neal had recorded off the radio.

Eventually she'd lost her virginity to him.

That was after his many protests when he insisted that he'd seen it all before and it wasn't such a big deal.

But to Claire it was a big deal.

Neal had booked a B&B to make the whole occasion more romantic.

But to Claire's bitter disappointment, when they arrived he produced a half-price voucher.

The landlady had scrutinized it as if trying to remember when the hell it had been issued.

She pointed out that breakfast wasn't actually included in the special offer.

Claire out of sheer mortification had offered to pay for breakfast but Neal had already spotted a little newsagent around the corner where he insisted they could grab something in the morning.

That night he was in and out before you could ask 'Are you in yet?'

Claire had lain awake in the dark listening to Neal's infuriating snores.

Everything seemed to go downhill after that. Every little thing he did annoyed her, from bumming cigarettes off people in the UCD bar, to turning up at every medical function for the free glass of wine. But only when she got a hand-picked bunch of flowers for Valentine's did she finally decide to call it a day. Claire gave a little shudder at the memory.

There was nothing worse than a penny-pincher.

The dress fitted perfectly. Claire gave a little twirl in front of the full-length mirror. Andrew clapped his baby hands showing his approval.

'You look stunning,' the assistant crowed.

Claire believed her. Simon would want to eat her in this.

'I'll take it,' she grinned. 'I'll just have to get my husband to come in and pay for it. Can I leave a deposit?'

'Of course,' the assistant beamed. It wasn't every day she made a five-hundred-pound sale. This week had been a particularly good one though. Sure wasn't it only yesterday she'd sold the exact same dress to that awfully pushy Reddin woman. That silver dress was really turning out to be a winner. Perhaps she should order in a few more.

Claire handed over a crisp fifty-pound note. As she did so, she felt a wave of sudden nausea wash over her. The assistant watched in alarm as Claire's face turned a curious shade of green.

'Are you all right?'

Claire clasped a hand over her mouth and shook her head violently.

'Quick, the bathroom's over there.'

Claire ran to the back of the shop, flung open the tiny bathroom door and reached the toilet bowl just in time. She collapsed to her knees, the tears streaming down her cheeks. She suddenly felt terribly weak.

The assistant was handing her man-size tissues through the door. Eventually Claire emerged and was handed a glass of water.

'I'm so sorry,' she apologized. 'I don't know what came over me.'

'Don't worry about it,' the assistant said kindly. 'Are you pregnant?'

Claire faced the shop assistant in alarm. 'No,' she practically shrieked.

'Oh.'

'I'm sorry, I didn't mean to react like that . . . it's just, oh God, it doesn't seem possible, I . . .'

'Listen, you don't have to explain yourself.' The assistant was beginning to look extremely uncomfortable. 'Go home now and have a nice cup of tea. I'll hold the dress for you.'

Typical Irish woman, Claire thought as she left the shop. A cup of tea was the answer to everything. She wondered what had made her so sick. The omelette she'd had for breakfast had tasted a bit funny.

Passing a chemist Claire hesitated for a second. Should she or shouldn't she? It was ridiculous really. Herself and Simon hadn't made love in nearly two months. Suddenly a thought struck her. Two months? Claire had missed her last period. She hadn't given it much thought as she was pretty irregular anyway.

Slowly she reversed the buggy into the chemist.

The test was blue, for positive.

Claire was in shock. This was so unplanned. So

unplanned. Vaguely she was able to remember the night of conception. She'd been exhausted as far as she could remember and Simon had been slightly drunk and unusually horny. She'd basically told him to get on with it.

What a dreadful way to conceive a life!

She wondered how long she was gone. Thank God she was still slim enough to wear the dress.

She reached for the phone. She'd have to ring her mum straightaway. Halfway through the digits she stopped. Surely Simon should be the first to know. He'd helped make the baby after all.

I've a feeling this one's a girl; she patted her stomach and waited for Simon to answer his mobile.

'Hello?' It was a female voice. Uh oh, Claire thought, she must have dialled the wrong number.

'Er . . . is Simon there?'

'He just popped out for a minute. I'll get him to ring you back or shall I take a message? It's Shelley by the way.'

Shelley? It didn't sound like her. Her voice wasn't quite as cocky as usual. And no, she didn't want to leave a message. *Unless of course Shelley would like to pass on the message to Simon that his wife was expecting a baby.*

'Thank you no, Shelley, I'll ring back.'

She pressed *end* with a sigh. It was ironic really, wasn't it? She was pregnant with Simon's child and he was out cavorting with another woman. Great. The doorbell rang loudly. Sugar, that must be Alice already. She'd completely forgotten about her calling around. Well, it was too late to send her away.

'Alice, you look fantastic,' Claire said as she opened the door. 'Come on in.'

Alice, a small mousy woman with a large nose and a generous smile, stepped into the hallway and gave Claire a hug. 'It's good to see you,' she beamed. 'You haven't changed a bit.'

Alice followed Claire into the kitchen and sat on one of the stools. 'This is a great place you have here. You're lucky.'

It was funny, Claire thought, everybody went on about how lucky she was. But if she was so lucky why was her husband not at home this evening? Why hadn't he phoned her back at all?

'Where's Andrew?' Alice wanted to know.

'He's in bed,' Claire replied. 'Would you like to see him?'

'You bet.'

Alice had obviously picked up some key sayings in New York.

The two women tiptoed into Andrew's room. He was sleeping soundly and looked unbelievably cute.

'I'd love a child,' Alice said with a hint of sadness.

Claire felt a wave of guilt pass over her. No wonder Alice thought she was lucky. She lived in a beautiful comfortable home and had a gorgeous healthy child. What did Alice have? Nothing but a failed marriage and an obviously painful history back in America. It would be hard for her to start all over again in an Ireland that had changed drastically over the last few years. God, she was making Claire feel very ungrateful indeed.

'So, what would you like to drink?' Claire opened the fridge. 'How about a nice glass of white wine?'

'That would be lovely,' Alice smiled.

Claire poured one for herself. She'd have just the one. God it was going to be hard to give up the drink. It had become her friend.

'So,' She settled herself on the stool opposite Alice, 'what happened?'

'My husband ran off with our next-door neighbour . . . John.'

'Excuse me?'

'John.'

'You mean . . .'

'Yes, you see he wasn't always absolutely sure he was gay, apparently. I guess being married to me made his mind up.'

'You're having me on.'

'I wish I was. Well, at least there weren't any children involved. I think that's a blessing.'

'So John and your . . .'

'And my husband are now living together. They moved to San Fran to start a new life together.'

'You poor thing.'

'Yes well, these things happen, don't they? Thing is you never really think they're going to happen to you.'

'No, I suppose not,' Claire replied quietly. God, she couldn't even contemplate Simon leaving her for someone like, say . . . Jake. The idea was absurd.

'So how have people reacted here?'

'To be honest, I haven't told that many people. It's not the kind of thing you want to shout from the roof tops.'

'I understand.'

'Do you?'

'No,' Claire said truthfully. 'No not really. In fact I can't even begin to understand what you're going through.'

Jesus, meeting people like Alice really put her own life in perspective. Suddenly Claire felt like a monster. She demanded so much out of life. But Simon hadn't left her or anything. And she hadn't any proof that anything was going on between himself and Shelley. Except for that kiss. The kiss. How could anybody explain that away?

God, she didn't know what to think. She couldn't just pack up and leave. Tonight she was going to sit down and talk properly with Simon. That's what was wrong with their marriage. Neither of them communicated any more.

Men weren't great talkers. Everybody knew that. It was a well-known fact. You couldn't go around holding it against them.

Claire sipped a little of her wine and began to cheer up. Everything would sort itself out. Yes, everything would work out in the end.

'Are you going to Victoria's party?' Claire poured Alice a second glass of wine.

'That blasted party,' Alice frowned, 'I've thought of nothing else for the past few weeks. I'm dreading it.'

'Why bother turning up so?'

'I wouldn't give her the satisfaction of not turning up.'

'So she wasn't your favourite person either?'

'She was horrible,' Alice fumed.

'How did she get away with it?'

'Oh, because her parents poured money into the school.'

'Terrible, wasn't it?'

'She used to call me Malice,' said Alice.

'Don't worry, she had a name for everybody.'

'Do you remember when I left school at the end of fifth year to go to Spain for a year? She told everybody that I was pregnant.'

'No way.'

'It's hard to believe, isn't it?' Alice sipped her wine thoughtfully. 'I mean I shouldn't be bothered by any of this at my age. After all, we're all grown-ups now. She probably isn't so bad these days.'

'Indeed she is,' Claire said crossly. 'I met her recently and she's still the same old cow.'

'We should all boycott her silly party,' Alice said

suddenly. 'I mean it's not like anyone else really wants to go.'

'I've already thought of that,' Claire chuckled. 'But in a way I wouldn't mind going along to have a look at the house. I believe it's out of this world. I shouldn't really be admitting that. It's like those social diaries at the back of Irish magazines. You ridicule them and pretend you don't give a damn about who wore what to the opening of those silly things but somehow when you're standing alone in the shop and you think nobody's looking, you can't help sneaking a quick look.'

'And you usually recognize somebody you can't stand,' Alice laughed.

'Yeah and you're thinking "Why did they bother taking a picture of *her*?"'

There was a pause.

'We'll go along and have a laugh anyway,' Claire said. 'I've already put a deposit on a ridiculously expensive dress so I'm kind of committed.'

'Shame on you.'

'I've lots of other lovely dresses that you might want to try on,' Claire offered delicately, aware that Alice's financial situation might not be the best following her speedy return from the States.

'Thanks, Claire, I just might take you up on that.'

'Please come back and see me again soon,' Claire stood up. 'When Andrew's awake. My husband might even put in a surprise appearance,' she grimaced.

'I'm sure I'll see him at the party,' Alice said brightly. 'Just remember,' she warned, 'a good man is hard to find.'

'So they say.' Claire got Alice's coat for her. 'And I believe them.'

Now that Alice was gone the house seemed very quiet indeed. Claire was alone with her thoughts once more. Negative thoughts too. Why hadn't her husband phoned back? Perhaps Shelley had had the audacity not to inform him of her call.

Claire badly needed to talk to him. She wanted him to hold her and assure her that everything would work out fine. She had to tell him about the baby.

'Where are you Simon?' she cried with exasperation.

Chapter Thirty-five

Claire awoke to the sound of the front door opening. The electric red digits on the alarm clock read 11:15. She slipped out of bed and into her comfy slippers. Pulling her old velour dressing gown on she made her way downstairs.

She still couldn't believe what she was about to tell Simon. To think that in seven months' time Andrew would have a little brother or sister!

The lamp in the kitchen was switched on. The television sound was low. Simon was lying on the sofa, his eyes half closed. He looked wrecked.

Claire wondered what was up. Simon hadn't even bothered taking off his scarf. Maybe the stock market had slumped and Simon was taking it personally. Claire didn't know much about stock markets but knew there were good and bad days.

Today must have been one of the bad ones.

'Hi.' She stood at the door.

'Hi, Claire.' He managed just a faint smile.

'Are you hungry? There's lasagne in the fridge. It would only take a few moments to heat up.'

'No thanks,' Simon shook his head, 'I'm not hungry.'

He looked worryingly strained. Claire sat down beside him in the sofa and took his hand. It was freezing and she rubbed it between her two palms. 'The electric blanket's on if you feel like going upstairs. Or I could run a bath. Would you like that?'

'Maybe I'll have a bath so.'

'I'll run it for you.'

'I need to tell you something, Claire,' he said and the flat tone of his voice disturbed her.

Why was he looking at her so oddly?

'I've something to tell you too,' her voice wavered.

Simon put his head in his hands, 'Jesus, Claire, I'm at a loose end and I don't know what to do.'

'What is it?' Claire asked, her mind suddenly paralysed with fear. 'What's bothering you, Simon?'

'It's Shelley,' he said finally. 'She's pregnant.'

Chapter Thirty-six

'Darren, what are you doing here?'

'Ssh,' he interrupted her with a kiss. 'Can I come in?'

'Er . . . yes . . . I . . . God, this is such an unexpected surprise.'

Anna led him into the sitting room, thanking God that out of boredom she'd cleaned it during the ad breaks of *The Late Late Show*. He sat down on the bright yellow sofa which clashed slightly with his orange shirt.

He stretched out his long legs in front of him.

'So this is your pad, eh?' Darren looked around the room with interest.

'Yep.' Anna struggled to think of something interesting to say but her mind remained blank.

'I couldn't wait till next weekend to see you,' Darren smiled, reminding her of a film star.

Next weekend? Hang on, that was the weekend of the party. Should she bring it up now? No, better wait until later. No point scaring him off.

'Well, I'm flattered,' she said instead, sitting down beside him. 'I'm glad to see you too.'

'Are you?'

'Yes,' she said shyly, 'I've been thinking about you. Have . . . have you been thinking about me too?'

'God, if only you knew, Anna Allstone,' he pulled her towards him, 'I've never met anybody like you. I think you're incredible.'

Anna snuggled into his broad chest, her cheek resting against it, listening to the steady rhythm of his heart. If there was ever such a thing as a perfect moment this was it. Afraid to look at him for fear of doing something daft like bursting into tears, she simply murmured, 'That's the nicest thing anyone's ever said to me.'

She didn't care about Victoria's silly party any more. She'd go along with Darren and not give a hoot about the chandeliers and champagne. As long as Darren was by her side, everything else would pale in comparison.

'Are you tired?' Darren gently stroked the back of her neck.

'Mmmm.'

'Do you want to lie down for a while?'

'Oh I don't know about that.'

'Nothing will happen that you don't want to happen.'

Now where had she heard that before?

He stood up and stretched provocatively. 'Come on,' he winked at her.

'Okay,' she said in a little voice and took the arm that was extended to her.

Their lovemaking wasn't earth shattering. The room didn't vibrate with explosive passion. Fireworks didn't suddenly light up Galway Bay. But as far as Anna was concerned it was perfect. Everything seemed just so right.

He took care to find out what she liked, what turned her on. There was no rush, he insisted. They'd all the time in the world to get to know each other's bodies.

He knew all the right things to say, Anna thought fondly. Even though *she* knew they didn't have all the time in the world. Tomorrow, Saturday, would be a very busy day in the store.

In the morning Anna's alarm clock blasted them out of it.

'I've a friend in Galway who I'm going to visit today,' Darren called from the shower. 'So how about I hang around after that and we can do something? How would you like to have dinner in Moran's?'

Anna thought she'd like it very much. Moran's was a delightful traditional pub on the weir with a thatched roof. She couldn't have chosen a more romantic spot herself.

'And I'll book a room in a five-star hotel for afterwards. A room with a view.'

'You're unbelievable,' Anna shook her head in wonder at him. 'What did I do to deserve you?'

Chapter Thirty-seven

Claire sat opposite her husband and stared at him as if in a trance. Right now her head was spinning and she desperately needed to find the right switch to turn it off. Why was her husband's face as white as a sheet? How was Shelley pregnant? As far as Claire could recall there wasn't any particular man in Shelley's life except . . .

'Simon?'

'Yes, Claire,' he sighed.

'Who's the father of Shelley's baby?'

'Oh Claire, does it really matter?'

She cleared her throat angrily. 'Yes it does.'

'She doesn't want me to tell anybody,' he said with a firmness in his voice. 'She's not coming back to work, that's all I know.'

'Why not?' Claire could feel her temperature rising rapidly. What the hell was going on?

Simon's eyes eventually met hers. He stretched out his hand and placed it on hers.

'Claire,' he said, 'if you were pregnant with your boss's child would you come back to the office?'

Claire disengaged her hand from Simon's and with the other hand slapped his face hard.

'What the hell . . . ?' he spluttered.

'How dare you?' she screamed. 'What are you trying to tell me here? Stop playing these mind games with me. Do you hear? STOP IT!'

'Jesus, Claire,' Simon looked alarmed, 'the baby isn't mine. It's John's, remember John who called over here one night with Richard and Jake?'

'I remember,' Claire said, her head still spinning. She didn't know whether to feel angry, shocked or relieved. She sat down on the sofa again, trying to put the pieces of this bloody confusing jigsaw together in her head. 'So,' she said eventually, 'excuse me for being so naïve here but what has all this got to do with you?'

'It's just that Shelley's leaving has thrown me. You know Shelley, she practically ran my life. How am I going to cope?'

'I'm sure you'll find someone else to go drinking with,' Claire replied acidly.

'It's not that. Jesus,' Simon sounded exasperated, 'Shelley knew me inside out.'

'I don't want to hear it.'

'I mean professionally. *Of course* I mean professionally. Okay we flirted occasionally but that was just a bit of fun. I'd never actually *do* anything about it. And by the way, Claire, that kiss was a cover up. She wanted people in work to think there was something going on between us so they wouldn't suspect anything was going on between herself and John. I just got caught up in the middle of it all. I couldn't believe that you actually saw her kiss me. Now you might believe me about what was really going on.'

'Well, it did look pretty fishy to me. You can't blame me for losing it. But I shouldn't have resorted to spying on you. I don't want us ever to have that lack of trust between us again.'

'Yeah well, I know I was going out and getting pissed too much. I suppose work was getting to me and I thought staying out all night drinking would solve my problems. But I guess I'm sick of waking up on other people's floors with a hangover. I should have done that as a student and got it out of my system like a normal bloke.'

Claire laughed, 'It's not a great feeling, is it?'

'Nope, come here to me and give me a big hug.'

Claire sat down on her husband's knee. 'So do you think you'll be able to get another PA or what?'

'It'll be difficult,' Simon admitted. 'A lot of them just like to come in and look at the clock or while away the hours painting their nails. Most of the temps don't last the day.'

'I could do it,' Claire said suddenly, 'I mean, you could train me in.'

'Are you serious?'

'Why not? I want to get back into the work place anyway. But the thing is I could only do it for a few months.'

'How come?'

'I'm pregnant.'

'What!'

Claire couldn't keep the smile off her face. 'Yes, I was just waiting for the right moment to tell you.'

'I can't believe it!'

'Are you pleased?'

'Pleased? Jesus, Claire, I'm over the moon.' He placed a hand over her tummy. 'This is the best possible news you could give me.' Claire relaxed. And then cried. The tears just wouldn't stop flowing down her cheeks. Everything was going to work out. She was so happy she almost felt guilty. Guilty that she'd despised Shelley so much. Guilty that the father of Shelley's baby wouldn't be holding her this very minute, while the tears streamed down her cheeks, telling her he was the happiest man alive. Guilty for suspecting Simon of a crime he didn't commit.

Thank God they were going to be a real family again.

Thank God.

Chapter Thirty-eight

'Are you the manager?' An irate customer drummed a handful of knuckles on the counter in front of Anna.

'Yes,' Anna said, bracing herself for a full tirade.

'I bought these slippers three months ago and . . .' Blah, blah, blah.

'We'll refund you the price of the slippers,' Anna replied wearily, wishing she could tell the angry red-faced woman to fuck off with herself.

The store was crammed with frantic late-night shoppers. Seven-thirty couldn't come fast enough for Anna. She wanted all these people to go away and leave her alone. In fact she wanted them to exit the world altogether so that herself and Darren could have it all to themselves. She adored the man. He was definitely her prince charming.

The Ferrari was waiting at the dot of seven-thirty. Anna slipped into the passenger seat with her little overnight bag, full of anticipation of the night yet to come.

It was still bright with no sign of rain, which was

a miracle for Galway. Darren turned on the engine and they headed for Moran's.

Moran's was buzzing with tourists and locals. Anna relaxed, enjoyed her seafood and drank in the ambient atmosphere. Back at the hotel, their lovemaking was more passionate than the night before. More urgent. More frantic. They practically ripped the clothes off each other between glasses of champagne and room service.

For the second night, Anna slept peacefully in Darren's arms, this time comforted by the fact that she didn't have to set the alarm clock.

She woke just after ten to find the bed empty. She heard the sound of running water from the bathroom.

'Can I join you?' she stood in the doorway naked.

'Hey, come on in,' he called, 'I'll allow you to scrub my back.'

She stepped into the bath and let him work a lather of soap over her. The hot water sluiced over them. Then she did the same to him. She loved all this. Being part of a couple. A real couple. She was fed up with the games. Leave the players to the other women in the world. She wanted a real man. She *had* a real man.

Afterwards as they sat on the huge bed, drying each other off, Anna told Darren that she'd never felt this happy. She confided that she'd all but given up on finding Mr Right.

'There's a lot of dodgy men out there,' Darren agreed. 'You have to be careful.'

'Then again you can't be too wary,' Anna countered. 'After all you were a dodgy stranger at the airport.'

'True,' Darren laughed.

'So tell me,' Anna tousled Darren's damp hair playfully, 'have you had many girlfriends?'

'Not really,' he answered uncomfortably. 'Now,' he said, swiftly changing the subject and giving her bare bottom a playful slap, 'are you getting dressed or what?'

'Yeah, yeah, leave me alone,' Anna said lazily. 'But seriously though, have you ever been like really madly in love with anybody?'

'I don't like to think too much about the past,' Darren said.

After lunch, Darren insisted on hitting the road. Anna was disappointed. What was the rush all about?

'I want to hit the road before the traffic,' Darren explained and then kissed her lips tenderly.

'I'll be up in Dublin on Tuesday,' Anna said eagerly. 'I've Tuesday as well as Saturday and Sunday off this week to make up for last week's workload. So we'll be able to see lots of each other,' she enthused.

'Well, I'll see what I can do. I've a load of meetings and stuff to get through next week so I can't make any plans just yet.'

'What about the weekend?' Anna knew she should quit while she was ahead but somehow couldn't find the lid to quash her motormouth.

'Saturday, no – Friday? Yeah, we'll definitely do something on Friday.'

'I was hoping we could meet up on Saturday,' Anna gushed. 'Some of my friends are meeting up and I was thinking . . .'

'I'll see what I can do.' Darren silenced her with a kiss.

And then he was gone.

Anna was glad when Aoife finally returned home that evening. She'd spent the whole day moping about the place, switching on the TV and then switching it off again. She'd watered Aoife's plants at least three times and had made endless cups of tea she didn't even feel like drinking. Why had Darren shot back up to Dublin when he could have spent the whole day with her?

Had she said something or what? Maybe it was because he'd seen her without her make-up. Maybe he felt she was hurrying things along too much. Then again *he* was the one saying he was mad about *her*. It was baffling.

Unfortunately Aoife insisted she couldn't chat for very long. She said she was already feeling guilty for taking the rest of the weekend off and now she intended to put her head down and slog for a few hours.

She showed a slight polite interest in Anna's weekend before disappearing off to her room. Anna was left abandoned in the sitting room with the heavy black phone choosing to remain irritatingly silent.

Maybe she should ring Darren and thank him for the fabulous weekend.

Just a teeny weeny call.

No way, a stern voice boomed inside her head. *Haven't you learned your lesson yet, you thick eejit? Go out. Get busy. Do something useful, you clown.*

Okay, okay, I back down, Anna succumbed to the angry voice. She put on a heavy bomber jacket and a pair of sneakers and set off to march the prom.

There was no point in worrying about trivial things.

Darren was *mad* about her.

He'd *said* so.

Chapter Thirty-nine

'Mrs Murphy has agreed to look after Andrew on a regular part-time basis,' Claire told her husband happily.

They were walking in the Wicklow Mountains, Claire pushing Andrew's buggy, Simon struggling with Blackie's lead. Like an ad for Flora, Claire thought. When Simon had suggested Dún Laoighaire pier, Claire had swiftly suggested the mountains. It wouldn't do to bump into Tom just now. Claire was determined to take her little secret to the grave. Sure, what would be the point in telling Simon anything now? It would only upset him.

Their marriage might not survive it.

'That's great news,' Simon smiled and bent down to release their over-excited dog from his straining lead. 'You're a star.'

'To be honest, I'm a bit nervous about going back to the workplace again.'

'You'll be fine,' Simon assured her. 'You've brains to burn. You've an honours degree, for God's sake.'

'Well, that's true,' Claire admitted. 'Oh, I'm just being silly, aren't I?'

'You'll be a massive support to me.'

'What will we call the baby?' She suddenly didn't want to be talking about work any more.

'If it's a boy we could call him Simon, after me?'

'Oh God, no. One Simon is enough,' Claire laughed.

'I don't care if you call him Arnold Schwarzeneggar. As long as the baby is healthy, I'll be one happy man.'

On Monday evening she tried on her new dress.

'Stunning.' Simon couldn't hide his admiration. 'You look sensational. Every man in the room will be hitting on you.'

'As long as you're hitting on me too, I don't care,' Claire twirled to give the dress its full effect. 'As long as you're after me that's all that counts.'

The doorbell rang.

'Oh, that must be Anna. I'll get it.' Claire made for the door and flung it open.

'Are you going out?' Anna looked startled.

'No, silly, this is what I'm wearing to the party. Come in. Do you like it?'

'Wow, it's amazing.'

'What are you wearing yourself, Anna?'

'Me? Oh I haven't a clue. What I'm going to wear is actually the least of my worries. Oh hi, Simon. Long time, no see.'

'Hi, Anna. Now if you two ladies will excuse

me, I'm sure you've loads of things to be gossiping about.'

'Well, he looks happy,' Anna said brightly and pulled up a chair for herself.

'He's every right to be,' Claire grinned and instinctively moved her hand across her still impossibly flat stomach.

'Is there something I should know?' Anna asked warily.

'God, where do I start?'

Claire told Anna about the pregnancy, about going back to work, and about Shelley. Anna listened, gobsmacked.

Claire had blossomed since she'd last met her.

Being pregnant suited her.

Still, rather her than me, Anna decided as Claire started to give a vivid description of her latest bout of morning sickness.

In turn, Anna spilled the beans on her new relationship.

'He sounds almost too good,' Claire said.

'I can live with too good,' Anna replied.

'But what about Mark?'

'What about him?'

'Don't you still hold a candle for him?'

'No,' Anna said firmly, 'I never held a candle or anything for him.'

'I dunno about that,' Claire teased.

'Oh shut up, will you?'

'So when are you meeting this fella again?'

'His name's Darren,' Anna said huffily.

'Does he know you've the day off?'

'Yep.'

'Well, give him a ring now so. It's only nine o'clock.'

'But suppose he wants to meet up tonight?'

'Well then you tell him you won't be able to,' Claire insisted. 'We're meeting Alice and Olive.'

'Olive Sharkey?'

'Yeah, Alice ran into her and she's dying to meet up.'

'You have *got* to be joking,' Anna fumed. 'She was Victoria's buddy in school. Don't you remember her? The ultimate yes woman.'

'I'm sure she's changed,' Claire said diplomatically. 'We've all changed in lots of ways, you know.'

'Right, anyway I don't think I'll ring Darren tonight. I'm a bit wrecked after my journey from Galway.'

'Whatever you think. Well, I'm ready when you are. Actually come in and have a peek at Andrew while I'm getting changed. He's got so big.'

Claire and Anna arrived at Coopers Restaurant early. Alice turned up fifteen minutes later. She seemed thrilled to see Anna. 'I hear you've a new man in your life,' she enthused. 'I want *all* the gory details later.'

'God, I'd be here all night,' Anna laughed good-naturedly. She was careful not to ask Alice how *her* love life was. Claire had her well warned.

'Olive won't be here till ten. She does yoga on a Monday evening,' Alice explained.

'Does she still follow Victoria around the place?' Anna was blunt. 'Last time I saw her she was peeping out of the back pages of *Ireland's People* with Victoria. It was the opening of some new clothes shop, I think.'

'Well, she still loves to go out, I know,' Alice explained. 'Her husband is very much the stay-at-home type. He's not gone on the whole social scene.'

'God, he sounds the opposite to Simon. No wonder she's so looking forward to coming out with us,' said Claire. 'Oh look, there's Olive.'

'Hi, girls.' Olive made her way down the steps to the others. She waved almost nervously.

'Hi, Olive,' the girls waved back.

'Sorry I'm so late. Oh you should have gone ahead and ordered without me. Thanks, I'll have a glass of Bud,' she told the waiter.

'You look fantastic, Olive,' Claire beamed.

'Yes you do,' Anna agreed. She wasn't sure if she trusted Olive. Olive had been wary of ever being seen talking to Anna in school. Anna hadn't been 'cool' enough.

They ordered their starters and a bottle of red and white. Anna's tummy was grumbling. Another busy day in the store had left no time again for eating.

'So is everybody looking forward to the party?' Olive looked from one face to another.

'Very much so,' Anna lied.

'Victoria was saying that she realized not everybody will have a partner to bring along but that they're welcome to come on their own anyway,' Olive said, mainly for Alice's benefit but Anna thought the comment was aimed towards her and felt a surge of annoyance.

'I would have thought it a better idea to leave the men out of it altogether,' said Alice. 'After all, it was a girls' boarding school run by nuns. Men were strictly forbidden.'

Everybody laughed. The wine was poured.

'But if the men were banned we wouldn't get to see all the telly hubbies.' Anna held her glass up. 'Cheers, girls.'

'Now, now, we'll have no bitching,' Claire tutted. 'Remember we all grew up together.'

'Like one big happy family not,' Alice said.

'So what does Victoria do all day?' Anna couldn't help asking.

Olive shrugged. 'Shop, I suppose. Look in the mirror? I'm not really sure, to be honest.'

'Aren't you two joined at the hip any more?'

'No, we had our operation a while ago. I'm free now.'

'So you saw through her in the end,' Alice muttered. 'Everybody does eventually.'

The starters arrived. Anna tucked into her salad. The evening was turning out to be a bit of fun after all. Olive wasn't so bad. People changed. You had to give them the benefit of the doubt. Maybe even Victoria wouldn't be so horrendous either.

'Do you still keep in touch with Mark Landon?' Alice asked during the course of the meal.

'Well, I haven't seen him since I went to Galway but he used to live across the road from me in Ranelagh.'

'Did he? Lucky you. I always thought Mark was divine,' Alice sighed. 'Is he not married?'

'No,' Anna put her knife and fork down. 'No, he is not.'

'Funny, I thought a man like that would have been snapped up long ago.'

Chapter Forty

It was strange waking up in her old bedroom. Anna stretched lazily on the bed and rolled over. Oh, the joy of not having to get up at the crack of dawn!

The first thing she had to do today was ring Darren.

He'd be expecting her call.

And anyway he'd no way of contacting her.

Grandad was sipping tea in the kitchen. 'Would you like a cup? The kettle's boiled,' he croaked.

'Thank you.' She fetched herself a tea bag.

'Are you married yet, Anna?'

'I don't have time,' she answered.

'You're no spring chicken, you know.' He nibbled on a plain digestive.

She made no reply. Grandad could be quite insensitive when he wanted to be.

She went out to the hall, dialling Darren's number before she could change her mind.

He answered promptly.

'Darren?'

'Hey, gorgeous.'

'I'm in Dublin.'

'Great, what are you up to?'

'Nothing much and yourself?'

'I'm up to my eyeballs in business meetings today.'

'Oh.' Anna was disappointed.

'I'm afraid I won't be able to see you this evening.'

'I see.'

'Are you mad at me?'

'No, not at all, I understand. You're keeping the weekend free for me though, aren't you?'

'Sure, I'll call you.'

'I'll look forward to it.' Anna put the phone down.

So much for that. Anna was upset. Surely he wasn't that busy? It wasn't as if she was in Dublin every week. Surely he could have fitted her somewhere into his busy schedule? What was going on? Was he losing interest already? Hadn't they just spent the most magical weekend together? Maybe she shouldn't have slept with him. Maybe that was the reason he seemed to be going off her. Men were sometimes a bit funny after sex. They saw you in a different light once the mystery had disappeared.

But it had seemed so right. It had felt so right.

Snap out of it, Anna, she told herself. He's busy, that's all there is to it. Sure wasn't she the very one who was constantly snowed under with work commitments? She of all people should be more understanding. Besides there were things to be done. A dress had to be bought for this blasted party.

The traffic into town would be manic, Anna reckoned. So she took the bus. She stood at the bus stop outside Stillorgan shopping centre and waited for a 46A. As long as Darren showed up at the party that was the main thing. And he would. Of course he would.

Eventually a bus stopped. Anna hopped on, taking a seat upstairs. The sun was shining. Life didn't seem so bad after all. She'd really have to stop being a pessimist. Not all men were bastards. Only some of them.

Just the ones that Anna had the misfortune to cross paths with.

At Grafton Street, she hopped off and ambled down the main street along with the hundreds of shoppers. In Brown Thomas she bumped into Olive trying on a cream strapless evening dress.

'Hi there,' Anna said making her jump.

'Hey, Anna.' Olive's face broke into a smile. 'You're in the same dilemma as me, I take it.'

'At this stage I feel like turning up in a pair of old jeans,' Anna laughed.

'Same here. What do you think of this?'

'It's stunning,' Anna said truthfully.

'Almost a month's wages.'

'But you only live once,' Anna reminded her.

'You're right, I'll take it.'

'Want to grab a coffee?'

'Sure,' Olive grinned.

It was funny, Anna thought as herself and Olive chatted easily about life in the coffee shop in Brown Thomas; she'd lived under the same roof as the girl for six years and had never really had a proper conversation with her.

'Do you know something, Olive?' she confided, 'You're so different now to what you were like in school.'

'In what way?' Olive seemed surprised.

'Well, don't take this the wrong way or anything, but I thought you were quite nasty in school. You laughed every time Victoria bullied anyone.'

'God, that's terrible.' Olive looked contrite. 'If I laughed it was only because I was afraid of Victoria. It wasn't like I thought anything she ever did was funny.'

'I'm dreading going to the reunion. I mean, if it was in anybody else's house I wouldn't mind so much.'

'We're all in the same boat,' Olive almost whispered. 'I don't particularly want to go along either. But I'd say the night will be interesting. I don't really know what to expect.'

'Is the house nice?'

'Amazing,' Olive sighed.

'Lucky girl, eh?'

'Do you know something?' Olive said after a while. 'You might find this hard to believe but I actually envied you in school.'

'Me?'

'Yeah, you were so independent and did your own thing, you know?'

'God, that's funny that you think that.'

'I was the sad case following Victoria and those around hoping to be accepted. You were so strong.'

'Not inside I wasn't.' Anna gave a slight shudder. She didn't like to think about it too much.

'Anyway, enough about school. What are your plans for the rest of the day?'

'I have to find a dress for starters,' Anna nibbled on her scone, 'and then, I dunno . . . I might call round to Claire's.'

'Don't you have to be back in work tomorrow?'

'Yeah, but not until lunch time. I'll drive down in the morning.'

'Are you meeting that sexy man of yours?'

'Not this evening,' Anna tried to keep her voice light.

'I'm sure I'll see him at the party.' Olive stood up and brushed the crumbs off her skirt. 'By the way you should give Alice a ring. She's dying to go out. She really is.'

'Well, maybe I will,' Anna smiled.

'So,' Alice met her later in the bar of The Morrison Hotel, 'describe it.'

They sat in the corner and ordered two vodkas and diet Cokes.

'It's short and black but completely different to

Olive's and it's got these chiffon sleeves. Cost a bomb but I'll worry about that later.'

'It sounds bliss. What's Darren wearing?'

'I don't even know if he's coming,' Anna sighed.

'Nonsense,' Alice argued. But what did *she* know about anything? 'So, do you want to go dancing?'

'Tonight?' Anna looked surprised. 'Sure nothing's open on a Tuesday.'

'Tomango's is.'

'God, well there's a blast from the past!'

'Let's go for the laugh.'

'I'll kill you for doing this to me,' Anna groaned.

'You're only young once,' Alice said as she hauled her out of her seat.

'I *was* young once,' Anna said.

Alice was determined to live it up on the dance floor. She shook her hands wildly to songs like 'I will survive' and 'It's raining men'. The music was brilliant and the place was packed with people having fun. But somehow, Anna felt, if Darren had been with her, the night would have been slightly more fun. What was wrong with her? Would she never be able to enjoy a girls' night out ever again? This was insane!

'How on earth are we going to get home?' Anna asked Alice at about 2 a.m. 'Stillorgan is miles and miles away.'

'Look out for somebody drinking water,' Alice suggested. 'They're usually the non-drinkers. One of them will bring us as far as town.'

'Oh I dunno about that,' Anna hesitated.

'Go on,' Alice urged. 'It's a tried and tested method.'

Anna glanced around the room trying to spot the non-drinkers. Eventually she approached a man with a pint glass full of water.

'Is that water you're drinking?' She fluttered her eyelashes at him.

'Yesh shis, I'm trying to shober up fore I get home,' he said. 'Want shome?'

'No thanks,' Anna muttered and walked away.

'No luck?' Alice asked her. 'Okay, let me try.'

Five minutes later she returned with a man.

And, more importantly, a lift.

His name was Nigel.

'Are you sure you don't mind about this?' Anna tried not to show her delight *too* much.

'Not at all,' the guy assured her. 'Sure, I was bringing my friend Jack home anyway.'

The 'lift' was a navy van so Anna and Alice had to climb in the back and sit among a pile of boxes. Jack was intrigued with the 'birds' in the back. He'd been trying unsuccessfully to score all night while Nigel had effortlessly picked up two!

Jack reluctantly got out of the car in O'Connell Street. Alice was dropped off a little further on.

'Where are *you* going?' Nigel asked Anna.

'I'm fine here,' Anna said.

'But where do you live?'

'Er . . . Stillorgan.'

'Get into the front so, I'll drive you,' Nigel insisted.

Anna took a good look at him. He didn't look like the type of guy who would strangle you and then discard your body in one of those wheelie bins. And it wasn't like he had even approached the girls in the first place. And it was pretty cold outside too. She didn't much want to stand at a taxi rank.

Ah she was probably safe enough!

'Did you have a good night anyway?' Nigel was very chatty.

'Great, I never left the dance floor.'

'So I noticed,' he said as Anna froze.

So he *had* been watching her. Oh God. Maybe he'd been simply biding his time. Just waiting for his chance to pounce. She took another look at him so she'd be able to describe him later to the Gardai. Curly red hair. Round face. Pert nose. Friendly smile. God, he didn't exactly *look* like a criminal, did he?

Nevertheless, Anna breathed a short sigh of relief when they finally reached Stillorgan. Thankfully she'd remembered her keys. She went to get out of the van.

'I never got your name,' said Nigel.

'Anna,' she said quietly. 'It's Anna.'

'That's a nice name.'

'Thanks. And er, thanks very much for the lift, it was so good of you to go ... er so far out of your way.'

'Not a bother, Listen, Anna, do you think I could

have your number? I'd really like to meet up with you again.'

'Well it's just . . .' *Jesus, how was she going to get out of this?* ' . . . it's just I have a boyfriend actually.'

'Just a quick drink,' Nigel insisted. *A quick drink? I don't think so.*

'Sure,' Anna relented. 'Give me your number. I'll ring you.'

She watched guiltily as Nigel scribbled his number on the inside of an empty cigarette carton, knowing full well she'd never ring him.

'Thanks again,' she said putting the carton in her bag. 'Goodnight.'

It was always the way, wasn't it, Anna thought as she sat in the kitchen drinking a glass of anything-to-try-to-keep-the-hangover-to-a-minimum water. The guys you were not interested in were interested in you. And the guys you adored treated you like shit. Why was life like that? Why was it all so bloody unfair?

Poor Nigel would be waiting for her call over the coming days until it became obvious she was never going to ring. In the meantime *she* would wait patiently for Darren's call. Her phone would sit in dead silence like a big black monster. And she would pick it up at least five times an hour just to make sure it was working.

And it would be.

It always was.

Chapter Forty-one

'Did anyone ring for me, Aoife?' Anna burst through the door of the apartment.

'No,' Aoife said gently, but the dreaded word alone seemed to cut through the room like a poisoned spear.

'Oh right.' Anna was subdued. 'And you were here all the time, were you?'

'Well, I went to the shops just the once. Er . . . he might have been trying to get through then.'

'Yeah, maybe you're right,' Anna said, her voice dropped, catching emotion as it did so. She had never felt so let down in her life. The party was only days away and it now looked like her escort would be a definite no-show. Why, she wondered. What had she done wrong? If she knew, it would all be a lot easier to understand.

'There's probably a good reason why he hasn't phoned,' Aoife said encouragingly. 'But that isn't to say he won't, you know.'

But no amount of kind words or positive thinking

could disguise the fact that Darren hadn't bothered his ass dialling her number.

'Would you like to see my new dress?' Anna tried to change subjects. *The one I'm going to turn up in. Alone.*

The following day dragged for Anna. Nothing made sense any more. What was God playing at up there? Some people asked for miracles and got them. All she'd wanted was a suitable man for the night. That was all. That and her health, of course. And her own business maybe one day. And happiness for all her friends and family. And to have no more homeless teenagers on the streets. Of course all those things were far more important than getting some idiot of a man to bring along to the party. Yes really, she should stop feeling sorry for herself.

'Miss Browne wants to see you in her office,' said Lorraine, one of the shop girls.

Anna made her way upstairs. What wonderful treasures would Miss Browne have in store for her? And who cared anyway? How was she supposed to be interested in sales and budgets at a time like this?

'Sit down, Anna,' Miss Browne motioned to the empty seat opposite her desk.

Anna obeyed. What was all this leading to?

'Firstly I'd like to congratulate you on your performance since your arrival. Your standards are very high and you've certainly proved your capabilities in my absence.'

'Thank you,' Anna said stiffly. There was a *but* in here somewhere. There had to be. Miss Browne wasn't in the habit of waffling on for nothing.

'Anyway to cut straight to the point,' the manager continued, 'unfortunately we're going to lose you now. They always seem to take the good ones away, I'm afraid.'

'What do you mean?' Anna was becoming extremely hot under the collar. *Could somebody please open a window?*

'Head office would like to try you in your own store. As you know, we're branching into the UK market at the moment.'

'That's right.' Anna felt faint. Her own store. GOD!

'The store is just outside London,' Miss Browne continued. 'It's brand-new with completely new staff and we really believe you have it in you to manage it.'

'Er, gosh . . . I don't know what to say.'

'You don't have to give us your answer just yet. You have until Monday to think about it. That gives you the whole weekend.'

The weekend! The party . . . oh God . . . manager of a new store . . . OH GOD!

'No phone calls?'

'No.' Aoife looked guilty as if it was *her* fault Darren hadn't rung. 'But sure you know yourself men have absolutely no conception of time.'

'Yeah yeah.' Anna flopped onto the small sofa. Tonight she should have been celebrating her promotion. So why was she so pissed off? After all why had she thought Darren would turn out any better than the others?

It was typical. She'd always given men the undeserved benefit of the doubt. They were all the same though. Only the names changed. She wished she hadn't slept with him. The thought of it was making her feel about as cheap as a used car. But worst of all was that Anna knew deep down, that if the phone rang now with Darren's voice at the end of it, she'd forgive him.

But as the next couple of days wore on, there was no pretending that Darren was going to ring. He'd made his escape through the Emergency Exit. That was the end of him. Bye bye. She'd been a weekend fling. That's all there was to it. A toy that he'd tired of. *Bastard*.

Anna went through the motions at work, trying to make herself as busy as possible. She'd go to England. She'd swim over if she had to. Anything to get out of this country for a while. She'd make a new start in England. Nobody would know her over there. Anna Allstone. The babe! A girl who took no shit from men. Yeah right!

Maybe she should give the *Guinness Book of Records* a call. Did they have a category for *Most Dumped Woman*? It was worth a try. Hey, it might even make her famous. She might start getting invited to chat shows to share her story with all her 'sisters' out there.

Ah sure, what was the point in moping? Who wanted to be part of a boring old couple anyway? The only reason Darren had seemed exciting was because she hadn't really known him. All men were pretty interesting at first. Then you found out they were the same selfish git as the last fella. He still went out on a Friday with the lads, coming in bollixed afterwards, looking for a shag. And in the morning he'd wake up with a chronic hangover and ransack your flat for food. After that he'd sit on your sofa, and smoke your cigarettes while watching one rugby match after another on your TV.

At least Anna didn't have to put up with any of that. She was looking forward to getting herself a snazzy one-bedroomed apartment in London. She could paint it a crazy-looking pink and fill her bathroom with make-up and all kinds of perfumes and face masks. She could leave the lid off the toothpaste and the toilet paper on the floor. God, it was going to be mad fun altogether!

Now she was beginning to cheer up. Who needed men anyway? Anna only had to look around Lolta's to see that all the top female managers were single. Yeah, that was a fact. They didn't waste precious hours alone with the radio, guzzling back wine and reminiscing on long-lost love. No way. They were too busy working and climbing the corporate ladder along with their male colleagues.

Instead of watching the phone they eyed sales reports, promotion possibilities and their competitors. And even though they didn't have somebody to hug them in the evening, they could hug themselves in the knowledge that they'd a hefty bank balance and nobody to wreck their head over unironed shirts and uncooked meals.

Single women could watch *Pretty Woman*, *Dirty Dancing* and *Pretty in Pink* over and over again if they wanted to. They could dance around the room to Destiny's Child or eat an entire box of Milk Tray just because they felt like it and didn't need some eejit of a man going to the ends of the earth to deliver the damn box.

Best of all, single women didn't have to put up with men hinting that although they'd a great figure, they'd have an even *better* figure if they just went to the gym.

She was better off, Anna decided. She was now free to live life the way she wanted to. When her holidays came up she could head off to wherever she pleased and chat up who ever she wanted instead of having to go to some boring resort and rub cream on some man's hairy back.

Oh yes, being single was pretty fantastic.

Chapter Forty-two

Anna drove from Galway to Dublin with a heavy heart. It was difficult to concentrate on the road. Okay, she was single now and had accepted that but it was still hard to completely banish Darren from her thoughts. She'd left several messages on his mobile. But no return calls followed. Nothing. He'd simply disappeared off the face of the earth.

She was glad to be leaving Galway for the weekend. Aoife was becoming distraught, persecuted by Anna's persistent questions. *Has he not rung yet? Were you here all day? Do you think he could have been trying when you were on the phone to your mother?* Because even though Anna had come to terms with being single again, some doubts still niggled. Like maybe Darren had mislaid her number? Maybe his mobile phone had been stolen? Maybe he'd been sent to America on urgent business? Or been involved in a terrible accident and was lying on a life-support machine somewhere. There were a lot of maybes. But nothing could alter the fact that tomorrow was the big reunion and she'd be going alone. She'd had three months to get herself just one miserable man for this event and had failed. Unbelievable!

She could always ask Mark, she supposed, as she drew up to McDonald's to break the journey. Mark would definitely come along and look the part. In fact he'd probably be honoured. And if she was completely honest with herself, *although she'd rather die than admit it to anyone*, deep down she secretly believed Mark had always kind of fancied her. He'd just probably never plucked up the courage to tell her how he really felt. He was probably afraid of rejection. Just like she was. She stopped the car. She was tired of driving. She was tired full stop. Tired of all the pretence. Tired of the games. Tired of ten years of denying how she really felt about Mark. It was time to stop messing about. It all made sense really when she thought about it. Of course Mark fancied her. That was the reason why his relationships never worked out. Those girls were never enough for a guy like Mark Landon. He needed a vivacious woman. He needed her. Anna was the woman for him. So why had it taken a harsh rejection from a player like Darren for her to see the light?

Thank God Darren had disappeared. That was the best thing that could have happened to her. This was fate. The more she thought about it the more everything made sense. She started up the car again. She wouldn't be able to reach Dublin fast enough.

Should she ask him to the party tonight or leave it until tomorrow? Maybe it would be best not to ask him straightaway. The shock might be too great for him!

'Hello, love.'

'Hi, Mum'. Anna dragged her suitcase into the hallway and let her mother kiss the top of her head.

'We're so pleased for you.' Mrs Allstone grinned from ear to ear. 'We've told everybody about your promotion. All the neighbours and cousins know. I don't think we left anybody out.' She gave a little laugh.

'Thanks,' Anna produced a smile.

'Your brother was delighted for you, of course.'

'Was he?' Anna asked, surprised.

'And he's just announced his engagement.'

'Wonderful,' Anna said. 'And what a coincidence that both events should be announced in the one week,' she couldn't refrain from adding.

'Now,' her mother said, ignoring the comment, 'come into the kitchen, I've baked you a chocolate devil cake. Your favourite.'

My favourite when I was about six years old, not now, Anna thought and obediently followed her mother into the kitchen.

'Congratulations.' Her grandfather almost spilled his tea. 'When are you getting married?'

'I'm not,' Anna muttered. 'I've been promoted.'

'Oh,' said her grandfather, immediately losing interest. He was of the old school, where a woman dutifully got married and didn't entertain daft ideas that entailed going off to England to run a store.

'Sit down and get a few digestives into you, you're skin and bone.'

'Do you think so?' Anna felt like hugging him.

'Are you looking forward to tomorrow?' Her mother cut a generous slice of cake.

'Not really,' Anna admitted. She wasn't exactly looking forward to meeting Victoria and her cronies but she was looking forward to having Mark on her arm. To think it had taken all this time for her to realize he was definitely the one.

'Do you want to tell me about it?' her mother said as she sat down.

'I'm bringing Mark Landon,' Anna told her. 'It's just that, I dunno . . . I'm not into this reunion thing at all.'

'But surely you don't have to bring someone,' her mother seemed surprised, 'I thought it was a reunion just for the girls.'

'I wish it was, but Victoria has invited partners as well.'

'I'm sure Mark will be delighted to escort you. He's a lovely, lovely chap. Handsome too.'

Anna couldn't believe her mother remembered Mark so well. She'd invited him to her debutante school graduation dance and had been a bundle of nerves before he arrived. She remembered her mother telling her to take deep breaths and to 'be herself'.

Mark had been the perfect gentleman, arriving with a pretty orchid and a huge box of *Milk Tray* chocolates. He'd stood patiently with Anna as her father took the usual fifty compulsory photographs and introduced him to the neighbours as 'Anna's young friend'.

He'd told her she looked beautiful, even though she felt like a waltzing Matilda in her big ballooning beige ball gown, and most importantly he'd ignored Victoria when she ditched her own poor escort in a failed attempt to get off with Mark.

That night had probably been the happiest night of her life. Mark had lavished attention upon her, making sure she'd enough to drink, pulling out chairs for her, dragging her onto the dance floor. But when he tried to kiss her at the end of the night, she'd turned away in case he was just feeling sorry for her and was kissing her out of pity.

'I wasn't going to invite him,' Anna admitted. 'But to be perfectly honest there's nobody else I'd rather bring.'

'Well, I always thought he was a perfect gentle-man,' her mother assured her. 'You two always made a great couple.'

'You've never said that before.'

'Ah, you see,' her mother smiled, 'I knew that if you thought *I* liked him you'd do your best to get rid of him.'

'But do you think he liked me? Even then?'

'Darling, the boy was *crazy* about you.'

For the first time in her life Anna felt like hugging her mother.

As she sat alone in her old room listening to an old tape of Madonna's and staring at a poster of Patrick Swayze that she'd never bothered to take down, Anna pondered on her mother's words. Had it really been that obvious? Had everybody known Mark was mad about her? Why hadn't anybody said anything? Now that she was definitely going to England a relationship between them wouldn't be so easy. But then again, didn't they say that true love conquered all? Somehow they'd be able to work it out.

It was late now. Her parents and grandad were downstairs watching *The Late Late Show*. Mark wouldn't be in this late on a Friday night, would he?

Well, she might as well drive down to Ranelagh and see if she could catch him now. So what if he was going out? All she wanted was a few minutes to invite him to the party. She slapped a bit of foundation on both cheeks, said goodbye to her parents and got into her car. Jesus, was she mad or what? Don't think about it, she thought. Don't think about it or you'll definitely change your mind.

She drove down the dual carriageway, her heart pounding. She tried to imagine Mark's face when she told him how she really felt. Would he automatically sweep her up in his arms or would he take a minute to let it all sink in? God, it was exciting and at the same time terrifying. What if he insisted on following her to London? Or insist that she take another job in Dublin to be near him? Anna wasn't sure she could do that. She'd worked too hard for this new position. Herself and Mark would really have to think this through properly.

She turned left at the lights in Donnybrook, up Eglinton Road and right towards Ranelagh. Please let him be in, she begged. Please, please let him be in tonight.

Slowly she drove past his front gate. A light was on in the front room. She parked the car a little further down the road and walked back, towards his house. She peered over the hedge. There was Mark sitting on the sofa watching the TV. *Here goes*, she told herself and took a deep breath. It's now or never.

'ANNAAA!!!' a loud voice boomed in her ear.

'Jesus, Grainne, you frightened the living daylights out of me.'

'Aoife said you'd be up this weekend. I'm thrilled you came to see us. Have you been waiting out here long? You must be freezing.'

'No, not too long,' Anna said, thanking God, it was dark and Grainne couldn't see her face go crimson.

'Come in,' she said. 'It's just me in the flat. Sandra and Rich are out.'

'Sandra and Rich!'

'Oh Jesus.' Grainne's hand flew to her mouth. 'I forgot you didn't know. Sandra will murder me, so she will. She wanted to tell you herself so there'd be no hard feelings.'

'Don't worry, there's no hard feelings,' Anna laughed. Jesus, Sandra deserved a medal to put up with him. But different courses for horses and all that. 'Is she getting on well with him?'

'Yes, apart from him being constantly broke,' Grainne laughed.

'But he's an actor,' Anna said ironically.

'So we keep hearing.' Grainne opened the big green door. 'Come in.'

'Do you ever see Steve?'

'Not any more unfortunately,' said Grainne. 'He's studying his brains out. Pity, he's a fine thing, you know.'

She followed Grainne up to the top of the house, past her old flat.

'Who's in there now?' she asked quietly.

'Some weirdo,' Grainne said. 'He's always complaining about our noise. He must have no life, that's all I can say.'

Anna sat down on a kitchen chair and accepted Grainne's offer of a beer. She couldn't believe she still hadn't got to talk to Mark yet. The longer she left it, the harder it would be.

She really had to talk to him. It wasn't such a big deal. He was mad about her. Everyone said so. Even her mum. And of course Claire had been saying it for years.

'Rich has a contact that can get us parts in *Fair City*,' Grainne broke her from her train of thought.

'What kind of parts?' Anna eyed her suspiciously.

'Well, sitting in the background of the pub pretending to talk, you know. Will I tell him you're interested?'

'There's not much point,' Anna sighed, 'if I'm going to England.'

'Maybe he could get you put on *Coronation Street* or *EastEnders*?'

Anna laughed. 'Do you not think if Rich was that well connected, he'd get himself a job on one of those soaps?'

'I s'pose,' Grainne agreed.

'Grainne?'

'Mmm?'

'Do you know Mark across the road?'

'The good-looking fella?'

'That's the one.'

'Well, not personally no.'

'But you know who I'm talking about?'

'Sure.'

'Have you seen him recently with a girlfriend?'

Grainne frowned. 'No,' she shook her head, 'no, I don't think so. Why, does he have one? It's very hard to tell. He's always with someone, isn't he? I wouldn't mind him myself. He's feckin gorgeous.'

'I wonder has he anyone now, though . . . anyone special like?'

'Why don't you go over and ask him?'

'No way. What do you think I am?'

'Well, it would put an end to the speculation,' Grainne was pragmatic.

The dull feeling inside Anna was growing all the time. Grainne was right. If she went across the road and rang his bell, then she'd know for sure if he was single at the moment. If he wasn't, then what? Oh God, she couldn't do this without any preparation.

'Go,' Grainne urged. 'It won't be as bad as you think.'

'Right.' Anna got to her feet. *Anything to get Grainne off her case*. 'But if I'm not back in five minutes you're to come and rescue me.'

'Sure,' Grainne promised. 'By the way, not being nosy or anything, but have ya the hots for him? I mean, are you going to ask him out or what?'

Anna took a deep breath. 'Something like that. Wish me luck, okay?' she said, fidgeting with her fingers.

She skipped outside into the darkness, determined not to be overwhelmed by all this. Even Grainne didn't seem to think it was much of a deal.

She walked boldly up Mark Landon's path, her heart pounding at a furious pace. She wasn't a bit worried. Of course she wasn't. At the end of the day Mark would probably be over the moon. But as she pressed a trembling finger on the modern doorbell, her stomach a flurry of butterflies, she asked herself, 'Anna Allstone, what the hell do you think you're doing?' She stood uneasily in the doorway, riddled with nerves, and waited for approaching footsteps.

Nobody came to answer the door.

Maybe he didn't hear the bell. After all, the TV was on. It would probably drown out the sound of the doorbell. She went to ring again but something intervened. Waves of panic swept over her, making her turn on her heel and walk swiftly back down the path.

'Chicken,' Grainne accused back in the flat.

'It wasn't a good time,' Anna argued.

'Well, if you can live without knowing, that's fine.' Grainne grimaced. 'Personally it wouldn't be me.'

'Could you not ask him for me?' Anna asked in a small voice.

'Me? Sure he'd think I was a nutter. Can you imagine me stomping across there demanding to know his romantic situation? Don't be silly, Anna.'

Grainne's words hounded her as she tossed and turned in her old bed later that evening. She was silly, wasn't she? The management at Lolta's didn't think so but she knew she was. She hid it well at work. She flounced around with her sales charts and her power suits. But deep down, Anna Allstone wasn't as brave as everyone thought. She still feared Victoria's cutting tongue and dreaded an entire evening in her showcase home. She still chose to drive home to the safety of her parents' house rather than pour her feelings out to Mark.

She sat up in bed suddenly craving a cigarette. Her parents still didn't know she smoked. She dragged herself to the window, opened it wide and lit herself one. She stared out into the night. This was where she used to sit and wonder about all those guys in college that she loved. Guys that didn't love her back. If someone had told her then, that in ten years' time, she'd be sitting in this exact same position, worrying about more or less the same kind of thing, she probably would have topped herself!

Tonight had been her chance. Sometimes you got one shot at something. Then the moment passed. And you never got it back.

She took a long hard drag, taking care to lean out of the window to prevent the smoke sneaking back into her bedroom. She'd kept this secret for fifteen years, no point in letting the folks find out now.

She remembered feeling a bit like this in summer camp centuries ago. She'd fancied a lad called Martin O'Kelly with blond hair. He looked like the twins from BROS. All the girls used to make a beeline for him at the ladies' choice at the ceilithe.

Anna remembered walking ever so slowly across the hall floor, her hands sweating, her face the colour of her red sleeveless jumper. But just before she reached him, she lost her nerve and asked his rather ugly friend to dance instead.

The friend had thrown back his big curly mousy head and roared with laughter.

Anna had stood facing him, rooted to the spot and realized that whatever happened to her during the rest of her life, nothing, but nothing, would ever be as humiliating as this.

'Well, will you dance with my friend so?' Anna had said in a desperate bid to conceal her mortification.

'Which one is she?' the ugly guy had sneered.

Anna turned and, to her horror, realized that every other girl in the room was dancing. Everybody except her.

'Is your friend better looking than you?'

'Forget it,' Anna had told him and walked away as the hoots of laughter grew louder behind her back.

So the following morning, when she jumped into the shallow end of the swimming pool and broke her foot, she didn't feel any pain. No pain at all. In fact she was elated that she wouldn't have to ask anybody else to dance.

She'd sat through the rest of the ceilithe with her crutches on her lap, thrilled that everybody felt sorry for her, delighted that she didn't have to do anything but sit there and gratefully accept the sympathy.

That's why on the very last night, when she eventually got talking to the hard-to-get Martin, she was surprised to find him very down to earth. He told her he thought she was pretty. He said he was sorry he hadn't had the chance to talk to her before. He told her it was a pity her foot was sore so she couldn't dance with him. And that night back in the dormitory, she'd bawled and bawled. Her friends had circled around her and asked what was wrong. And she told them it was because it was the last night and she was so sad that she wouldn't be seeing them again. But the truth was, she was devastated that Martin had fancied her all along and nobody had told her. She was heartbroken because she knew that the following day his parents would drive up from Cork to collect him and she'd never, ever see him again. If only she'd asked him to dance that first night instead of that other fecking eejit. If only she'd followed her heart that first night.

If only . . .

But that was a long time ago. She was a child then. She hadn't known any better. This was different. She was thirty now.

Chapter Forty-three

'It's great to see you again, Anna. I'm so glad you rang. I've missed you, believe it or not.'

They were sitting in the BT2 coffee shop looking down on the throngs of shoppers hurrying through Grafton Street and colliding with bewildered tourists trying to take photos.

'I've missed you too, Mark.' Anna smiled at him. She *had* missed him. At least she could admit it now without feeling like it was something to be ashamed of. 'Galway's great but it's not the same without you around to spy on me all the time.'

'Ah, that's so sweet.' Mark gave a big cheesy grin.

The coffee shop was crowded. Anna hoped that nobody would overhear what she was about to say to Mark. Suddenly she didn't feel that this was the right time or place to be discussing anything serious. Wasn't it so much easier to discuss feelings and things with a load of alcohol in you?

Anna had a three o'clock appointment with the hairdresser. She had to get this over with fast. All

of a sudden she had a much better idea. It would
be so much simpler just to ask him to the party
now and then snog him afterwards at the party
or whatever. Then it wouldn't be so intense. She
said nothing for a few minutes. Then she took a
deep breath.

'Mark?'

'Uh huh?'

'It's my school reunion tonight.'

'Ah.' He leaned forward and stared deep into her
eyes. She wanted to kiss him there and then. God,
how had she resisted him all these years? 'So it all
makes sense now.'

'What do you mean?' Anna was confused.

'I thought for a moment there that you had come
all the way home just to meet me for coffee. I should
have known there was something else going on,' he
said with a glint in his eye.

'Well, I wanted to see you too.'

'Ah thanks.'

'The thing is, Mark . . .'

'Jesus, isn't that Johnny down there?'

'Where?'

'There, see over there. He's put on about two
stone. Must have given up the rugby. It often
happens.'

'Right.' Anna was getting impatient.

'Go on anyway, you were saying something.'

'I want you to come with me.'

'Where?'

'To the reunion.'

'You're joking.'

'I'm not. Partners have been invited.'

'That's stupid. It's not really a reunion then, is it? I mean, a reunion is supposed to be about catching up and that.'

'Well, it's really more of a party. That's why partners are being invited.'

'And you want me to be your partner for the night?' Mark asked, a look of complete puzzlement on his face. 'Sure, nobody would believe that.' He broke into spontaneous laughter, 'You and me? That's ridiculous, Anna. I just wouldn't be able to pull it off. I mean, what would you want me to do? Hold your hand?' He laughed again.

Anna felt a surge of intense irritation. She looked at her watch. It was a quarter to three. She didn't have time for games now. 'Yes or no?'

'No,' he said. 'Sorry, Anna.'

If he'd slapped her face, she couldn't have been more shocked. Her heart sank below sea level. She felt herself become warm and then hotter and even hotter as the humiliation became almost too unbearable to endure.

'Why not?' She tried to sound casual but failed miserably.

'If I'd got a bit more notice maybe . . .'

Oh the bastard! 'What are you doing tonight then?' Christ, she sounded like her mother.

'Oh, one of the girls in work got tickets for

something in the Gaiety ... some comedy, don't ask me the name of it.'

'Can't you say no?'

'No.'

'Well, she must be really special.' Anna knew she sounded spiteful although she didn't mean it. She was heartbroken. And in shock. Mark had just turned her down. This was real pain. She'd never get over this. Never. Until the day she died she'd never ever recover from this.

'She's a nice girl. Nice looking too. Anyway I said I'd go, so that's it.'

'And she's a friend, is she? Like me?'

'She is at the moment ... but after tonight, who knows? You know me, Anna. I'd find it way too hard to remain friends with an attractive woman.'

Anna stared, too shocked to say anything. Had he any idea what he was saying to her? She'd been his friend for ten fecking years! He must think she was a horrendous old boot!

'Are you rushing off or what?' he asked as she stood up.

'I'm afraid I have to get going.' Keep your cool, she told herself as she carefully buttoned her coat. You'll get over this rejection somehow, like you got over Darren, Steve, Emmet, Rich and all the others. You'll get over it. God knows how, but you will.

'Oh, that's a pity. We didn't get to have much of a chat.' He stood up too. 'Listen, you enjoy yourself tonight, do you hear?'

'Yes,' Anna said, distraught. This was a night-mare. It really was.

'And remember to keep in touch, Anna, you really are a really *really* good friend.'

'And you, Mark,' she picked up her handbag and looked him straight in the eye, 'are a fuck-ing prick.'

'I just cannot believe you said that,' Claire gasped.

'Well, I did,' Anna said tonelessly into the payphone at the door of the hairdressers. 'I just lost it.'

'I just can't believe you said that.'

'Would you stop saying you can't believe what *I* said? What about what *he* said?'

'What did he say exactly?'

'More or less that he wouldn't touch me if I was the last woman on earth.'

'Are you sure you didn't take him up wrong? Are you sure he wasn't just getting back at you for all the times you said you were too busy for him?'

'This is different, Claire, this is so different. I'll talk to you later, they're calling me over to the basin.'

'So you're definitely coming to the reunion any-way?'

'Of course I am. You know me – made of steel, I am.' Anna replaced the receiver as a lone hot tear slid down her cheek.

She wasn't going to do anything drastic. No hair chopping or anything. Women always did that when they were suddenly dumped. But not Anna. She was going to be strong and go for a few subtle highlights, and a blow-dry. After all, it was bad enough, turning up alone without looking like she'd double-crossed a lawnmower.

'Are you going anywhere nice?' asked Mandy, the super skinny hairdresser with the luminous pink hair.

'Yes,' Anna muttered, not exactly anxious to explain her business over the noise of the hairdryer.

'With your fella, is it?'

'No, just out with the girls actually.'

'Oh, is it a hen's? I was at one last night. Me head's still killing me. It was brilliant though. Debbie had this big L sign stuck to her bra and this stripper turned up . . .'

Anna let her ramble on without commenting, determined she'd never ever have anything so ghastly as a hen night. Mind you, what chance was there of her ever having a hen night anyway? Ha! She couldn't even get herself a miserable date. Not even with Mark who'd no problem dating half of Dublin but had a major problem being seen with her. She tried to take no notice as Mandy yanked her hair to within an inch of its life and nearly burned the top of her head twice. Beauty meant pain. You had to suffer. Not that she realistically thought she'd ever suffer as much as she was doing now.

'That's lovely,' she said, glancing in the round mirror held to the back of her head.

'Have a good night,' Mandy stuck her tip in the back of her skin-tight jeans. 'Don't go too mad.'

Don't worry, I won't, Anna thought. The only madness about tonight was the fact that she was turning up alone. A fruitless three-month search for Mr Right for the night had come to nothing. She had to admit the couple of hours in the hairdresser had done her the world of good even though she hadn't actually stopped reeling from her earlier conversation with Mark. Imagine! All this time she'd thought him so charming. And to think that all he'd ever felt for her was sympathy. Good friend, me arse!

Next stop was the sunbed room. She shot through the open door hoping that nobody she knew had spotted her.

'Hi, Anna,' the chocolate-coloured, white-haired receptionist beamed. 'If you'd like to have a seat. One of the beds should be free soon.'

Anna took a seat beside a young guy who looked like he was probably in a boy band. He didn't seem remotely perturbed about sitting in a sunroom. Imagine being that cocky, Anna marvelled.

Suddenly a door swung open and a red-faced, red-haired girl came out apologetically. God, she wasn't brown at all, Anna thought sympathetically. What a waste of money.

The boy-band boy sauntered in, hands in his combat pockets, whistling a tune. Anna stared after him intrigued. She hoped the person in the other sunbed would hurry up. Come on, how long did it take one person to get dressed?

The door swung open again. Anna automatically rose to her feet. About flippin' time! She almost collided into the sallow-skinned man coming out.

'Sorry,' he muttered without looking up.

'Rich? Is that you?'

'Anna!' He looked like a startled rabbit.

'Rich, how nice to see you.' She gave him a wide smile. 'You've got a great colour.'

'Er thanks, Anna. It's good to, er, see you.'

'Likewise.'

God, he looked so uncomfortable, it was great.

'Listen, Anna, I'd love to stay and chat but I'm rushing off to an audition.'

'They're looking for someone dark, right?'

'Er . . . right.'

'Okay, bye then. And congratulations?'

'Why?'

'Oh you know,' Anna smiled at his discomfort. 'You and Sandra.'

'Oh yeah. You're okay about that, aren't you?'

'I'm fine. Well, see you.' She disappeared into the sunroom and closed the door firmly shut. 'Are you okay?' Anna mimicked as she undressed. God, the bloody nerve! Who did men think they were?

She was well rid of him anyway, she thought as she relaxed into the heat. Wasn't he supposed to be broke? Huh! Obviously not too broke for the old sunbed sessions. Men, they were a complete waste of time.

Just as she was beginning to truly relax, the sunbed snapped itself off. Sugar. She'd enjoyed lying there sniggering at the memory of Rich's face. At least it had taken her mind off Mark somewhat. She redressed quickly, hoping the sunbed hadn't completely ruined her hair.

She ambled up Grafton Street drinking in the lively atmosphere. How Dublin had changed over the past few years. Apparently it was now the 'in' place in Europe. People of all nationalities came for weekends to party, party, party.

But they weren't going to Victoria's party. No, you'd have to be an eejit to go to that. They came to have fun in Temple Bar and stagger the streets at 2 a.m. singing Ole, Ole, Ole.

How things had changed. Years ago, the only tourists you'd see would be a few Americans dressed from head to toe in green for fear of standing out. Anna had thought they were all extremely rich. People, you know, who'd left a depressed Ireland by boat and had made a fortune over in places like Boston and New York. She'd always thought they were mad to come back to visit Ireland where it rained all the time and was as boring as hell.

A glance at her watch stopped Anna from daydreaming further. It was past five. In three hours she'd be at the party. Oh God, oh God, oh God!

Back in her bedroom Anna squeezed her size twelve figure into her clingy black dress, sucked in her tummy, turned sideways and took a long hard look at herself in the full-length mirror. Oh God, would she pass? Would people recognize Anna Allstone? Or would they simply take pity on her, still single after all these years? Poor old Anna. Imagine! She actually fancied her chances with Mark Landon. As if.

She sat down on the bed and cradled her head in her hands. She couldn't go through with this, she couldn't. Anna was the worst actress in the world. She couldn't possibly pull this off without a hitch. What was she going to do?

She didn't have to go, of course. It wasn't as if someone was holding a gun to her head. She was a free agent.

It wouldn't matter if she didn't turn up. She was a nonentity. Nobody would care if Anna Allstone didn't show her face.

Stay at home if you want to, she told herself. Go to bed. Go to bed and then tomorrow you can wake up and it will all be over.

She could tell Claire she'd got food poisoning. Food poisoning! Yeah, right. As if Claire would fall for that. Cop on, Anna. You're a successful career woman with the whole world at your feet. Grow up and act your thirty years.

She needed help. Some Dutch courage. A brandy would help her nerves, wouldn't it? Just a tiny brandy. It couldn't hurt.

Right, where was she going to get it? Booting round to the off licence was out of the question.

Surely there was some stacked away in her parents' sideboard?

She sneaked downstairs, feeling sixteen again. She stopped by the sideboard, praying to God her old man wouldn't pounce from the kitchen demanding an explanation. She gently eased open the little mahogany door. It creaked loudly. God, it probably hadn't been opened since last Christmas.

An unopened bottle of vodka stood by the half bottle of brandy. Did Anna imagine it, or was the vodka just screaming to be opened?

Suddenly, she grabbed it and tiptoed back up the stairs, her heart beating a little faster than normal. She felt like a naughty child who'd just nicked the Christmas tin of Quality Street. She sat back down on the bed and studied the unopened bottle. She had to get a mixer. She was nervous, but not *that* nervous. The vodka couldn't be drunk straight.

'Oh, Anna, you look as pretty as a picture,' Mrs Allstone gushed as her daughter tottered into the kitchen in four-inch shoes. 'Doesn't she, James?'

Her father looked at her. 'She could do with a little less muck on her face.'

'Thanks, Dad,' Anna sighed. Jesus, some things never changed.

'The frock is a bit short,' Grandad grumbled.

'Could everybody please give me a break?' Anna wailed. 'I only came down to get myself some coke. I'm parched with the thirst.'

'There's coke in the fridge, dear,' said Anna's mother. 'Get yourself a glass.'

'I think I'll take the bottle up with me,' Anna avoided her eye, 'I really am very thirsty.'

Back once more in the privacy of her own room, Anna poured herself a generous measure of vodka and coloured it with a drop of coke. What was she like? Eh? Drinking vodka all by herself at seven o'clock in the evening. Jesus, it was still bright outside.

She took a sip. It burned her throat, nearly killing her. And then another one. Ah, that was better. She took another peep in the mirror. Maybe she didn't look so bad after all. Her hair had a *because I'm worth it* shine and the sunbed had given her cheeks a healthy just-back-from-the-sun glow.

The dress had cost a small fortune. Anna had nothing to be ashamed of. She was up there with the best of them. She took another gulp of vodka. In fact she looked quite pretty. Even her mother had said so. Her mother didn't throw compliments out easily. What had she said again? As pretty as a picture. Well, that depended on what picture you were looking at really. As long as it wasn't a picture of a pig's arse, Anna chuckled and drank some more vodka. Jesus, this was hot stuff.

She drank some more. Where had her parents got this stuff from anyway? It must have been a Christmas present. God, what a waste. Well, it wasn't going to waste now, that was sure. Anna was thoroughly enjoying it. 'Cheers' she told her reflection. The reflection smiled back at her. She looked pretty fab, although she said it herself. Pretty fab indeed. Victoria Reddin, eat your heart out!

A knock on the door startled her. Panicked, she ran to her wardrobe and put the half-full bottle at the bottom of it. Half-full! Jesus, had she really drunk that much?

'Who is it?' she called.

'It's Dad. Do you want a lift to this place or what?'

'Oh thanks, Dad, that'd be great.'

She sat in the passenger seat of her father's car aware that her dress was riding up along her thighs. She placed her coat on her lap to avoid any comment.

God, it was still bright. Anna caught a glimpse of herself in the side mirror. Was it her imagination or did her make-up look like it had been caked on with a shovel?

Mr Allstone drove from Stillorgan to Blackrock at like ten miles per hour. Anytime tonight, Dad please, Anna thought as she crossed her legs tightly underneath her coat. Why hadn't she gone to the toilet before she left the house? Ha! She could just imagine her introduction. 'Hi, everybody, where's the loo?'

Sophisticated or what? But who cared? Anna didn't any more. It was just a stupid reunion thingy. Full of silly twits she went to school with. Who cared

about them? They had the problem, not her. Anna
Allstone was a big success with a hugely important
job in London. She was single out of choice. Any fool
could get a man. The world was crawling with them.
Why should Anna settle for second best? Why? She
was too fussy, that's what she was. Anna was one
fussy babe.

'Do you think this could be it?' Mr Allstone
turned the corner into Cherrylog Avenue.

'Well, judging by all the Beamers and Mercs it
must be,' Anna muttered. 'Let me out here, Daddy.
No seriously, you don't have to park right outside
the front door. Thanks, Daddy. Goodnight, bye.'

Anna walked unsteadily along the tree-lined gravel
drive, staring ahead. A uniformed man was directing
the cars into parking spaces. Who was that, Anna
wondered. The house was more like a hotel. Anna
wondered what it had cost. Easily a million. Probably more like two. A majestic stone mansion with
Georgian windows, flanked by a hard tennis court
on one side, an indoor swimming pool surrounded
by glass walls on the other. Wow! The Reddins must
be millionaires several times over. Anna suddenly
didn't feel as brave any more. All this was very
intimidating.

She mounted the stone steps and took a deep
breath. She hoped she wasn't the first to arrive.
Please let Claire and Simon be there already, she
silently begged. Oh please don't leave me in there
all on my own.

man chewing on a fat cigar. The man was bald
except for two tufts around both ears and he sported
a decidedly unpleasant sneer.

'Who's that Simon's talking to, Claire? Don't look
now, they're over there.'

Claire swung around. Could she be more obvious?

'Oh that's Aidan Levine, Carole's husband.'

'I don't believe it.' Anna was gobsmacked. 'I met
her earlier on and she'd the cheek to commiserate
with me on my being single.'

'Take no notice,' Claire laughed. 'This whole
party stinks of bull. No one seems to be having
any fun. The whole thing seems to be . . . I dunno . . .
staged or something.'

'Cheers.' Anna raised her glass and clinked it with
Claire's. 'To a most memorable night.'

'Count me in on that toast,' a small voice cut
in.

'Alice, you've arrived!' Anna gave her a hug. 'You
look super.'

'Do I?' Alice asked nervously. 'I almost didn't
come, you know.'

'Have you met Victoria yet?' Claire was curious.

'She just walked past me,' Alice whispered. 'I
don't think she had a clue who I was.'

'Oh, she's probably just up to high-do. It's very
stressful hosting a big reunion party like this,' Claire
said kindly, careful not to hurt Alice's feelings.
'Look, there's Olive over there!'

Olive, sitting on one of Victoria's antique chairs next to her rather conservative-looking husband, waved excitedly at the trio. A far cry from the old days, when she'd have been afraid of acknowledging them for fear of ruffling Victoria's feathers, Anna thought. It was funny really, she chuckled to herself, all the time she had wasted worrying about this silly party. How ridiculous. She was *glad* she hadn't brought anybody. It wasn't the type of party you dragged an unwilling escort along to. Now she was free to flutter around like a social butterfly without some man hanging on to her like a ball and chain for the night. She could get hammered if she wanted and nobody would notice. All that worrying for absolutely nothing!

Come to think of it, she was already well on her way to being hammered. Now on her third glass of champagne, she could almost feel the bubbles shooting to her head, dancing with her brain cells. She'd need to be careful. Victoria's bathroom was not the kind of place you'd like to vomit in.

She excused herself and made her way to the magnificent buffet spread. Every taste was catered for. God, she didn't know where to start.

'A bit of everything,' she instructed the caterer greedily. Well, she did have to eat, didn't she? There was nothing but alcohol in her stomach right now.

'I *knew* I'd find you near the food.'

Anna's heart sank as she heard a cold familiar voice cut the air.

'Anna Allstone, you haven't changed a bit.'

Facing her hostess, her plate overflowing with food, suddenly she didn't feel quite so hungry any more.

'Victoria, I can't believe you remember me so well.' Anna gave a rigid smile.

'Well, I admit the name didn't ring a bell when I first got the list of everybody's names,' she smirked. 'But I'd know your face anywhere.'

'How come?' Anna felt the muscles in her throat constrict with indignation.

'Sure you were sitting beside me in our end-of-year photo. I *loved* that photo. Mind you people said I looked *too* thin in it. Anyway, enjoy your food.' Victoria flashed a set of perfectly capped teeth. 'There's plenty of it. Second helpings, third if you like, there's no limit.'

'Thank you.' Anna suddenly found she was able to speak. 'If there's enough left over I might even put some in a bag, you know, to bring home and keep beside my bed in case I wake up during the night and feel hungry.'

'If you like.' Victoria looked mildly put out. She wasn't sure whether Anna was joking or not. Better to make her escape now, and anyway there were far more important people to chit-chat with. She couldn't see Anna Allstone as somebody who'd be of much use to her in the future. And after all that's what parties were for: securing future contacts.

'Well, excuse me for now,' she smiled falsely,

'I'm sure you'll have fun. I'm afraid there aren't too many available men here tonight – Carole told me about your situation – but you should have fun with the girls.'

'I'm sure I will,' Anna said through gritted teeth, 'and by the way, in case I don't talk to you again, I love the dress.'

'Thank you, I got it in—'

'Oh, I know where you got it,' Anna swiftly interrupted. 'In that boutique in Ranelagh, wasn't it? Claire couldn't believe her luck when she found hers in the bargain bin. Sure, as she said herself, you couldn't get a pair of jeans these days for fifty quid! Now, if you'll excuse me, I'm going to tuck into this fabulous food before it all runs out.'

She strolled off, leaving Victoria clutching the banqueting table, fuming. What was all that about a bargain bin? She'd never go back to that boutique again. How *dare* that idiot of a saleswoman charge five hundred pounds for the same dress she sold to that cheapskate Claire!

'What on earth did you say to Victoria?' Claire asked when she came back. 'She looks livid.'

'Oh, not a lot.' Anna popped a heaped spoon of dressed avocado into her mouth.

'You must have said something,' her friend insisted.

'Well, don't kill me,' Anna flashed a wicked grin, 'but I told her you only paid a few pounds for the same dress she's wearing.'

'Oh you bad girl,' Claire guffawed. 'Don't you know Victoria won't be able to enjoy the rest of the night now if she thinks she's wearing something cheap?'

'I don't care,' Anna shrugged. 'You know, I think that woman is either evil or incredibly stupid. I'm serious, Who does she think she is going round insulting people like that? Money doesn't give you a passport to be nasty.'

Olive joined them. 'Having a good night, girls?'

'I'm having a blast,' Anna answered. Was it her imagination or had the room begun to spin ever so slightly? Oh please don't let me collapse. She closed her eyes. And filled her lungs with cigar-filled air. Ah, that was better. What a perfect evening so far. Too perfect, even. She felt uneasy. Something was bound to go wrong.

'The food's great.' Olive's eyes shone. 'Did you try some?'

'Of course I did.' Anna grinned. 'You can take as much as you want, you know.'

'Right,' said Olive, puzzled. She wondered if Anna Allstone was a bit drunk. Her eyes were slightly pink and her make-up needed retouching. 'Have you met everyone? Orla and Suzie are sitting over there. They were commenting on how well you looked.'

'Were they?' Anna asked faintly. Did she look well? Did she? She didn't feel . . . in fact . . . ugh no, her stomach gave a violent rumble.

'Are you all right?' Claire clutched her arm.

'I'm fine.' Anna was beginning to sway. The room was hot. 'No need to call an ambulance or anything. I just need some fresh air.' She hiccuped loudly. 'Ooops, sorry, ha ha!'

'I'll bring her out,' she heard Claire tell the others. She felt herself being steered out of the drawing room. 'We'll be back in a mo.'

'Here, drink this.' Claire shoved a glass of iced water in her face. They stood on the front steps gazing at the vast front lawns. The cool night air was sobering. Anna gave a slight shiver. 'Can we go back inside now?'

'Not until you can walk properly,' Claire whispered fiercely. 'We've done well tonight, Anna. We've turned up looking great, our heads held high and that's the way we're going to leave. Now hurry up and drink this.'

Anna stared at her friend, her eyes wide with surprise and confusion. Was she really that drunk? God, Claire was being pretty hard on her. All she wanted was to have a bit of fun. That's all she wanted. 'I'll be fine.' She finished the water as Claire went off to get her another glass. 'I promise, I'll behave myself,' she hiccuped again, 'I promise.'

'Hello, good looking.'

Anna swung around to see who'd made the comment. *Oh hello, ugly.* It was Carole's unattractive hubby. *She* was nowhere to be found. 'Hi,' she said. Anna hoped he hadn't come over to bore her to tears for the night. Somehow he looked like he'd be quite a hard person to shrug off. He held out a hand for her to shake. It felt like a wet fish.

'Which one of the gang are you?'

I wasn't one of the gang, Anna thought. *I was actually one of the girls the gang picked on, didn't Carole tell you?*

'My name's Anna,' she said.

'Annnnnna,' he said meaningfully. *God, what a bore.* 'And who are you here with, Annnnnna?'

'Oh I'm just here with everyone,' she answered lightly.

'You mean you're not with anyone special?' he asked her cleavage.

'Nope.' Christ, he was beginning to make her skin crawl.

'Well, well, well.'

'It's a great party, isn't it?' Anna said to the ceiling. 'Victoria went to a lot of trouble, didn't she?'

'I'd say you've a few men hidden away somewhere. I wouldn't believe that someone as gorgeous as you is single.'

'The food is just lovely. And have you seen the garden? It's—'

'I'd say half the men here would do anything to get in your knickers.'

'Excuse me?' Anna looked visibly stunned.

'I'd say you're an animal in the scratcher.'

'Listen here, egghead,' Anna snapped, the effects of the alcohol suddenly giving her zero tolerance levels. 'I wouldn't go near you if you were single. But you're married, which makes you doubly unattractive, so piss off.'

'Jesus, no *wonder* you're still single.' His ugly red face became much uglier and much redder.

'Well, when I meet people like you I'm glad that I am. Poor Carole, she's the one who has to see your face every morning.'

'I was only trying to compliment you but obviously you're so unused to—'

'*There* you are, darling.' Carole suddenly appeared from nowhere. She grabbed her husband's hand and squeezed it possessively. 'I hope you're not boring poor Anna with stories about how well your computer business is going. It's a dot com.' She winked at Anna. 'I'm always telling him not to be talking about his successful business. I mean, I'm very much aware of the fact that not everybody has done as well as us from the old Celtic Tiger.' Another wink.

'Don't worry,' Anna gave a dangerous smile. 'We weren't talking about that *at all*. Not *at all*.'

'Oh.' Carole looked completely put out. 'Er . . . what were you talking about?'

'You tell her.' Anna grinned at the pair of them.

'I was just saying . . .' He began to cough as Carole's mouth set in a hard straight line. 'I was—'

'I'd better go off and mingle,' Anna interrupted airily. 'Don't ever let it be said that poor old Anna was the cause of a lovers' tiff.' Hee hee.

'Were you causing trouble again?' Claire was suddenly back with more water. 'I'm not sure if I liked the look on Carole's face just there.'

'I don't blame her for looking like that. You should have heard what her saddo husband was saying to me. *In his dreams!*'

'God, Carole doesn't seem to have caught such a good catch after all,' Claire said after hearing the nature of the conversation. 'The way she goes on you'd think she was married to Mel bloody Gibson. Actually, speaking of gorgeous men, have you seen Victoria's Vincent?'

'He's divine, isn't he?' Olive was back again. 'When God was giving out looks he must have been camping outside HMV all night to be first in the queue,' she swooned.

Where was this Vincent? Anna's eyes scanned the room. Where was this lovebeast they were all raving about? He couldn't be that wonderful if he'd married Victoria. No indeed, there must be something wrong with his brain, if not his looks. Nobody could marry that girl unless they were daft in the head.

'Someone introduce me,' she demanded. 'I'm dying to meet this Vinnie fella.'

'When he passes next, I'll grab him,' Olive giggled.

'More champagne?' a fresh-faced caterer appeared.

'I'd love one,' Alice smiled.

Claire shot a warning look at Anna as she eyed

the tray longingly. 'No thank you.' She spoke for them both.

'Meanie,' Anna muttered.

'Have you seen the birthday cake?' Olive asked. 'Both Vincent and Victoria were thirty last week. Their cake is amazing. It's got her face and his face on it.'

'Oh, wouldn't I love to be the one to cut it,' Anna muttered.

'Now, now,' Alice wagged an accusing finger, 'we'll have none of that.'

'Oh, there's Vincent.' Olive grabbed a passing six-footer and dragged him over to the small group. 'Vincent pet, I want to introduce you to a few people. You've met Claire, I know, but have you met Alice?'

'Alice and the tall blond man shook hands.

'And have you met Anna?'

He turned. She gave a sharp cry. People's conversations drew to an abrupt halt. It was as if they knew a drama was about to unfold. Vincent Reddin didn't react for a second. He just stared, disbelieving, disconnected. For one awful moment, Anna stood nailed to the deep, plush, crimson carpet in rigid shock. People's eyes were boring into her. This wasn't happening to her. It couldn't be.

This could not be happening to Anna Allstone. Things like this did not occur in real life. The silence that hung between them was unbearable.

'How do you do, Vincent,' she spoke eventually, sounding like ET. 'Or should I call you Darren?'

Sharp intakes of breath could be heard from Alice, Olive and Claire.

'Is Darren some kind of stage name or . . . let me see . . . could it possibly be short for Vincent?' she continued in a dangerous tone of voice.

'Listen, I can explain,' Vincent stammered and reached out to touch her.

'Get away from me!' she screamed and pushed him away.

She watched him sway. Somehow he lost his balance and, to Anna's horror, fell backwards into the crowd of guests.

'What the hell is going on here?' Victoria suddenly appeared out of nowhere, her thin features contorted with surprised rage.

'Don't ask me,' answered Anna numbly as if she'd simply been paid to deliver the lines. 'He's the one with the answers.'

'Well, I don't know what kind of drugs you are on, Anna Allstone, but leave my property now without any further trouble.'

'Don't worry, I was just going anyway.' Anna straightened herself up. 'Goodbye, Victoria. I hope you and your guests enjoy the rest of the evening. And goodbye, Darren,' she looked down on him contemptuously as he struggled to lift himself from the floor, 'or should I say Vincent? It's impossible to know, isn't it?'

How she turned on her four-inch heels and walked steadily out of that room with any ounce of dignity, she'd never know. But walk out with her head held high, she did. And Alice, Olive and Claire followed with their partners. And as it transpired later, so did many other guests when they quickly realized the party could only go downhill after that.

But although on the outside, Anna left Victoria's house with a tiny piece of pride, in the inside she was crumbling. She would never be able to face any of those people ever again. Without knowing her side of that story, they'd brand her as a tart and a home-wrecker.

People wouldn't forget Anna Allstone for a very long time. To think she'd actually slept with Victoria's husband. It was too unbearable to think about. She sat in silence in the back of Simon's car as he drove her to Stillorgan. She didn't want to talk about it, she insisted. She pushed Claire's comforting arm away, insisting she was fine. She'd get over it. She had nothing to feel guilty about. She wouldn't have gone near Vincent if she'd known the truth. He was a liar and a cheat and Victoria was welcome to him.

But Anna hardly slept that night. She lay in the dark, eyes heavy with exhaustion, her stomach tied up in heavy knots. Thank God, she was going to England. She'd never come back, not even for Christmas. At least in England nobody would know anything about her. No Darren over there. No

Mark. No nobody. Hot, hopeless tears slid down her cheeks, soaking her pillow. At that very moment, Anna almost wished she were dead.

Chapter Forty-four

Back in Galway, Anna tried to lose herself in her work. She rang head office and assured them she was prepared to take on this exciting and challenging role. They gave her ten days to get organized.

Anna began to lose track of time as she shot around Lolta's like a loose bullet trying to busy herself, and after a while she couldn't remember if it was a Wednesday or a Thursday.

Thankfully Lolta's were buying her plane ticket and setting up initial accommodation for her. Two less things she had to worry about.

Claire had phoned several times but Anna hadn't taken the calls. The last thing she wanted was a bloody post-mortem on the party. Eventually she took the phone off the hook.

The weather was becoming milder and Anna took to walking the prom in the evenings. She'd miss the sea when she went to England, she really would. It had a huge calming effect on her nerves. Striding up and down the seafront in the evenings she had plenty of time to relive every minute of the party. One good thing had come out of all this, she decided. She no longer envied Victoria Reddin's lavish lifestyle. Money couldn't buy happiness, security or love. It was a sorry substitute for a real life. Anna hadn't much, she admitted, but at least what she had was real. It was real.

Never again would she presume that rich people had a better quality of life. If she had millions of pounds and a sleazeball for a husband, she wouldn't want that package. Life was enough trouble.

But was there such a thing as a truly decent man? Or were they all ratbags given half a chance? It was hard to know. After all, men never introduced themselves as slimy gits, did they? No, they were all one-woman men until you caught them with somebody else. Was it because they were the weaker sex? That was a possibility. Yeah, that was a real possibility. Because when you thought about it, if the most powerful man in America was caught having 'sexual relations' with some ordinary smitten intern, what chance did the average Joe Soap have?

'Anna, is that you? Thank God I've finally caught you.'

'Hi, Claire.' Anna groaned inwardly. She didn't want to talk about the party. She didn't need therapy or to be set up with another one of Simon's friends to ease the pain. She was over Darren/Vincent. She didn't give a tinker's curse about him. Let him continue to be married to his sad little wife and conduct his seedy affairs with somebody else.

The party was the best thing that could have happened to her. Else she might have gone through life thinking happiness was in the passenger seat of some flashy sports car. Good luck to the Reddins and their silly circle of cronies. Anna wouldn't want to be them for anything in the world.

Her career was her own. Nobody had ever handed her anything. Her achievements were all due to sheer bloody hard work.

'Anna, I'm just ringing to say that I'll miss you dreadfully when you go over to England.'

'Ah Claire, it's only an hour away. I'm not going to the moon, you know.'

'I know.' Claire sounded all emotional.

'I'll probably see you more than I do now,' Anna said kindly.

'Yeah, listen, I know you don't want to talk about the party so I won't mention it.'

'Right,' Anna said, now kind of wanting to talk about it since Claire wasn't pushing it. 'I'm fine about it, honest.'

'Victoria knows about the affair.'

Affair? God, it sounded so sordid. Anna cringed. It sounded like they were doing it in dingy little hotels all around the country. But that was Dublin for you. Small place, small minds. People had nothing to do but gossip. It just showed how uneventful their own lives were. Affair indeed! An insignificant fling. That's all it had been.

'Is she standing by him?'

'Yes.'

Of course she is, Anna thought scornfully. She wouldn't blame *him*. Women like that never blamed their husbands. It was always the other woman. The temptress. Victoria would eventually convince herself that Anna must have got down on her hands and knees and begged him to give her one. Poor sad Anna Allstone who despite all her achievements, was still some old eejit desperate for a bit of nookie.

Of course, he would *swear* to Victoria that it had meant absolutely *nothing*, that he'd simply felt sorry for Anna and that nothing like that would ever happen again. He might even feign a few tears. And convince her that the fear of losing her was killing him.

And of course Victoria would forgive him, after a few tantrums followed by a week or two of keeping her bedroom door firmly locked. Because what would Victoria Reddin *do*, what would she *be* without her husband? A woman like that would rather die than be left on the already oversubscribed single shelf. That would be a fate worse than death for a woman whose life revolved around clothes and cocktail parties. Anna sighed. Women like that made it so much easier for men to win all the time. No wonder the world was in such a bloody mess!

'Ah well, it's all behind me now.'

'So you're not upset?'

'No.'

'Good.'

'And you're all set for the big move to England?'

'My first-class ticket won't be able to take me there fast enough.'

'First class? They must think highly of you in Lolta's.'

'Well, it's just as well somebody does,' Anna replied.

'And you're sure you're not just running away from it all?' Claire seemed concerned.

Running away from it all? Running away from *what*? It's not like she was leaving a hectic, fulfilled existence behind. Nobody would miss her. Anna wasn't feeling sorry for herself, she was simply being realistic. People usually didn't make it in business unless they travelled.

Ireland was way too small. Just a tiny dot on the map really. In fact, most people in the world had never even heard of Ireland.

Anna wondered if she'd become one of those non-resident Irish people who counted the days till Christmas to come home and have the maddest time ever, only to return to Britain at the start of a gloomy January, all depressed again. Because people who lived abroad and only came back once or twice a year constantly lived with the tourist-book impression of Ireland. Because they didn't stick around for the gloomy part, the post-Christmas months when people didn't go out at all. Because it was either too cold or wet or because you knew you wouldn't be able to get a taxi home.

Anna would join them now. The first thing she'd do in London was find an Irish pub and sit there moping over a glass of Guinness, singing 'The Green Green Grass of Home'. Well, maybe not. Actually, definitely not. She was going to make sure her new life was a huge success.

'No, I'm not running away,' Anna assured her friend. 'I'm being sent there, remember?'

'Well, I'll definitely come over and we'll go on a mad shopping spree,' Claire enthused.

'Definitely,' Anna said, realizing that Claire must have absolutely no idea how hard a store manager worked. Weekend shopping sprees? In her dreams!

'And you won't be too lonely, will you?' asked Claire, knowing that personally she'd rather die than head off to a big unfriendly city like London.

'Not at all. Anyway, Roger's over there if I ever need to see a member of my family in a hurry.'

'Oh, that's right,' Claire said, suddenly remembering that Anna had a brother somewhere. 'Your parents will probably visit you both so, you know, killing two birds and all that.'

'Try stopping them.'

'And what about Mark?'

'What about him?'

'Have you been in contact?'

'Of course not, Mark and myself are no longer friends. That's the way I want it.'

'I still think you two should clear the air.'

'Forget it, Claire. Mark had his chance.'

'Did he?' Claire sounded doubtful. 'Anna, you never gave him anything but abuse.'

'How do you mean?'

'You were always going on about other men and stuff and going on about him just being a friend, you know?'

'Is that a crime?'

'No, but you shouldn't have freaked out when he more or less played you at your own game.'

'Yeah well, I probably overreacted,' Anna admitted. 'But there's no way I'm ringing to apologize. No flippin' way.'

Eventually Claire got off the phone after a tearful goodbye. Anna thanked God she wasn't as emotional as Claire. Life wouldn't be worth living if everything was that traumatic. It was good Claire was going back to work, though, even if it was part time. She'd probably become semi-normal again. Anna slumped down in front of *Corrie* and opened a packet of chocolate fingers.

The phone rang. Ah Jesus, who was that now? People should know not to ring during *Coronation Street*. It was just so rude. Well, she wouldn't answer it. Sure, it was probably just her mother wondering had she packed yet. She could always ring back.

It rang and rang and rang.

All right, all right, hold your horses, I'm coming. Anna dragged herself off the couch. God, her mother could be so impatient sometimes.

'Hello?'

'Anna?'

It was a male voice. Anna felt a bolt of electricity shoot right through her. Oh Gawd, who the hell was this?

'Ye . . . es?'

'It's Mark.'

Mark! Jesus. Anna stared dizzily at the phone. He had some neck ringing her after all that had happened. Had she heard about the party from hell? Was he ringing to offer his condolences. A million and one things shot through her head. Why had he suddenly decided to ring her?

To wish her luck with the rest of her life? To apologize for pretending he fancied her for over a decade? Well, he could go to hell as far as she was concerned.

'Hi Mark, it's good to hear from you,' she said stiffly.

'And it's nice to hear you too,' he returned the compliment.

And suddenly it dawned on her. Mark was ringing with his fond farewells. He wanted to wish her luck with the rest of her life. That was it, of course it was.

'You're off soon, I hear.'

'That's right,' she tried to sound upbeat. She felt herself struggling like a fly in a web.

'Any chance of catching you before you go?'

'It's highly unlikely, I leave Monday.'

'Will you be around Sunday?'

'As it happens, I'll be at my parents Sunday night. It'll be like The Last Supper, knowing them.'

'I'll call around so,' Mark said, obviously ignoring the fact that she hadn't invited him. 'See you then, I'll look forward to it.'

But I won't, Anna thought as she twiddled the phone wire. The last thing she wanted was a parting chat with Mark. She hadn't forgiven him for insulting her over the whole reunion thing. In fact she didn't think she'd ever forgive him. He couldn't go on pretending everything was all right between them. She'd called him a prick the last time they'd met. Oh God, it was humiliating. 'Actually, Mark, I don't think it's a great idea,' she said with a calmness she didn't feel. 'I've just got far too much to organize for tomorrow. But I'll send you an e-mail from London, okay?'

'Right, if that's what you want,' Mark said very quietly. 'Well . . . good luck, Anna.'

Good luck? Anna stared at the dead phone. *Good luck?* She sat down on the bottom stair and burst into tears.

Chapter Forty-five

So that was it. She was finally leaving the country. Anna sat in the kitchen of her family home and tucked into the vegetarian lasagne her mother had baked especially.

'Of course, you'll only be a phone call away,' Mrs Allstone said encouragingly.

'And half of Ireland's living in England anyway, you're bound to bump into some of them,' her father added.

'I doubt it, England's not the type of place where you'd easily make friends.'

'Nonsense,' her dad said firmly. 'With your personality, Anna, you're bound to meet like-minded people.'

'I remember my brother Eamonn went to England,' Grandad said distantly. 'He never came back.'

'It was different in those days though,' Mrs Allstone interjected quickly. 'England's less than an hour by plane, isn't that right, Anna?'

'That's right.'

God, would they ever stop fussing over her like

this? It was making her all emotional. She was going to England, no big deal about it. Anna was a big girl now. She wasn't going to end up on the streets with no money, selling her body for drugs and living out of a cardboard box. This was simply a career move, not some huge drama. Anyway, why did everyone think she'd be lonely and down in the dumps in London? That wasn't Anna at all. Didn't anybody really know her at all? London was a cool place to live. Even Madonna lived there and she could afford to live anywhere. And Robbie Williams. And Geri Halliwell and all those really cool funky people. Anna couldn't *wait* to join them all over in London. She'd have to get a good map and find out exactly where the Met Bar and the Ivy restaurant were. God, it was going to be so much fun!

'Passport?'

'Yes.'

'Money?'

'Yes.'

'Contact lens solution?'

'Er . . . I think so.'

'First-class ticket?'

'Oh God, Mum, you're such a snob,' Anna laughed. 'Don't worry, I've got everything packed.'

'Are you sure now you don't want us to drive you to the airport?' Anna's mother had tears in her eyes.

'No, Mum, the bus stop is fine, it'll be quicker with the bus lanes and all.'

'You'll write?'

'I'll phone,' Anna laughed, 'Anyway I'll be home the weekend after next for Andrew's second birthday. I'll see you then.'

'Take care, Anna, we'll see you in two weeks,' Anna's Dad was a lot more practical.

At Donnybrook, the bus came along and as Anna paid her fare she heard a voice shout out 'Anna'.

She swung around. 'Nice one.' Her dad clicked on the camera. Thank *God* she hadn't let them take her all the way to the airport!

'Window or aisle?' The nicely made-up ground hostess processed her ticket.

'Oh, the aisle is fine,' Anna smiled. She wasn't going to be childish now and ask for a seat with a view.

'Your flight will be boarding from Boarding Area B, Gate 26,' the girl smiled back. 'Enjoy your flight.'

Anna skipped into Hughes & Hughes to buy a few rag mags to pass the time, but then decided to buy *The Times* (well, she really *had* to look the part). She also bought the latest Robyn Sisman before she left. Well, that was all. She might as well try to find her boarding gate. There was a queue of people waiting to go through security and people were clinging to each other exchanging tearful farewells. Thank God she hadn't let the folks come along, she reminded herself for the fiftieth time. She was about to join the queue when suddenly she remembered that –

hurrah – she'd a business ticket that allowed her to fast track past the plebs. Brilliant idea.

She headed for the security belt.

'Anna, ANNNAAAAA!'

She froze. Jesus, that voice. She turned. Slowly. As did everybody else.

Mark. Yes, oh Christ, it *was* Mark, on his knees. 'Anna, don't leave me. Don't get on that plane. All is forgiven,' he cried mockingly.

People began to titter. One man had to cover his mouth to smother uncontrollable laughter. *This is so SO not funny*, Anna winced. She felt like a complete twat standing there with her briefcase and *The Times* tucked under her arm, with Mark making two goons out of the pair of them.

'Get up,' she hissed, her cheeks crimson.

'Oh ma Gad that's so romantic,' said an enormous woman wearing a *Guinness is good for you* cap.

Someone took a photo. And it wasn't even her dad.

'I'll call security, Mark, I swear,' Anna said, but the only security man she could see was laughing his head off. 'I'll never forgive you for this.'

'Have you forgiven me for the other thing?'

'Nope.'

'Well then, I've nothing to lose.'

'Please get up,' Anna begged, 'you're making a show of me.'

'Only if you promise me something.'

'What?'

'Well, there's this reunion the lads are having. Will you come? As a friend?'

'No.'

'As a girlfriend?'

Her heart bungee-jumped. 'Oh yes.' *Oh hang on, Anna, calm down. Say something witty.* 'Just don't expect me to hold your hand.'

Mark got to his feet and gave a small bow to the crowd, no longer crying and hugging their loved ones.

'Are they getting married, Mommy?' a small boy asked the large lady with the *Guinness* cap.

'No, honey,' she sighed. 'That kinda thing only happens in movies.'

'I'll kill you,' Anna told Mark as he brushed the dirt off his knees.

'Well, it's better than ignoring me,' Mark admitted.

'How did you know what time I was coming out here?'

'Claire.'

'Claire! I'll kill her. What else was she saying to you?'

'Oh, you know, how much you loved me and all that.'

'She what?'

'Only messing.'

'Mark?'

'Yeah?'

'I've just thought of something.'

'Yeah?'

'You had your school reunion two years ago.'

'Oh God,' Mark put his hands to his head, 'did I? I forgot.'

'Mark?'

'Yeah?'

'Why did you really come out here?'

'Cos I want you to be my girlfriend,' he grinned.

'And that's it?'

'Yes, why?'

'Cos I have to go now, right now.'

'Okay, just give me my kiss.'

'Uh?'

'You're my bird, I'm entitled to a snog.'

'You're a tosser.'

'I know.' He leaned forward and drew her towards him. His strong lips were on hers. She never wanted this kiss to end. 'Did I ever tell you I think you're beautiful?' he murmured.

'Tell me next weekend.' Anna suddenly felt dizzyingly happy. This was too much to take in. She'd have to go away and analyse this, like, for ever. 'After all, it's taken you over a decade already and they're boarding my flight now.'

'What are we doing next weekend?'

'You're coming over to London.'

'Am I? Cool!'

'I'll see you then,' Anna grinned, her eyes shining.

Over a decade, Mark mused as he watched her disappear through security. Over a decade. Was it really that long? It was too long. *Far* too long. A year was a much more reasonable time frame. Yes, a year was good. And that's exactly how long he'd give himself to get her to come back home.